LIVE FREE OR DIE

DOMINIC LAGAN

Editions Gigouzac

http://stores.lulu.com/store.php?fAcctID=2192270

ISBN: 978-0-9561518-0-3

To Jill Sutton Wilkinson

"Is life so dear or peace so sweet as to be purchased at the price of chains and slavery? Forbid it, Almighty God! I know not what course others may take, but as for me, give me liberty or give me death!"

Patrick Henry

PROLOGUE

DEATH CERTIFICATE - CAPET

Temple Section, third year of the French Republic on the 22 Prairial, death of Louis Charles Capet, aged ten years two months, domiciled in Paris at the Temple towers, son of Louis Capet, last King of the French, and of Marie Antoinette of Austria. The deceased was born at Versailles and died the day before yesterday at three o'clock in the afternoon.

CHAPTER ONE

Wednesday, October 23rd, 1793

The second Bow Street runner paused and eyed the intruder speculatively. Trouble, he thought, and signalled to his mate. The latter, as if to say 'you deal with it', merely shrugged and continued his meticulous search of the terrified prisoner's dress.

"And what may we do for you, friend?" asked the redbreast, adroitly managing to combine both irony and amiability.

"I ain't yer friend," snapped back the newcomer, evidently having no use for either quality. He was an enormous man with ape-like arms and the unmistakably broken face of a prize-fighter.

"E's in 'ere," he called out to someone lingering in the next room.

When the second man entered, the policeman did as all policemen do. He looked at the man's shoes. A gentleman certainly, he guessed. Not pinchbeck buckles, but gold. Not an English gentleman, though, he thought, noting the raven black hair and slightly olive skin. Some kind of foreigner.

"My profoundest apologies for this interruption in your duties, gentlemen," the foreigner said, with no trace of an accent, accompanying this courtesy with a sardonic little bow. "May I introduce myself? I am de Born and this," indicating the hulk beside him, "is my ..." he hesitated, as if unsure of the correct word. " ... my colleague, Mr Benjamin Pingo."

De Born gazed around the room in disgust. Like most of the houses in Clare Market, the decor of the upstairs room at the *Bunch of Grapes* was a mixture of the shabby and the genteel. The walls were lined with the usual cheap prints of the usual kind - all in varying degrees of obscenity. The floor was strewn with greasy cushions, upon one of which sprawled a rough-looking trooper still in his high cavalry boots, his face trickling blood from a livid wound high on his cheek.

For a moment there was a silence, broken only by the sobs of the prisoner, who clutched pathetically at a torn décolletage.

When de Born spoke again, it was with considerably less courtesy. "The trooper may go, but this one," he said, pointing with his ivory topped stick in the direction of the sobbing, "is now my prisoner."

"We'll see about that," the runner said derisively.

He had hardly spoken, when Pingo's huge ham of a fist smashed into his solar plexus.

"No back-chat to 'is lordship if you please," Pingo said, surveying his handiwork with some satisfaction. Now on all fours, the policeman gushed a thin stream of vomit and gasped for breath. His partner drew his truncheon and backed away, bewildered by the unexpected violence.

Ignoring both men, de Born stood over the prisoner, in whose expression growing hope fought the memory of recent terror. De Born's face was a study in distaste.

"You are the Honourable Henry James Hood," he enquired formally, "eldest son of Lord Hood, First Naval Lord of the Admiralty?"

At the mention of his father's name the prisoner made a pitiful attempt to stand at attention, until he realized that a man wearing flame coloured taffeta and silk stockings, however fetching, is doomed to appear hopelessly undignified. Still sobbing, he simply nodded. Pingo promptly grasped Hood by the arm and hustled him out of the room, booting the scuttling trooper through the door as he did so.

"You will say nothing of these events to any person," de Born said to the gaping runner. "The prisoner is now in the custody of Mr Philip Stephens, Secretary to the Admiralty." With that he left the room, turning at the door only to give a sarcastic tip of his tricorne hat.

Outside, Pingo and the prisoner waited in a closed coach, its Russia leather curtains firmly fixed against the prying eyes of a small knot of onlookers who had gathered outside. De Born leaned into the doorway and discreetly instructed Pingo to take Hood back to his barracks and then return to the office in Whitehall. Before he stepped back from the carriage he glanced over to the far corner where Hood sat. His shoulders were still hunched, although he had ceased his weeping.

"Can you help me, Johnnie?" Hood asked timidly.

De Born's face softened a little. "Yes, you stupid bastard. I dare say I can."

Hood gave him a tiny smile. "Knew you would. Thanks."

De Born nodded his farewell and closed the carriage door.

Oblivious to the curious stares of the crowd, de Born strode down Clare Market, past the other bagnios, followed by a runt of a man wearing a shabby greatcoat and carrying a nasty looking cudgel of twisted wood. One end was formed into a gnarled club, the other sported a vicious spike. When he had reached Stanhope Street, de Born turned and signalled his companion to approach. "Keep close by me, McPheat, until we reach the Admiralty," he said to Pingo's repellent understudy. "And then wait for Benjamin's return."

McPheat wordlessly knuckled his forehead and fell into step behind his master.

Satisfied, de Born continued his progress, passing through Covent Garden and working his way towards the Strand. As he walked, he puzzled over the nature of such men as Hood. Irrumatio. De Born remembered the time he had come across the unfamiliar word in a volume of Juvenal. He could still see his father's face, rigid with embarrassment, as he described its meaning. 'The most base perversion a man could practise,' he had called it. And yet, thought de Born, he had known Harry Hood well at Winchester (where 'mollies' were hardly rare) and had liked him a good deal for his wit and *joie de vivre*. After all, he thought, if Harry wanted to do that to another man, why not let him? It wasn't as if he was doing anyone any harm - except, perhaps, to himself.

Reaching his destination, he reluctantly gave up the unequal struggle between his natural sympathy and his father's harsh admonitions, choosing instead to concentrate his mind on formulating and rehearsing his report.

*   *   *

'The Somerset' in the Strand was the favourite meeting place for naval officers and others connected with the Admiralty, in particular agents for the External Department, to which de Born belonged. As usual the waitresses made a fuss of de Born as he entered, alone, having left McPheat on guard outside to frighten passers-by with his feral scowl. With the quick perception of their calling, the girls soon melted away. This normally amiable young man, who teased them, admired their new ribbons and asked after their faithless lovers, was evidently in one of his black moods.

Ignoring the coffee-pot that was placed on the table in front of him, de Born ordered a mug of brandy, hesitated and ordered a pint of claret instead. He sat over his wine for an hour or more, brooding. The truth is, he thought bitterly, I'm just a glorified errand-boy. Whilst others in the Department roamed the Continent, winning glory and steady promotion, I'm stuck in London doing odd jobs for uncle Philip. Sometimes bodyguard, sometimes agent provocateur and mostly, as the afternoon's events proved, the one who had to clear up unpleasant messes left by others. He ordered another pint of claret.

Once or twice a colleague ventured to his table with an item of office gossip or an offer of another drink, but all were repulsed by the brevity and chilliness of their reception. De Born was an object of some mystery and not a little envy on the part of his friends - in reality more acquaintances than friends. No one minded that he was Mr Secretary Stephens' nephew - most of them owed their own positions to high-placed relatives; nor that he was titled - many of them were themselves the younger sons of peers. The envy was occasioned by the air of urbane ferocity that surrounded de Born. They envied the atmosphere of glamour that trailed after him, made up of his bodyguards, the hidden weapons he was known to carry, fast horses, those famous turquoise eyes that women admired, and were frightened of; an air of secrets and violence and money. Of course, he was a foreigner, which explained his dandyism, eccentric love of reading and the amazing fact that he never hunted. Yet the young bloods from the Admiralty and the Foreign Office universally both admired de Born and feared him a little, although if asked none could have explained exactly why it was so.

When de Born's father, the old marquis, had married Betsy Stephens, he had promised her that their first-born son would be brought up as an English Protestant gentleman. The promise was freely and gladly made, for the type of Englishman the marquis had met in his time as French Ambassador in London was the type he admired tremendously: solitary, hard, tight-lipped, stiff-necked, with vigorous intellects. In short, Scotsmen.

The average Englishman his son encountered, first at a dame-school in Sunbury, then at Winchester, with their drunken, boorish love of practical jokes and witty stories about farting, would have horrified the old marquis. Their bucolic lives, given over to hunting in muddy fields and breeding children in draughty houses, would have seemed to him no better than the lives of the peasants on his Guyenne estates. By the time de Born left the university at Edinburgh, he was already an outsider. He had become a freakish hybrid, made up of the asceticism of a Scottish intellectual, the severity of a French aristocrat and the dash and wit of a London dandy - each group instinctively recognizing that, although superficially he was like them, he was not truly of them. To be sure, women were intrigued and charmed, but their brothers were respectfully wary.

When yet another Admiralty clerk approached, bottle in hand, de Born decided that this wallow in self-pity had gone on quite long enough. He bestirred himself and marched out into the street. McPheat automatically fell into step five paces behind. As he drew alongside the statue of Charles I, de Born suddenly realized that not once in the last two hours had he thought about his report on the Hood arrest, and so he spent the remainder of his time between Charing Cross and the ante-room to his uncle's office in the Admiralty, mentally rehearsing his account of the events that had taken place that afternoon in the 'Bunch of Grapes'.

*   *   *

Philip Stephens was standing by a globe in the centre of his book-lined room, tracing a sea route with his finger whilst consulting a chart held high to catch the light from the tall windows at the other end of the gloomy office.

He was a small, plump, partridge-shaped man, bald without his wig. His cold, grey eyes were hooded, looking out over a beaky nose and the thin lips of a soul grown pitiless in His Majesty's service. Now in his late sixties, he retained the energetic bustle of his youth and his mind still had all the qualities of a steel trap, sharp, quick and deadly. He had recently undergone an operation for the stone. The astonished surgeon reported afterwards that, although he was seven minutes under the probing knife, not a murmur was heard from the tough little fellow. He was the only man in England who possessed de Born's unreserved respect.   Without looking up from his work, he motioned de Born to begin.

"Hood was taken from the runners two hours ago, and is now back in his barracks." He paused and Stephens looked up enquiringly. "He ... he was taken in the act," de Born muttered.

"Yes boy," Stephens said softly. "It was a sorry thing I asked you to do. However, young Hood has been kept from the disgrace of the Charing Cross pillory, while his Lordship will be greatly heartened by this news. And grateful too."

"But uncle," de Born protested. "This is hardly work for a gentleman, especially ... "

"Yes, yes," interrupted Stephens. "You think only the likes of Benjamin should dirty his hands with this sort of affair, while you, sir, should be catching Jacobins. Well, you are wrong. Clare Market is part of life, just as the fancy gaming rooms in St James Street are - and it is life, all of it, that you must learn about if you are to be of help to me in my work. Remember the words of your hero, it is by experience we learn."

De Born's suppressed irritation subsided. He owed this man and his wife almost everything. He had never known his English mother, who died giving him life. Her sister, his Aunt Anne, had become the only person to whom he could confide all his boyish troubles. She had always been there to mend his scrapes and soothe away his tears with a kiss and a loving smile. His father had been a remote figure, only glimpsed in the school holidays when de Born returned to the family estate, while uncle Philip had closely supervised his upbringing and education. Ever since the old marquis had been hacked down by the billhooks of a drunken peasant mob intent on destroying the manorial archives his father was so determinedly guarding, de Born had regarded Stephens as his sole mentor, and himself as a son to the childless couple.

His uncle had given him an allowance, paid his debts and, after he had sold his commission, secured a position for him in the Paris embassy. After what had happened there, Stephens had taken de Born into the External Department at the Admiralty to act as his personal agent. In the last year de Born had, under his uncle's tutelage, learnt more than in all his previous thirty-odd years, had been cosseted by his aunt and fiercely protected by Pingo and McPheat.

Abruptly he realized that his uncle was asking him a question.

"How would you feel, John, at the prospect of returning to France?" He studied de Born intently, looking for any sign of hesitation or fear.

"In wartime?" asked de Born, puzzled. "How is that possible?"

"Never mind the how of it, just answer my question, if you please," demanded Stephens.

De Born was keenly aware that his uncle's eyes were searching his face.

"Of course, sir, I am at your service." He felt a rush of excitement. And yet.

"May one enquire, sir, what task you would have me perform?" he asked with a poor pretence at sang-froid.

"Certain august personages are to be removed from their captivity and returned to England," Stephens said cryptically, still trying to divine the slightest reluctance on de Born's part. "You may be asked to assist this process."

At that moment, Stephens' secretary entered and told him that the gentlemen were now assembled and required his presence. Receiving no response, he added nervously, "The message reads 'forthwith'."

Stephens, seemingly content with de Born's response to his questions, sprang to his feet, asked the secretary whether his carriage was ready and, without waiting for an answer, swept out of the office - successively jamming on his wig and hat - along the hallway to the portico. There he paused at the coach's step and called out their destination to the coachman.

"Downing Street. And be quick."

*　*　*

As the carriage rumbled along Whitehall before turning jerkily into Downing Street, de Born's mind teemed with thoughts of Paris. That very morning all London had been agog at news of the Queen's execution in The Times and he knew from his boxing partners amongst the Foreign Office 'nursery' clerks that the city was now a dangerous place to be for its own inhabitants - never mind an émigré outlaw in the pay of the British. His excitement was already wearing off. Fear, remembered fear, was driving it away.

Even at that late hour, Downing Street was alive with the linkboys' lights, scurrying messengers, lounging footmen, anxious equerries and weary clerks. A crush of carriages was stationed from the end of the cul de sac right up to the door of Lord Sheffield's house. The drivers had set up a brazier by the Foreign Office and stood around gossiping about their betters and smoking their foul pipes, while their charges whinnied and stamped their hooves restlessly.

As they bustled into Number 10, de Born just had time to notice two gentlemen warming themselves by the fire in the hall. He noticed that his uncle gave the older of the two a sharp look. As they were making their way up the corridor, Stephens suddenly stopped.

"Remember, boy, speak only when you are spoken to directly. And not before. Keep your wits about you at all times - never lose concentration in the business at hand. If you are in any - " here he prodded de Born's arm for emphasis, - "any doubt, look to me for a lead."

Having been announced, they climbed the stairs to the first floor and entered a small, slightly shabby room containing a table, some chairs, a sécretaire and four men. Three of the men were seated at the table in front of the fireplace, while the fourth, in the uniform of a Light Dragoons colonel, stood with his back to them, gazing out over Horse Guards.

One of the men coughed gently and, the noise breaking his

reverie, the officer at the window turned, a silvery decoration at his breast gleaming in the candlelight. De Born looked at the Garter star and then quickly up to the face of its royal recipient. And a fat, handsome, dissipated, weak, sly face it was, with the ruddy cheeks, rheumy eyes and veined nose of a heavy drinker and the dyed, thinning curls of a roué. His high collar cut deeply into his double chin. The pungent aroma of his eau-de-Cologne flooded the room.

"With Your Royal Highness' permission, may I introduce my nephew, the marquis de Born," said Stephens, making his bow.

"I am very glad to meet you, Monsieur le marquis, very glad indeed. Your uncle tells me you are exactly what we require for this difficult task," said the Prince of Wales amiably.

De Born murmured his thanks, intrigued by this royal apparition, but very conscious that the real power in the room had not yet recognized his presence.

"Please do sit with the others. My complaint forces me to stand, but that's no reason for you to be inconvenienced, eh, Mr Secretary," the Prince said to Stephens, motioning them towards the table. De Born had not the faintest idea what possible complaint could result in such lèse-majesté, but knew with utter certainty that to enquire would be to attract the most glacial of all his uncle's repertoire of icy stares.

None of the trio rose to greet them. Indeed, two of them barely looked up from their papers, and then only to grunt a greeting at Stephens. The third, however, appraised de Born frankly. In contrast to the Prince's military finery, this man was simply dressed in a plain, dark blue coat and white stock. He was in his thirties, thin and, evident even when seated, tall. De Born had seen Pitt many times before in the House but never with the advantage of such proximity. He was shocked to see the lines of suffering and pain etched in the face of a man still only in his early thirties. The dark eyes gave him a look of determination and the cupid's bow mouth told of someone used to getting his own way. A plain, intelligent face, made forbidding only by the heavy scar on his cheek.

"You are most welcome, Monsieur le marquis," Pitt said in his odd, shy manner. "Please attend while the Foreign Secretary and I continue our business. We shall reach the reason for your attendance at this meeting presently. Pray continue, William," he said, turning to his right, whereupon Grenville took up his papers and began to read in a confident bark.

"On the 3rd of October last, forty of these Girondins were arrested, accused of conspiring against the unity and indivisibility of the Republic and against the liberty and safety of the French people. The Duke of Orléans was taken at the same time."

"What will his fate be?" asked Pitt.

"The fate of all damned regicides, I would hope," came an indignant voice from the window. Wearily Pitt signed Grenville to continue.

"You, sir," continued Grenville, inclining his head towards Pitt, "are unanimously declared the enemy of the human race by the Convention, but you will be glad to learn," here the Foreign Secretary gave a wintry smile, "that they stopped short of decreeing that every man had the right to assassinate you."

"Most gratifying," said Pitt, who had hardly taken his eyes off de Born since he sat at the table.

"What of the forces loyal to the crown?" asked the Prince.

"Sir, the loyalist forces in the Vendée were routed at Cholet on the 17th. Our agents, with what is left of General La Rochejaquelin's army, report two thousand executions at St Florent, four thousand at Nantes.

"These last," Grenville said in an even tone that belied the accompanying disgust in his eyes, "were executed - massacred, I should say - in mass drownings. At a place called Gonnord our agents observed General Crouzat's men order two hundred old people, together with a number of women and children, to kneel in front of a large pit they had been forced to dig themselves. They were then shot so as to tumble into their own graves. Those who attempted to flee were struck down by a mason's hammer." Grenville's glance at de Born was full of loathing. "It seems, Monsieur le marquis," Grenville spat, "that thirty of these children and two women were buried alive by your countrymen when the earth was shovelled into the pit."

For a few moments there was a profound silence in the room. De Born deliberately studied the inkstand on the baize-covered table, determined not to give the man the satisfaction of a response.

"Am I to believe that all internal resistance to these maniacs is effectively at an end?" asked Pitt, with a petulant frown.

"Yes, sir," said Grenville. "The French say that their Republic consists in the extermination of everything that opposes it. And by God they mean it."

De Born burned with indignation. His countrymen indeed. It was his countrymen that were doing the dying. It was his countrymen who had been deserted by the British when they failed to disembark the promised forces and *matériel* on the French coast earlier that year. He felt Stephens' restraining hand apply a firm, warning pressure to his arm.

Pitt was silent for what seemed to de Born like several minutes. His brother John, First Lord of the Admiralty, yawned and, drawing an ivory pick from a gold case, proceeded to excavate the noble dentition.

Grenville waited patiently while Pitt digested this news. "Turning to the body politic," he continued tentatively, waiting to see if he had

Pitt's full attention, "our agent on the Committee of Pub ..." and stopped abruptly with a quick look at de Born, aghast at his error.

So, thought de Born, we have a man at the very heart of the French government. Pitt's voice, like a whip-crack, interrupted his thoughts.

"You will not repeat that intelligence to anyone outside of this room," he said, staring hard at de Born.

"My word on it, sir," replied de Born hastily.

Satisfied, Pitt turned again to Grenville, who had by this time mastered his embarrassment. "What does our contact," he emphasised the word carefully, "say of the man d'Anton?"

"In brief, finished," Grenville said. "He dallies with his child bride in the country and spends our money with abandon, but his influence is on the wane, whilst that of Maximilien de Robespierre increases daily."

"Can we not bribe this fellow as we did with all the others?" asked John Pitt, in the lazy drawl familiar to de Born.

"Our man thinks not," said Grenville, irritated by the interruption. "In my opinion, we will not receive any co-operation in this matter from any member of the French government. If we are intent on removing the boy from Paris we must rely solely on our own efforts and resources."

At the mention of a child, de Born was perplexed. From his

uncle's words he had naturally assumed that 'august personages' referred either to the Prince of Wales' bosom friend, Sir William Codrington (the Prince's extraordinary presence had seemed to confirm the theory) or Colonel Richard Grenville, Pitt's cousin. Both had been taken the previous week by the French, as part of the wholesale arrest of British subjects for use as hostages. Who on earth could ... ? De Born's mind stopped dead. My God, he's talking of the ..

"Yes, de Born." Pitt had seen the direction his thoughts had been leading. "You have guessed it. We - you, in fact - are going to rescue the Dauphin."

CHAPTER TWO

Wednesday, October 23rd, 1793

De Born sat stunned. Only a few hours ago he had been engaged in a humiliating errand in the most sordid part of Covent Garden and now he was sitting in a Downing Street chamber whilst the heir to the throne and His Majesty's First Lord of the Treasury were calmly discussing with the Secretary of State for Foreign Affairs the abduction of the boy King of France. A boy, moreover, who was imprisoned in - of all places - Paris. He could feel the sweat gathering on his palms. As he wiped them on his breeches, he thought with regret of that bottle of brandy he had declined at The Somerset. Paris. They must be mad to think of sending him back there after what had happened. He shifted uncomfortably in his chair.

"You wish to say something?" asked Pitt.

"No sir, well, it's just ... " de Born struggled to get his mind working again after the shock. "Begging your pardon, sir, but - why?"

"Because those are your instructions," retorted Grenville, only to be cut short by a wave of Pitt's hand.

"No, William," Pitt said with a reproving frown at Grenville's boorishness. "This young man may be going to a place of great danger, even death. It is fitting that he should understand the reasons for it.

"It is important to grasp, de Born, that this war we are engaged upon is not pursued in order to restore the Bourbons to their throne," said Pitt, glancing for a moment towards the figure at the window, "nor to punish the French for their predilection for butchering women and children in the name of liberty. It is being pursued to check French aggression towards other sovereign states on the Continent, restore traditional frontiers; and to re-affirm the binding power of treaties entered into freely." De Born nodded in a manner he hoped showed an intelligent understanding of the situation. "Nevertheless, it is our duty to help those forces loyal to the Crown as best we can," Pitt continued, still staring at de Born as if appraising his response, "and to that end we need a figurehead that will bind these forces together."

"I understand perfectly, sir," said de Born. "But with respect, the Dauphin is a mere boy and, in addition, one who is kept in close confinement in the heart of the capital. Why not use his uncle, the comte de Provence, as the figurehead you desire? Monsieur is after all experienced in matters of state and is, furthermore, at liberty in Turin."

"Because," began Pitt before his voice was drowned out by the Prince's bellow of "Because mon cher cousin, that pusillanimous sack of lard, is a scheming, Janus-faced, untrustworthy liar."

"Because," Pitt began again quietly, "with his Royal Highness' indulgence, the late king's brother is not the heir to the throne and as such can never command the wholehearted support of those forces inimical to the revolutionary government."

"Are there perchance any other matters of which you wish to be informed?" enquired Grenville with heavy sarcasm.

"Yes My Lord," replied de Born evenly, determined not to surrender to Grenville's arrogance. "What intelligence does His Majesty's government possess as to the nature of the Dauphin's confinement and to the difficulties of extracting him from it?"

Pitt smiled at de Born's boldness and, for the first time that evening, de Born began to see the qualities of charm that commanded the loyalty of older men and which had made Pitt the greatest statesman in Europe. "We must endeavour to satisfy his lordship's curiosity, William," Pitt murmured and, leaning forward, grasped a small bell which lay on the table and gave it two sharp rings.

A cheerful-looking secretary with a quill stuck behind his ear thrust his head around a door behind the pillars at the end of the room.

"Andrew, be so good as to ask our visitors to attend us," said Pitt.

At the word 'visitors' Grenville raised an interrogatory eyebrow but, as Pitt seemed disinclined to elaborate, subsided sulkily into his seat.

The private secretary ushered in two gentlemen, who turned out to be the foreign-looking types who had been warming themselves by the hall fire. De Born noticed an instantaneous rise in the level of tension in the room. Grenville gave a violent start, while Lord Chatham shot an appraising glance at his brother and gave a long, languid whistle of surprise.

"I believe you know these gentlemen, General," Pitt said to the elder of the two, "with the possible exceptions of Colonel Cornwall," indicating, to de Born's surprise, the Prince of Wales, "and your fellow countryman, le marquis de Born."

The Prince's frigid nod disconcerted the visitor with the long pointed nose, full lips and arrogant eyes, who, turning to meet de Born's respectful bow, said simply, "My name is Dumouriez. This is my aide-de-camp, the Duc de Chartres."

De Born studied the couple as they took their seats at the table. He had read a great deal about Dumouriez in the journals. Of his stunning victories at Valmy and Jemappes commanding the French army. And his amazing desertion and subsequent flight to England. Somehow he had imagined a more dashing figure, much different from this lawyerish-looking individual with his long pointed nose and receding brow.

His aide, Louis-Philippe (son of the Duke of Orleans so recently damned by the Prince and the great, great grandson of King Louis XIII and therefore a first cousin removed of the boy in the Temple prison), was much less of a disappointment. The colourful uniform glaring out from under his travelling cloak was a riot of gilt frogging, bullion braid, gleaming high boots and spotless buckskin breeches.

Grenville could contain himself no longer. "Damme, I protest, sir. This is intolerable," he spluttered. "I personally ordered this man run out of the kingdom not six months ago and now I see him before me yet again. By whose orders was this renegade brought here, and why?"

"By mine," said the Prince haughtily, "and, since you are so concerned with motives, Grenville, you should know that the General was brought here at great expense, inconvenience and secrecy to answer the very question the marquis de Born has just posed."

Grenville's anger quickly subsided into a sullen silence in the face of the royal broadside. Pitt began his interrogation of the General, who still had not recovered from the frightful experience of a lowly Colonel snubbing the Foreign Secretary.

"How long have you been acquainted with the Duke of Normandy, known as the Dauphin of France?" asked Pitt.

Dumouriez and Louis-Philippe exchanged puzzled glances. Whatever they had expected, it was not this.

"I have been personally acquainted with His Most Christian Majesty, whom God preserve," began Dumouriez, only to be stopped by Pitt's raised hand.

"Indulge me, General, by not referring to the Dauphin as the King of France. He has not yet been crowned," Pitt said in his characteristically precise way.

"Nevertheless, M'sieu," said Dumouriez with a Gallic shrug.

"Nevertheless," Pitt replied stonily, "he is not recognized by His Britannic Majesty's government as the monarch of that unhappy land."

"As you will, sir," said Dumouriez, bewildered but anxious to placate Pitt's evident displeasure. "I saw the Dauphin many times when I attended the late King at Versailles, requiescat in pace," Dumouriez said, crossing himself.

"His portraits show the prince without distinguishing marks," Pitt said. "Does he have any peculiarities of face or limb by which he could be definitively identified?"

"Yes, sir," answered Dumouriez eagerly. "He has the marks of smallpox vaccinations high on both arms and the mark of an animal bite, a rabbit I believe, under his chin."

A faint jangle of spurs caught Pitt's attention.

"Does Your Grace wish to add something?" asked Pitt.

"If I may, sir," said Louis-Philippe, stiffening to attention. "The

Dauphin has a peculiarity known only to family members of which the General must perforce be unaware. His right ear is badly misshapen, the inferior lobe being much larger than is normal. Like mine" Louis-Philippe continued, pushing away a lock of hair to reveal the Capetian abnormality, "it is normally kept concealed by the length of his hair."

"We are in your debt, Duke," said Pitt with a gracious bow. Louis-Philippe beamed with obvious pleasure.

"Now, as to the Dauphin's confinement, General," continued Pitt. "What intelligence could you provide as to the circumstances of his confinement?"

"Before discussing this undoubtedly interesting and important subject," said Dumouriez, evidently still mystified by the turn the conversation had taken, "may I once again request that I be allowed to return to London openly, to reside here and be afforded such courtesies as befit my rank and station?"

At this de Born noticed Grenville's face growing crimson with rage.

"So that you can plot and conspire with your friends in the Convention behind our backs, no doubt," he hissed. "I'll see you in Hades first." Leaning over the table, Grenville slammed his open palm down to emphasize his words. "I shall not allow your treachery to your own country to be rewarded with the opportunity to practise the same treason here in London."

"It was not treachery, My Lord," replied Dumouriez angrily, yet unable to keep the defensive note out of his voice. "I was calumniated by an odious cabal of Jacobin criminals who plotted the fall of the generals and more especially mine own. When they kept my brother officers in that filthy jail to Septembrise them at their leisure, I was forced to leave."

"Septembrise, General, what do you mean?" asked the 'Colonel', puzzled by the unfamiliar expression.

De Born suddenly felt the blood pounding in his temples at the memory of September 1792. He desperately wanted a drink. There was a decanter on the table but he did not dare to help himself.

"He means murder, sir," he burst out, before Dumouriez had a chance to answer. "The expression derives from the jail massacres in Paris last year."

"Let us not be diverted, gentlemen, from the topic under discussion by talk of these unsavoury matters," Pitt said silkily, irritated that the meeting had plunged off the path he had so carefully constructed.

De Born could bear it no longer. Provoked by Grenville's insults, Dumouriez' oily and treacherous speeches and above all by the sudden memory of those awful September days, his control finally snapped.

"Unsavoury, Mr Pitt? Unsavoury?" He could feel Stephens' eyes boring into him, but he could not stop. "Would you call it 'unsavoury' if your wife were to be treated as I saw the Princess de Lamballe treated in La Force prison? Forced to climb a mound of freshly slaughtered corpses. Raped and disembowelled whilst still alive. Her tripes used as ribbons for hats." The ugly words kept pouring out. "Her head then hacked off with a butcher's knife and set upon a pike to be paraded in the streets."

For a moment Pitt was silent, his gaze directed to his long, bony hands steepled before him. "I am in fact unmarried, de Born," he said coldly, "but that does not prevent me from understanding your distress at witnessing such a vile barbarity. Nor would I wish to leave the impression that the murder of those innocents is a matter for anything other than the severest condemnation." The other men nodded automatically and murmured their agreement. "God, I trust, will deal with their murderers; I must deal with the living." He was very angry.

"I apologise, sir," said de Born stiffly, ashamed that his feelings had overwhelmed him and conscious that he had in one fell swoop smashed a unique opportunity to re-establish his career.

"You must forgive my nephew, sir," said Stephens. "He did not mean to imply that you ... " His voice trailed away.

Pitt's expression softened. "You do not have to defend your

nephew, Philip," he said, looking fondly at the older man. "Indeed, his sentiments do him credit. We have all too easily become too inured to this bestial violence that surrounds us. He at least remains outraged by the outrageous and sickened by the sickening."

Stephens bowed in gratitude.

"Now gentlemen," said Pitt briskly, "shall we return to the matter in hand? Do we have your assurances, General, that you are not, as the Lord Grenville suggests, in league with the revolutionary government in Paris?"

"Mr Pitt, surely you do not give credence to such bizarre suggestions?" replied Dumouriez, glancing disdainfully at the still furious Grenville. *"Quand même,* to bring an end to these vile disorders which cover all France in mourning and to destroy the odious tyranny of these monstrous anarchists, it may occasionally be necessary to treat with some of these criminals - purely on a temporary basis, you understand."

As Dumouriez appealed to each man at the table de Born caught a blast of his fetid breath.

Pitt rose from his chair and advanced on Dumouriez in a cold fury. "I had thought, General, that your motive for coming here was to help us in our efforts to bring an end to the crimes and calamities that menace France. I see now that you seek only your own advantage. *Tant pis!* To prolong your stay in this kingdom will perhaps present you and your suite with too many inconveniences. Perhaps you would feel more comfortable in, say, Vienna."

"But sir, I'd planned to ... " Dumouriez' panicky speech was interrupted by the Prince, who, forgetting yet again his role as a lowly officer in the previous play-acting, reverted to his natural hauteur.

"You have our permission to withdraw, General."

Bewildered and dejected, Dumouriez nodded and, forgetting to bow, trailed miserably out of the room. Louis-Philippe executed a magnificent salute which took in the whole company, grinned knowingly at the Prince, whom he had recognized instantly, and exited smartly in a clattering of boot-heels and clanking spurs.

"Your pardon, sir," the Prince said in a low voice to Pitt. "My idea of bringing Dumouriez here was in error, as indeed you forecast. I see now that a man who will desert his country when at war makes a poor ally."

"Your Royal Highness is too hard on himself," Pitt said magnanimously. "Besides, we gained valuable intelligence concerning a sure identification of the Dauphin, is that not so, de Born?"

"Indeed it is, sir," said de Born, grateful to have been brought back into the discussion. "Yet, with respect, my question remains unanswered. How securely is the Dauphin held, and what difficulties may be encountered in such a rescue?"

"It seems there is only one true way to discover these facts," said Pitt. "You must go to Paris and discover the answers yourself. I have heard from your uncle how you rescued the Marquise de Tourzel and her daughter from 'La Force' prison and I am confident that your courage, quick wits and daring will be sufficient to complete the task. Are we agreed, My Lords?" Receiving a curt nod from Grenville and an indolent yawn from his brother, Pitt rose and shook de Born's hand. "I wish you good fortune, Monsieur le marquis."

Abruptly, with a scraping of chairs being pushed back from the table, the meeting was over.

As de Born made his bow he was surprised when the Prince grasped his hand and shook it heartily. "Good fortune attend you, de Born. His Majesty takes a keen interest in this venture, you know. Do not disappoint him, what? what?" laughing at his own expert mimicry of his father.

As he left the Cabinet chamber de Born glanced back to find Pitt still watching him. In his eyes there was a strange expression. Anxiety, thought de Born. Only later did he realize it was pity.

*   *   *

Stephens led the way to the door at the rear of Number Ten. De Born looked ruefully at the stiff, angry back of his uncle. What a fool I am, he thought. I make an enemy of the Foreign Affairs Secretary, insult the First Lord of the Treasury and embarrass my uncle in front of the Heir Apparent and the First Lord of the Admiralty - all in the space of a single hour. I still can't keep my nightmares about Paris from intruding into my waking thoughts, and I never seem to know when to shut up and just let others talk. When will I ever learn?

This bout of self-flagellation ceased at the garden door, when he saw Pingo and McPheat, torches in hand, waiting in the mist from the canal in St James Park that enveloped Horse Guards.

"No time for dawdling," said Stephens, urging de Born to catch up. "Nor self-recrimination either. You sail from Portsmouth on the Justinian tomorrow night."

Taking a red leather portfolio from Pingo, he extracted a heavy linen document sealed with the Admiralty anchor and gave it to de Born. "Take this to Tellson's Bank at Temple Bar tomorrow morning and see Mr Jarvis Lorry. He will furnish you with the necessary funds. Remember, John, on no account are you to attempt the rescue of the Dauphin without reporting all the circumstances back to me first," Stephens emphasized. "No heroics or dashes for glory, eh?"

De Born nodded soberly in acknowledgement.

"Having entered Paris, you will go to *Le Chat Gris* in the Rue Béranger every day at 11 o'clock until you are contacted. Remember, boy," Stephens said, "you are to wait until he approaches you and not vice versa. He will ask you if you are a 'travelling man'. Answer him, 'Yes I am' - those words exactly, mind. He will ask, 'Where are you travelling?' You will answer, 'From west to east.' He will then hold his right hand waist high and palm down, like this," Stephens said, demonstrating, "as if swearing on a Bible. You will raise your left hand in acknowledgement, like this. This man may be trusted absolutely.

"Lastly," said Stephens, turning to Pingo, who held the portfolio out to him again, "take this and wear it always." He pressed something cold and round into de Born's hand. Looking down he saw that it was a curious kind of antique amulet. On the face he could just make out an all-seeing eye atop a pyramid surrounded by the letters TGAOTU in old-fashioned script.

"It was your father's," Stephens told him. "He told me once that he dreamt it would save your life one day. If you are ever in danger, show it and say this word." He glanced at Pingo, who moved off discreetly, and, leaning forward, whispered it into de Born's ear. De Born smelt his familiar odour of snuff and old age .

"You have your orders. Trust in God and the Board of Admiralty and all will be well." He took de Born's hand in his. It felt dry and warm. "Goodbye John. I too am relying on you."

De Born stood for a few moments watching him walk stiffly towards the Admiralty, until the light from Pingo's torch and the sound of his uncle's cane tapping on the cobbles died in the gloom, then turned for home.

That night he dreamed yet again of La Force.

CHAPTER THREE

Thursday, October 24th, 1793

The girl who entered de Born's bedroom on tip-toe was about fourteen, dark-haired with china blue eyes. She placed a tray containing a pot of chocolate and two rolls onto a dumb waiter by the fireplace, removing an untouched meal and a claret jug as she did so. She checked the jug's contents and frowned when she saw it was completely empty. Then she stood for a moment looking at the narrow camp bed, craning to see more than the portion of black hair that was poking above the covers. The clock on the mantel struck the quarter chime, which seemed to galvanize the girl into action. She went to the window and opened the shutters with the maximum of banging wood and clanging iron until a muffled noise was heard from the bed. At this she grinned impishly and tripped out of the room, slamming the door shut with a tremendous crash for good measure. De Born, who had heard his landlady's daughter long before she even reached his bedroom, smiled. Little minx. He swung himself out of the bed, put on a robe of scarlet damask and poured his chocolate.

The room was large and airy, with two windows facing onto Pickering Court. Apart from the bed and the dumb waiter, it contained a walnut bachelor chest, on whose brushing slide stood a double medallion portrait in miniature of a man and a woman dressed in the fashion of thirty years before, a solitary candlestick and a woman's pyrope garnet ring. Arrayed around the walls were a wash-stand, linen press, tray-top commode and an iron strong-box.

A door led off the bedroom to a room of similar size painted with ochre. Similarly neat and austere, it contained a single library chair, a tripod table, a Canterbury full of old copies of The Spectator, and an imposing sécretaire bookcase. A copy of Paine's Rights of Man was open on the flap, half of its pages cut. The bookcase contained works, mostly in French or Latin, of history or political philosophy. Herodotus, Josephus, Tacitus, of course, and Dio Cassius stood next to Hobbes, Locke, Harington and Voltaire. Here and there was an oddity like della Porta's classic work on codes and cyphers. On the walls there was an untitled watercolour of what looked like a French château, two Gillrays - both extremely disrespectful to the royal family, and a stick barometer.

De Born wandered into the sitting room, chewing the bread, and stood looking out of the window, running over the previous day's meeting and playing absent-mindedly with the amulet hanging from his neck, repeatedly twisting it to and fro. The previous night's enthusiasm had now disappeared completely. If he were to be caught, which he judged more likely than not, his fate was certain - torture then summary execution. If he failed to get the boy out and back to London, his career was finished, uncle or no uncle. He went over to the bookcase and reached for a flask of Cognac concealed behind Hobbes' Leviathan. After a few moments gazing at it, he put it back in its place and locked the bookcase doors.

* * *

Leaving through the paved yard in front of the house, he paused to listen to the familiar sounds of his landlady, the redoubtable signora Carloni, alternately beating a turkey rug and the amply proportioned behind of Luca, her ne'er-do-well progeny and brother of the impish Gabriella. He would miss their intimate gossips in the snug, steamy kitchen full of hanging onions and flitches, her cheerful homicide of the English language and her determined but fruitless struggle to rid the house of fleas and bed bugs by the liberal application of turpentine. Catching her eye through the window, he blew her an extravagant kiss and, in a sweeping gesture of his arm against an imaginary derrière, encouraged her in her retributory tasks.

Emerging from the dark corridor leading onto St James Street, the low October sunlight dazzled de Born momentarily. As his eyes accustomed themselves to the white glare he saw Pingo and McPheat desist their lounging by Lock's and fall into step. As always, Pingo went afore, clearing a path with just his chilling glare, and the stoat-like McPheat followed aft, rhythmically swinging his ever-present hercules and muttering vague threats and imprecations against all and sundry.

Ever since he was relieved of his duties at the Paris embassy the previous year, following the prison massacres, de Born's two bodyguards had shadowed him day and night. He had been uncomfortable with this arrangement at first, but his uncle's insistence on taking precautions and the salutary effect of a shooting incident on Rotten Row had convinced de Born. The reports that Robespierre had personally ordered his assassination were, it seemed, true. For the past few weeks de Born had been unable to shrug off the feeling that he was being watched - studied, even. Pingo swore blind that they were not, but once or twice de Born had turned sharply to see someone all too attentively interested in a haberdasher's window or a newspaper.

Pingo was an imposing and much recognized figure on the city's streets. A challenger for the British championship, he had been brutally beaten only after a lengthy and bloody contest with the Jew Mendoza, after which Stephens had hired him to protect de Born. McPheat had been caught one foggy night, grappling for loot from the Gordon riots in the St James Square basin, and had been offered transportation or Admiralty service. Separately they were formidable: Pingo's sledgehammer fists and McPheat's vicious expertise with the club were both legend. Together they were invincible protection against the French government's hired assassins. On the street the trio were generally given a wide berth. De Born was obviously someone of note. It was not just his clothes, although he was easily spotted for a man of fashion, but more his fluid, easy walk - not lordly or arrogant, as one might expect, but strikingly self-confident. His air of self-containment was also very evident to the onlooker. Indeed, people invariably apologised for speaking to him first, as though they were needlessly breaking into some private meditation of great importance. While Pingo and McPheat worked up a sweat, pushing and shoving, swearing and threatening their way through the crowds, de Born was the calm eye-spot, leaving in his wake a trail of disappointed ladies whom he had not recognized, jealous gallants, interested pick-pockets and affronted citizens whose feathers Pingo had ruffled or whose delicate feelings McPheat had trampled.

"Well, nephew," said Pingo out of the corner of his mouth. "Where to today?"

De Born, who had long since ceased to rise to Pingo's satirical references concerning the iniquities of nepotism, merely grinned and then, fingering his chin, ordered "Truefitts. I need a shave."

They walked up towards Bond Street, ignoring the blandishments of the brawny men at the sedan chair stand. In the middle of the street chariots rattled, brewers' sledges growled and an unending stream of carriages, chaises and drays rolled by. At every step, above the hum and din of a hundred voices, de Born could hear the piercing cries of the street-sellers and the whores, the chimes of church towers, the clatter of horses' hooves on the cobbles, the newspaper sellers' trumpets and the postman's bell. These fought to be heard against the cacophony of organs and fiddles and hurdy-gurdies which echoed off the grand facades of the yellow-brick houses. On the corner of King Street the roaring of the knife-grinder's stone and the braying of his donkey mixed with the snarls of fighting dogs and the shouts of club servants wagering on the result.

Outside Kelsey's floated the sweet smell of roasting apples, mixing in with the pungency of horse shit, damp clothes, stale sweat, spilt beer, soot, cat's meat, rotting vegetables and sea-coal fires. Everywhere was energy, purpose and speed. As they drew closer to Bond Street de Born felt something of his old self, the one before Paris, coming alive again. He decided that he would not take another drink until he got back from Paris.

*　　*　　*

His welcome at Truefitt's was genuinely warm. De Born had the knack of dealing with all manner of servants; he was comfortable in his own station and his friendliness was neither forced nor patronising, but based on his insatiable curiosity concerning the lives of everyone who surrounded him. Besides, he tipped well.

As he sat down in the proffered chair his eye was caught by a print stuck on a nail above the window. Noticing his gaze, the barber took it down and gave it to him for a closer look. It showed Talma, the famous Parisian actor in the role of Titus in Voltaire's 'Brutus'. His hair was dressed in the Roman fashion, short and without powder. De Born was seized by a sudden inspiration.

"This style is all the fashion in Paris, I suppose?" he asked idly.

"Indeed yes, Monsieur le marquis," replied the barber. "Amongst *le bon ton* it is the very height of *à la mode*." De Born winced at his atrocious accent.

"I feel very Republican today," he said. "Pray style my hair in the same manner."

Emerging later to be greeted by an impudent wink from Pingo and

McPheat's puzzled squint, he felt a little self-conscious and jammed his hat down harder. Yet, after some admiring looks from the ladies in Conduit Street, his enthusiasm grew for pursuing this stratagem further.

"Through Vigo Lane to Sproat's," he said, answering Pingo's unasked question, "and then on to Tellson's."

As usual, Sproat the tailor stood at his window on the corner of Swallow Street lasciviously eyeing the daughters of the gentry and respectfully raising his hat to their mothers. At de Born's approach he flung open the door with a flourish and expressed himself 'astoundingly delighted and amazedly honoured' by the presence of his visitor. At least, that is what de Born thought he said. Sproat's Pictish brogue was sometimes so thick that for all de Born knew he may just as well have been damning his eyes and heartily wishing him dead.

Inside, a single coal in the grate struggled to warm the room, which felt to de Born considerably colder than the street.

"Can you copy this?" he asked, thrusting at Sproat a page from the Paris journal he had borrowed from the barber.

"Aye m'lud," said Sproat, peering doubtfully at the page in question, "but ye ken that this is nae the fashion?"

"Indeed?" replied de Born. "Perhaps I shall make it so."

"Aye well, nae doot," shrugged Sproat, used to the eccentricities of aristocratic whelps.

Smirking to himself as he left, de Born set off in a chair for Tellson's at Temple Bar, where he presented his uncle's letter to the ponderous Mr Jarvis Lorry.

"French gold louis and paper assignats, I see, My Lord," said the man of business, eyeing him with curiosity.

"Payments to emigrés, I believe, Mr Lorry," de Born said, assuming the air of a man who neither knew nor cared what the money was for.

"Just so," said Mr Lorry politely, but his look communicated his disbelief both in de Born's professed ignorance and in his feeble story.

Handing the heavy canvas bag to Pingo, who on receipt assumed an even more ferocious expression the better to guard it, de Born retraced his steps until he reached the Hay Market. Stopping by a doorway beside Fribourg & Treyer, he entered what seemed from its exterior to be unoccupied and shuttered premises, leaving McPheat on guard outside. Inside was an empty, oak-panelled room which led by way of an uncovered yard to a workshop at the rear. There he found Whitehead, the gunsmith, talking seriously to his foreman.

De Born set about explaining his requirements. The gun should be very light, be suitable for close-quarter work and easy to conceal. Whitehead frowned on hearing the last point and began to pace up and down the yard, his snowy thatch (which had finally given truth to his name) bobbing up and down as he argued with himself. At last his expression brightened and he began to make a rapid sketch on the back of a waste piece of card.

Initially de Born could not follow the meaning of the lines until all of a sudden his eyes widened in surprise at the gunsmith's solution. On the card he saw the outline of a walking stick, the handle being at right-angles to the length of the cane. Whitehead chuckled, partly at his own cleverness, partly at his customer's delighted reaction.

"Propelled by air, not powder, that's the secret," he said proudly. "The trigger folds against the stick like so, while the handle acts as the pump reservoir. It takes small shot - I'll supply you with a special mould, although you could use sling shot at a pinch. It's deadly if fired at the unprotected head from within a yard. At a clothed body it will wound severely, but only if the gun is near - or, better still, touching - the torso."

"When can I have it?" de Born asked.

"Next week, say?" replied Mr Whitehead.

"Not good enough. It must be tomorrow," insisted de Born.

Sensing his determination, Whitehead shrugged and assented. "It will cost treble, My Lord," he warned, bowing him out of the shop, "but it will be ready in the forenoon."

* * *

Thoroughly satisfied with the day's work, de Born pulled out a handsome Breguet *perpetuelle* and, seeing it was close on four o'clock, made for 'La Toque Blanche', the 'ordinary' in Suffolk Street run by French emigrés.

De Born generally avoided the company of his fellow citizens as they were now called. Many were spies, and most of those that weren't he considered worthless, aristo trash. Endlessly whingeing over their fate and always quick to complain about their hosts, they were invariably foppish, arrogant, stupid, titled nobodies who made de Born ashamed of his native land. The English had no time for them either, although they happily ogled their pretty, empty-headed women. Emigrés also bothered de Born in a more fundamental and important way. If this worthless collection of guillotine fodder represented the ancien régime, who could possibly argue that it should be restored? The old way of life had been reduced to a boy in the Temple prison - who was to be a pawn of the British - and the boy's two uncles, both plainly unfit to rule. To oppose the murderous tyranny of the Jacobins may be the obvious course of action for a free-born Frenchman, thought de

Born, but when they fell, what then should replace them? It was a familiar internal debate, invariably sparked off by the sight of emigrés, and one he disliked intensely as it was never resolved.

He made an exception of avoiding the French when it came to this particular restaurant. He opened the street door and his nostrils were immediately invaded by the reason why. These were the smells of his native *coin*. Morels, cèpes and girolles doused in walnut oil. Goose necks stuffed with spicy sausage-meat. Chicken stewed in inky wine from Cahors. Wild boar smoked and sliced with shallots. White confits of truffled duck and whole goose livers, glistening palest pink from the corn gavage. Great pungent bûches of Castillonès chèvre. Rising above all this was the celestial aroma of the king - he corrected himself - nay emperor of flavours (and horror of all right-thinking Englishmen) - roasting Limousin garlic.

Here de Born was again in the lost country of childhood. Running to the kitchen of his father's château at Born. Hiding from his tutor inside the great box settles in the ingle-nook. Stealing chicken legs from the cauldron that hung suspended from the iron wall-cranes and teasing the red-faced, roly-poly, perspiring cook.

Here at 'La Toque Blanche' even the coffee was good, a miracle in London, where all the cooks in the metropolis were engaged in a gigantic conspiracy to see who could produce the foulest-tasting liquid possible and still have the English call it coffee.

After dinner he returned to Pickering Court and took out a large portmanteau from the strong-box. Emptying its contents onto the bed he checked them thoroughly one by one. He spent some time cleaning and oiling a naval dirk, which he normally carried fitted into a groove inside a specially adapted pair of riding boots. The dirk had a 'Marmeluke' hilt which unscrewed to reveal a hollow wherein lay a tiny compass and a vial of prussic acid. The boots themselves had hollow heels. The left contained gold coins and the right a snare, plus hook and line.

Opening a small pouch, he checked the levels of the two bottles it contained, both labelled 'lavender water'. They were in fact filled with Jay's sympathetic stain and reagent respectively. This was not the customary method of concealed writing used by the External Department, but one recommended to a grateful de Born by a friend in the Alien Department at the Home Office.

Also in the pouch was a copy of Entick's *New Spelling Dictionary*, which was used for special coded messages of great significance by employing the standard 'page and line' method. In de Born's view, the 'Julius Caesar' code still used by many agents was suitable only for brief notes of no great import.

Next was a thin leather case containing rows of brass buttons left over from his time at the Paris embassy, all bearing some Republican symbol. Each one was hollow, with a detachable top large enough to carry a silk map or a rice-paper note. For a moment de Born stood debating with himself until, deciding he could trust to the close mouth of the tailor, he went to the window and tossed the case down to Pingo, telling him to go back to Sproat and instruct the tailor to attach the buttons to that morning's creation. Humming an air from 'Solomon' softly to himself, he carefully repacked all the objects, together with the canvas money-bag, into the portmanteau. At the last moment he threw in some extra items: a portable door lock, an American-made set of brass knuckles, a leather-bound spy glass and a minute 'overcoat' pistol. Then he locked the portmanteau and stowed it in the strong-box.

*　　*　　*

His last night in London was passed much as any other night. He went up to Brooks's (he had refused to join White's as smoking was forbidden there) and played Pope Joan with a few acquaintances from the Foreign Office. After losing a few guineas, he sauntered into the dining room for a light supper. Fox was dining with Talleyrand and carrying on a conversation with his deaf mute bastard in sign language.

The sight of one of the most ardent English supporters of the Revolution provoked de Born to contemplate what might happen to his adopted country. De Born wondered how these noble gamblers would fare if the London mob ever took it into its very small head to storm the Palace and cry revolution. Would John Bull erect a guillotine in Berkeley Square? Would the village parson be reviled and beaten? Would Fox call his valet 'citizen'? Somehow de Born doubted it. Although truly only a tolerated outsider, he had come to admire the English for their dull honesty, robust independence, even their infuriating air of superiority. When he thought of the day labourers and goose girls on his father's estates, with their bovine, sullen resentment and the squalor of their wretched huts, and then compared them with the breezy ploughmen and spirited dairymaids on his uncle's land in their sturdy cottages, he no longer thought (as once he had) that England would inevitably follow its neighbour into chaos. Here they called their King 'Old Nobbs' and delighted in stories of his love for writing letters to farming journals. In their cups de Born's gambling partners may call him 'Johnny Crapaud' and 'frog-eater', but this was just thoughtless high spirits and only those with a very thin skin would have taken offence. If he called them 'rosbifs', or 'goddams' in return, they just laughed the harder and called for yet another bottle of port to toast their new name.

That night de Born was restless and loathe to leave for his bed, so he persuaded some of the company to make up a party for the play at Drury Lane. Although he hated the noise of the pit and the suffocating heat of its crowded flesh, his spirit needed a distraction and maybe a glimpse of Polly Wilkes (daughter of the notorious '45' Wilkes), a lively, pretty young thing he had been pursuing for weeks - as yet in vain. In the event, as the play was damnably dull, Polly nowhere to be seen and his friends beastly drunk, de Born slipped away early, hailed a chair, dismissed Pingo and went home to bed.

He was woken the next morning by the rain rattling at his window. The early part of the day was taken up with packing his clothes, including Sproat's chef-d'oeuvre and taking delivery of the Whitehead gun-stick, which he tested successfully against the trunk of the old linden tree that grew in the courtyard. A postchaise having been hired, he set off for Portsmouth with Pingo beside him and McPheat acting as an extra postillion.

After a dreary journey through the rain under an ever worsening sky, de Born's party arrived at the Justinian tired, hungry and irritable. They were greeted by a lanky, raw-boned midshipman, who conducted them with the captain's compliments to a neat cabin where a meal of overdone beefsteak and mealy boiled potatoes was laid out. Eventually they were under way with the wind set fair but into a choppy sea. After an hour had passed the captain arrived with a sealed Admiralty package and asked, somewhat stiffly de Born thought, for a signature on the receipt. His refusal to stay and share de Born's supper was even colder. De Born became uncomfortably aware that the captain evidently thought that he should have better things to do than convey foreigners in the pay of the Espionage Service about the Channel. With a last glare of distaste for Pingo, he wished de Born a brusque good night and stamped off, swearing violently at the marine posted outside de Born's door.

The packet contained, as de Born had expected, his papers and a note from his uncle. He was now Charles Cheftel, a notaire from Villeréal, a small market town he knew well, close to Château Born itself. The accompanying note from his uncle explained that, due to the haste in which they were prepared and the ever-changing laws and regulations in wartime France, de Born was not to rely overmuch on these papers and to seek replacements in the same name as soon as he was established in Paris. Having carefully stowed them in his portmanteau, de Born went up on deck. This turned out to be an error of Homeric proportions. Below the motion of the ship had seemed comparatively regular, even soothing. Upstairs (de Born was vaguely aware that this was not a correct usage aboard one of His Majesty's vessels) the Justinian seemed to have taken on all the characteristics of a cork flung carelessly onto a heaving swell. Before he knew it, he was bent double over the rail and parting company from his supper. Above him came the distant but distinct laughter of the watch officers. Not wishing to stand about being the butt of such epauletted scorn, de Born retired to his cabin and dozed fitfully.

At Jersey he was transferred by gig to a corvette belonging to the secret royalist network called 'La Correspondance'. As the crew drew away from the Justinian he waved a laconic farewell to Pingo and McPheat standing at the gunwhale. It had been arranged that while McPheat would return to Portsmouth, Pingo would go on to Ostend and there wait until de Born should arrive, with or without the boy.

As dawn broke de Born saw a faint smudge of grey on the near horizon. He hugged the heavy boat cloak around him even closer. He could see the outline of a church spire poking up out of the mist about four miles to port. It was Mont St Michel. He was home.

CHAPTER FOUR

Quintidi, 5 Brumaire, Year II

As he stood on the lonely shingle beach looking up to the dunes, de Born felt the first familiar stirrings of tension in his stomach. He reached down into his coat pocket and felt the comforting shape of his flask. What lay beyond the sand was a land where nearly every hand was against him, and where he could trust no one. He took the flask out of his pocket and unscrewed the top. The slightest slip and the enemy would have him by the throat; yet, if he won through, the glory, more than could be imagined, was his alone. He watched as the Cognac dribbled into the sand at his feet. All or nothing.

He sat on a boulder and watched the unhurried preparations of the burly Breton peasants in their goatskin vests as they roped his portmanteau and trunk onto an uncomplaining mule. While at their work they chatted quietly to each other and he was amused to hear their surprise at seeing their visitor was a *milor' anglais* who looked so much like a good Frenchman.

Turning to the nearest man, he asked, "Do all Bretons chatter like dairymaids about their guests?" and received a shy, delighted smile in return. "A true French patriot among us," they called happily to one another in the darkness and ascended the narrow, winding path through the dunes to a barn on the outskirts of St Malo.

There, saddled horses had been provided for de Born and his two armed guides. The little group set off immediately for a succession of safe houses belonging to La Correspondance positioned at regular intervals along rarely used cart-tracks. Before each stop one guide would go the last furlong alone and, when near the house, make the 'toot-toot' call of the hoopoe. If there was no reply the party would move on and seek what shelter was available in the neighbouring woods and hedgerows.

At first the fact he was a lord, and the hardness they saw in his eyes, made the guides bashful in his presence. But soon the inevitable camaraderie of the journey and the small signs of nervous tension de Born displayed, in particular the incessant playing with the amulet around his neck, encouraged a greater degree of familiarity. What de Born learnt about the war from these conversations was depressing and discouraging, and it did nothing to resolve his debate as to the war's object. The boy in the Temple obviously meant little to the Bretons, who took orders only from their local leaders. Provence they considered a coward for deserting his brother and, at the mention of Artois' name, they merely spat on the ground in silent contempt. The war had bestialized them. All they respected now was revenge and blood, fear and death.

*   *   *

By the second night, de Born, who had not sat a horse for two months, was sorely chafed. Seeing his awkward gait, the farmer's wife insisted, to his great embarrassment and to the amusement of his guides, that he drop his breeches so she could administer handfuls of goose grease to the afflicted parts. At each farmhouse the welcome was the same. The farmer's wife would force gargantuan helpings on the men, while the farmer asked how the rebellion fared. The eldest son would solemnly guard the stable yard where they slept, and in the morning the giggling daughters of the house would bring them hot shaving water. Payment was always firmly refused.

The early November weather was unusually mild that year and, as each day passed, de Born felt some of the tension experienced on setting foot in France begin to fade and he started to take more interest in his surroundings.

Signs of the civil war were everywhere. Burnt-out cottages lined the route, some with their charred beams still smoking. Occasionally they would hear the furtive sounds of dispossessed peasants retreating from their approach, or catch a glimpse of a frightened old man hiding amongst the trees, too old and too tired to run. The lazy glides of the buzzards circling overhead announced an abundance of carrion lying on the forest floor, some of it human. Yet game abounded, with no one to shoot or trap it. De Born saw hares and foxes, even the odd badger. He heard the jays chattering to one another and the sparrowhawks' triumphant ululations as they swooped furiously onto their prey in the forest clearings.

*   *   *

It was with something of a shock that de Born greeted the news that his guides were to leave him. They had reached Chartres, where he was to wait for the Bordeaux-Paris diligence. Seeing a derelict wood-cutter's cabin near the track, de Born took the opportunity to change his travel-stained clothes. After handing his coat and breeches to one of the guides to be burnt, he put on Sproat's magnificent creation and emerged from the cabin to startled applause. He was now the very model of the provincial dandy come to Paris on important business. His stock had been replaced with an outrageously large cravat, over which he had a horizontally striped candy coat and lime knee breeches with delicate velvet pumps, all of which was topped off with a smart new bicorne hat.

In this guise he watched regretfully as his two brave companions turned for home and then set off, leading the mule, for the post inn which lay next to the town square.

The Paris diligence was late, but after an anxious hour de Born heard the yard ring with hooves and the postillions shouting for food. Securing a place in between a fat brewer from Poitiers and an officer convalescent from the Neerwinden campaign, de Born settled down to sleep.

It seemed no time before he was awoken by an unshaven National Guard sergeant thrusting his head inside the coach and demanding everyone's papers. They had reached Paris.

"Why aren't you wearing a cockade, citizen?" asked the soldier sharply, gesturing at de Born's hat.

Desperately, de Born manufactured a thin-sounding tale of losing it in the straw on the carriage floor. On hearing the accent de Born had assumed to match his new identity, full of the nasal twang of the south-west, the sergeant relaxed and volunteered that he himself came from Bergerac and it was good to hear French spoken properly 'after all these gabbling Parisians'. After a friendly warning that 'everyone must obey the law, even us Périgordins', he gave de Born the tricolour cockade from his own hat and waved a somewhat shaken de Born through the gate where the diligence was waiting. He realized that in the pleasant amble through the countryside his vigilance had relaxed too far. He had read reports of the new law enforcing the wearing of this revolutionary symbol on pain of imprisonment, but had simply forgotten to obtain one. It was just the sort of slip an amateur would make and he was furious with himself.

On leaving the coach, de Born sought lodgings in the Temple section, far from his old haunts. While there were few people left in Paris who would recognize him and recall his service at the embassy, he was in no mood to take chances. By afternoon he had secured rooms in the Rue Béranger near to the rendez-vous at *Le Chat Gris*.

That night de Born lay on his lumpy, straw-filled mattress listening to the sounds of the house. Next door a couple fought and then copulated noisily. Upstairs an old man hawked and spat at precise intervals as he paced the floor. Cold and restless, de Born finally drifted off to sleep, only to dream of Grenville chasing Dumouriez through Brooks's with a mason's hammer, while the Prince of Wales huzzah'd and kissed a pliant Polly Wilkes.

*   *   *

At 11 o'clock the next day, de Born went as ordered to *Le Chat
Gris*. This turned out to be a run-down tavern beside a slaughter house
full of hulking young men in blood-stained leather overalls, most
wearing red liberty caps, drinking brandy and complaining about the
price of tobacco.

All talk ceased as the stranger entered, heads turning sharply to
examine this dandy in the unlikely-looking clothes. Inwardly cursing
whichever idiot picked this unsuitable meeting place, de Born
shouldered his way to the bar and faced the surly-looking landlord.

"A private word with you, citizen," he said, pressing a gold louis
into the man's hairy paw.

"I am to wait here for a certain lady," he said with an exaggerated
wink. "The lady in question is not yet unencumbered of her husband,
d'ye see?" Again the wink. Slowly enlightenment spread over the
landlord's face and, with an anxious glance towards a hatchet-faced
woman counting coins at the other end of the counter, he whispered
that he would 'see the citizen was not disturbed until the lady arrives'.

As de Born settled down with an ancient copy of *Père Duchesne*
for company, the landlord returned to his cronies and, from his

gestures, de Born could see that he was explaining the circumstances of de Born's visit. The slaughtermen nodded sagely and one or two turned to de Born, winked slyly in turn and raised their glasses.

After an hour de Born, seemingly downcast, rose and, signalling his regret to the company - who shot him sympathetic looks, he left and walked down the Rue du Temple towards the centre of the city.

Everywhere he saw the gifts of war, hunger and resentment. As he listened to the women in the bread queues, each one clutching their precious ration cards, the name of hatred most frequently on their lips was not 'aristo' but '*accapareur*', the rich merchants who bought up and hoarded provisions as they came into the city and then sold them at inflated prices.

Outside a grocer's he heard one old man complaining loudly to anyone who would listen, "Sugar once 20 sou, now four livres - long live the Republic!" Food could be got, but only at a price. He followed one street seller and saw her discreetly lift the corner of the linen sheets in her basket, revealing to her customer the eggs and butter bought illegally from the stall-keepers in the market.

Beggars, vagrants and deserters were common, even on the main streets, but he saw only a few able-bodied men under twenty-five as the general conscription had taken them into the army - save, that is, for the ones who had mutilated themselves to escape military service. The people's faces were pinched with hunger and their clothes shabby and patched. From the number of shuttered and untenanted shops he saw, only those who had Army contracts and the fortune-tellers seemed to be making any money. Near the Pont Neuf, de Born saw soldiers break up a near riot that had started when a potato cart had overturned and a mad scramble to pillage it had got out of hand. And this, thought de Born, for a food that before the war was thought to be fit only for pigs.

A diseased darkness seemed to hover over the city, full of the smell of blood, the muted noise of terror. De Born felt he was being sucked into a whirlpool of danger, at the centre of which was oblivion.

*   *   *

At first de Born was tense to the point of nausea. Every eye seemed to be on him, but gradually, remembering the old saw of his uncle's that 'only pick-pockets see pick-pockets everywhere', he steeled himself to talk to people, asking the way of several and noting that (apart from some amused looks at his coat) they accepted him easily. He went into the markets and recorded the prices. He went into the coffee houses and observed the fashions, new slang expressions and the topics of the day. He studied the official notices carefully and then bought several newspapers and sat in a restaurant in the Place Vendôme absorbing the news and reflecting on how much he missed the comforting presence of Pingo and McPheat.

Attracted by the sound of drums and raised voices coming from the Rue St Honoré, he paid his bill and went out to discover what the commotion was all about. He was just in time to see several red-painted tumbrels turn the corner into the street leading to the Place de la Révolution. As he caught the tail end of the deathly procession he could see that the last cart was full of young Breton peasant girls, calm and seemingly unafraid, dressed in white. One older girl stood upright, bracing herself against the side of the cart as it lurched over the cobbles. She prayed aloud, while the others knelt and kissed their rosaries.

The skies suddenly darkened and a wintry squall sprinkled large drops of rain onto the cart. In seconds the girl was soaked, her white shift clinging slickly to her body, revealing her pink nipples and the dark smudge between her legs. Bystanders on the pavement watched them go by in silence; a few looked on with pity, most just looked away.

In the square a sizeable crowd of poissardes and washerwomen, loafers and street peddlers had built up: and the wine-sellers were doing a roaring trade. De Born heard two men placing wagers on the order in which the prisoners were to die. The area immediately around the scaffold was crowded with civic functionaries, officers of the court, clerks, messengers, militia and all the majestic apparatus which gave a bogus legality to the Terror.

Studying the crowd with his back to the guillotine, de Born saw the thrilled anticipation on their faces. At each ugly noise their expressions hardened in concentration. Thud - as the victim was thrown onto the plank. Thud - as the neck clamp was flicked into place. Thud - as the swish of the heavy blade ended its fall.

As each of the men in the first tumbrel died, one of the executioners' valets threw the headless corpses into a large red basket. Another tossed the heads into a basin, where they floated in the accumulated blood. As he did so there were cries of complaint from the spectators in the front row, whom he had inadvertently splashed with blood.

As the cart with the peasant girls pulled up to the scaffold, de Born saw an elderly man raise his hand in absolution. The girls bowed their heads in repentance, holding each other's hand. One or two of the very young ones were crying now. All of them looked frightened and bewildered, all save the praying girl.

He hurried away towards the Tuileries. One of the onlookers, a sans-culotte coal heaver swigging from a straw-covered flask, roughly took hold of his arm.

"What, ain't you staying to see these fucking Breton tarts sneeze into the sack?" he sneered. For a moment de Born stood speechless, in the grip of a killing rage, literally shaking with fury. Then with a cry of disgust he pushed the drunk away and ran into the Tuileries gardens. As he sat, listening despite himself to the satisfied shouts of the crowd as their pathetic victims succumbed to revolutionary justice, he felt a strange wetness on his face.

Putting his hand up to wipe it away, he was astonished to discover that, for the first time since he was a boy, there were tears running down his cheeks.

That night his dreams were full of blood.

*   *   *

The following day the routine was repeated. A visit to *Le Chat Gris*, where he bought a round of drinks for the slaughtermen and paid unlikely compliments to the landlord's wife. After a while he was approached by a wiry, bandy-legged little man who sat down at his table and passed the time of day. De Born mentally rehearsed the password sequence.

"Perhaps, citizen, you would care to own a sacred relic of King Louis?" the newcomer whispered, pulling a small square of linen from his pocket. "This was dipped in his blood by Sanson himself, you know." He pointed to one corner of the cloth, which was stained a rusty brown.

Over the man's shoulder de Born could see the landlord making frantic warning signals. Offering to buy the man a drink, de Born took the opportunity to go over to the counter.

"Citizen, be careful," said the landlord, in great agitation. "This man is a notorious spy for the police. Tell him nothing of yourself and praise the government."

De Born turned back to the man still seated at his table. "Citizen landlord," he said in a loud voice. "Fetch a policeman. This man is a royalist and a traitor to the people."

For a second the room was silent, until the landlord and the slaughtermen burst out laughing in admiration of de Born's stratagem. After a savage look at de Born, the spy scuttled out and the tavern patrons clustered around de Born, clapping him heartily on the back and re-telling the joke to each other.

The 'lady' not choosing to appear that morning, de Born resumed his reconnaissance of the city. As he left the tavern he thought he saw, out of the corner of his eye, a figure detach itself from the crowd around the meat stall on the opposite side of the street.

De Born hurried to the drapers on the corner of the Rue Béranger.

Reflected in one of the panes he saw his companion from the tavern. He was being followed. De Born gratefully remembered Pingo's training and sought out the nearest long, straight street. As he had hoped, this forced the spy to hang back for fear of discovery. About half way, de Born stopped and took out from his coat pocket a piece of paper. He carefully tore this into tiny pieces and, looking around him as if to check for watchers, scattered the pieces in the gutter and walked swiftly away. As he reached the end of the street he looked back and saw to his satisfaction the police spy on his hands and knees scrabbling for each piece of paper. Doubling back, de Born made for his lodgings, where he thought it prudent to remain until morning. He felt his confidence returning.

*   *   *

The weather being clement, de Born took up his station next day on a low bench outside the tavern. He sat watching the passers-by, idly daydreaming of Pickering Court and La Signora. Through the crowd of girls selling lavender water by the Boucherat fountain he saw an old man, a herbal drinks seller, puffing furiously on a long clay pipe clenched between his teeth. He was dressed in a ragged, dusty brown coat with patch pockets and creased grey velour trousers. He wore huge sabots and around his neck there hung a wooden tray held by ropes. His face was an explosion of grey whiskers but the forehead was curiously unlined for one so advanced in years.

He ambled in a stooping gait across the street, calling out his wares, until eventually he stood leaning against the wall next to de Born's bench.

"Take your hat off, you blockhead," hissed a voice which startled de Born out of his daydreaming.

"You're wearing your cockade on the wrong side, you eejit, take it off," came the voice again, even more urgently.

As de Born's hand went automatically to remove the offending hat, he suddenly realized that the voice had spoken to him in English.

CHAPTER FIVE

Duodi, 12 Brumaire, Year II

"Count to twenty, slowly mind, and then follow me," said the voice. "And for Jesus' sake stop staring at me as if you were a recently deflowered virgin."

As the old drinks-seller began to move off de Born thought furiously whether or not he should follow. After all, the voice had not recited even a part of the password sequence. What if this was yet another police spy? As if reading his mind, the street-seller paused level with him and muttered out of the side of his mouth, "And I'll be buggered if I'm going to stand about in the street chanting all that Masonic malarkey and waving me hands about. I'm off. You may please yourself."

That bloody cockade again, de Born thought as he sat counting. Leaving a few sou on the bench in payment for his drink, he sauntered off after the rapidly retreating back of his irascible contact.

Turning the corner into Rue Charlot he nearly bumped into his prey, who merely said, "Jesus, Mary and Joseph," in a disgusted manner and added, "Go to your lodgings and wait."

His visitor strode in energetically, looked about him, stuck out his hand and said, "Richard Ferris. Call me Dick, everybody does." He took off his coat and lay down on the bed.

Taking a chair and placing it opposite Ferris, de Born studied him closely. He could see now that his hair and beard had been floured to make him look older and he was in reality only about forty or so. He was slightly taller than de Born, well over six feet, with broad muscular arms and strong white hands. His dark eyes stood out from his very fine, pale skin, the eyes of a dissolute but good-natured rogue, and his mouth was wide and sensual.

"Cat got your tongue has it?" he asked, a little unsettled by de Born's silent inventory.

"Not at all," replied de Born evenly. "I was just wondering whether you were the 'eejit' who picked *Le Chat Gris* as the meeting place."

Ferris laughed, showing his large yellow teeth. "*Touché*, Admiralty man. And how did the fellows in the tavern like your coat?" he laughed again, but good-naturedly.

Aware he was being teased, but suddenly not minding, de Born smiled back at him.

"Madame admired it tremendously," he said.

"Did she indeed?" said Ferris. "A conquest and you not back in Paris two minutes." Connaught judging by the brogue, thought de Born, who had once had a groom from Ballinasloe.

Ferris got up abruptly and walked over to the table by the window and set his tray down. Feeling along the side of the box he pushed a peg into the wood revealing its false bottom. Out of this he took a small red card covered in official type.

"This is your *carte de surété*, As a provincial you need one to stay in Paris. Wear it in your hatband at all times. I've already filled it out in your name. Here's your ration card for bread." He handed de Born a piece of buff card. "And the one for fuel. Have you got the money?"

De Born nodded and went to his portmanteau, opened it and gave Ferris the canvas bag. Breaking the seal and looking inside, Ferris whistled. "Enough to bribe an army in here. Here, let me take charge of the assignats. I'll have them changed into gold by some black sheep I know. I might get a third of their face value if I'm lucky. But why the fortune in specie?"

"You mean you don't know the object of this venture?" asked de Born, amazed at the other's ignorance.

"Haven't the smallest notion, old cock," replied Ferris, going back to the bed and lying down with his hands behind his head.

De Born told him.

*   *   *

For the first time since their meeting, de Born felt that Ferris was at a loss.

"Have they all gone mad in Whitehall?" he asked. "You'll never get that boy out of the Temple, not with all the saints behind you and a cartload of Mr Pitt's gold. And even if you did, he wouldn't unite that rabble any more than I would."

"Do I take it you won't help me?" said de Born.

"No, I'm game, but you better know just what you - we - are taking on," replied Ferris. "Have you pen and paper?"

De Born fetched some from a shelf above the table and set it down. Ferris' hand dwarfed the quill as he made a series of rapid lines.

"Imagine a square formed by the Rue du Temple to the west, Rue de Bretagne in the south, Rue Béranger, where we are now, to the north and the Rue Charlot closing the square to the east.

"Inside the square are three different sets of buildings: the palace of the *ci-devant* comte d'Artois; the old Commanderie of the Knights Templar - chapter house, cloisters, church and so on; and lastly a vast collection of private houses, courtyards, alleyways and gardens. My guess is that there would be about four thousand souls who live or work in the Temple precincts.

"There is only one way in to the tower where the Dauphin is kept and that's through the palace courtyard, then past what's called the Little Tower and then on to what they call the Great Tower. The boy is held somewhere in there."

"Where?" asked de Born.

"That I don't know," replied Ferris. "I've only been in the Temple once and that was two years ago, long before the royal family were shut up there."

"How do we find out?" asked de Born.

"Well, we'll need a friend on the inside, someone who knows the ground and can come and go easily. There is one possibility, Cléry, the old king's valet de chambre. He looks after the boy now and occasionally is allowed out to see his wife."

"Will he help us?" asked de Born.

"I doubt it," replied Ferris. "If he's caught talking to us, he's a dead man. However, it's worth a try; indeed, I don't see we have any other choice."

"How do we approach this man?" asked de Born.

"The only way is for me to sell my herbals in the Rue de Bretagne and contact him when he emerges on one of his conjugal visits," replied

Ferris.

"Meanwhile, I'm famished. What say you and I go for dinner and I'll tell you how to stay alive in this hell-hole. Upon my honour, I'll be glad to get out of these rags for one night. Have you anything to lend me that doesn't look like it was made for a pair of withdrawing-room curtains?" he asked, still smirking at de Born's coat.

De Born went to his trunk and fished out a sober black coat and matching breeches, plus some white silk hose and leather shoes. "Try these," he said. "Incidentally, what does a recently deflowered virgin look like?"

*   *   *

Ferris insisted that they should dine at Procope and, against his better judgement, de Born allowed himself to be persuaded. He was still nervous of being recognized, even with his hair *au Talma* and minus the luxuriant moustachios he had sported in his time at the embassy.

Heeding Ferris' warning that they should speak French to each other at all times, de Born stepped into the crowded restaurant. The smoky interior remained the same to his eye, even if the clientele had altered radically - which, thought de Born, was certainly the mot juste, given the current mix of revolutionary journalists and Jacobin politicians. Ferris strolled through the series of cramped rooms until he came to a larger room which was at the disposition of the owners' more notable customers, of whom Ferris seemed to be one.

Taking their seats, de Born noted to his left a figure that was somehow familiar. He had a pale, pock-marked, young-looking face with thin lips. His eyes were obscured by a pair of green-tinted steel-framed spectacles and even more unusually he still wore his hair curled and powdered. Despite the fact he was peeling an orange, he was neatly gloved and dressed in a superbly cut dark violet coat, immaculate nankeen breeches and high heels. With a shock de Born realized he was looking straight at the dapper Devil himself. Maximilien Marie Isidore de Robespierre.

Evidently he was nearing the end of his meal for, after only a short while, he and his dining companion stood up preparatory to leaving, heads turning in the room to follow their exit. The room fell silent. Robespierre paused for a moment to allow his ever-present *bouledogues*, their coats bulging with huge hunting knives, to go ahead of him. De Born took the opportunity to examine the face of Robespierre's partner. Aged about thirty, he was an untidy-looking, sloppily dressed plump little man with staring blue eyes under an unkempt shock of long, thinning straw-blond hair framing a heavy, big-nosed, thick-lipped face. He looked very angry and was slightly unsteady on his feet.

De Born nudged Ferris.

"Who's the little fellow with Robespierre?"

"Pierre-Gaspard Chaumette, the *Procureur-syndic* of the Paris Commune," replied Ferris, looking round at the figure coming towards him. "Calls himself Anaxagoras after some old Greek philosopher. Bit odd seeing those two together, especially in public. Robespierre usually eats at Venua's."

Chaumette's eyes met de Born's. Something stirred in Chaumette's expression. Not exactly recognition, thought de Born, puzzled, but something akin to it. For a heart-stopping moment de Born thought he had been discovered. Then Chaumette's eyes moved on to stare at Ferris. I'm getting ridiculously jumpy, thought de Born, forcing himself to relax.

As the room settled down again after the departure of its two illustrious patrons, Ferris carefully outlined the current political situation for de Born, pausing only to gulp down copious draughts of Sillery champagne and eating partridge with his hands.

From his position of power at the Committee of Public Safety and in the absence of Danton, Ferris explained, Robespierre was unassailable. While he tolerated Chaumette's 'de-Christianisation' campaign and the 'Cult of Reason', it was generally thought that Robespierre was against the excesses of vandalisme and the accompanying outrages against the clergy. With both the enragé extremists and the Girondin moderates out of the way, courtesy of the national razor, Robespierre was plotting to rid himself of his only competitors for power by suspending the Commune itself.

Meanwhile, the Terror mounted. The hunting down and slaughter of the Vendéan peasants continued and the jails were full as a result of the Law of Suspects.

Police spies and paid informers were everywhere, warned Ferris, eavesdropping in hairdressers, billiard rooms, cafés and the public baths.

"People forget the Terror during the day when they are busy, but at night the streets are deserted and they listen for the Commissioner's footsteps on the cobbles. No one opens their shutters to see what the knocking at a neighbour's door means. No one feels safe. No one is safe. Look at the faces on the street. Stupor. Apathy. Resignation. No one dares speak his mind. No one is true to themselves. Neighbours denounce each other to pay off old scores. People are arrested for raising their hats. Not using *tu-toi*. Looking 'smart'. The Revolution has become a policeman's dream. They slaughter priests in prisons and a hundred yards away the good people affect ignorance lest they be butchered in their turn. And meanwhile the city drowns in blood."

By now Ferris was a little drunk.

"I'm fed up with all this talk of these bloody crooks and imbeciles," he said with a sweep of his hand to take in the room, beginning a long, rambling account of his life and adventures. Born the illegitimate son of a local Squireen (to whom he bore no ill-will), and his Catholic scullery-girl (to whom he very much did), Ferris had been brought up as a son of the house, but in the pastoral care of the parish priest. He had attended the Irish College in Paris but had been 'asked to leave' for brawling and then, through his father's influence, obtained a commission in the Connaught Rangers. This episode also ended ingloriously when he impersonated a nun for a wager during an inspection of the local convent by a visiting general.

"Faith, I think he was quite taken with me, what with my lovely eyes a-fluttering and my neat little wimple," said Ferris, his eyes streaming with tears at the happy memory. Having chased a mistress to Paris he had got into debt and began to pay his way with journalism for the London newspapers. "That's when I fell in with one of you fellas from the External Department. Money's not bad. That's how I can afford to eat here," he said, defensively de Born thought. "But the bloody risks I have to take for it. Ah *merde*. How about a bottle of

Armagnac, eh?" He waved at a nearby waiter. "Tell me about yourself," asked Ferris, filling de Born's glass. "Got a woman?"

"No one special," replied de Born, experiencing a brief pang at the thought of Polly Wilkes.

"Pity," said Ferris. "Nothing like the love of a good woman, as my old da' used to say."

"Love?" queried de Born, feeling very superior to this Irishman.

"Well, it's not as fine as gold, I grant you," admitted Ferris. "But it's the next best thing."

De Born merely shrugged and changed the subject. He was surprised to discover that a man so seemingly sophisticated as Ferris could believe in a concept so childish and irrational as 'love', just as if he were one of those foolish serving girls at The Somerset. The de Borns had, like all of their class always married for land. He had never met anyone who had married for this 'love', although he knew men who had become infatuated with their mistresses.

De Born was by now tired and a little alarmed by the increasing volume of Ferris' reminiscences. By promising him more brandy he wheedled him back to the lodgings, where Ferris slumped down on the bed and instantly began snoring. Spreading a blanket over his legs, de Born settled down in the chair to sleep. The last thing he remembered before he dropped off was the look in Chaumette's eyes. If not recognition, what?

*   *   *

De Born was awoken as dawn was breaking by a peculiar rustling sound. In the early light he could just make out Ferris over by the window. The portmanteau, which he had carefully locked, was lying on the table, open. Ferris was counting the paper *assignats*, which accounted for the noise. He didn't seem at all drunk now. After a while some instinct made him turn and look towards de Born's chair, but the Frenchman being too quick for him, had shut his eyes before Ferris could discover he was awake. The rustling started again and de Born sneaked another look. Ferris had such an odd expression on his face. Not greed - more like a hungry man looking wistfully through a restaurant window. Soon de Born fell asleep again, but the rustling of paper continued for some time.

Early next morning Ferris retrieved his tray and street-vendor's clothes and proceeded to his vigil at the Temple gate. Before leaving he instructed de Born on their communications.

"If you receive a message from me with this signet seal upside down, you are discovered and must flee on the instant." De Born nodded. "If you receive a message to come to a house and you see a Salem cross in blue chalked on the door, do not enter but stand some way off and observe events." Ferris studied him intently until he was satisfied de Born understood. "Otherwise, use your judgement - although I suppose that if you had any, you wouldn't be here at all."

There was nothing for it but to wait, so de Born settled down with Rousseau's autobiography until Ferris returned. It was two days later when his door burst open and the big Irishman came in with the news that he had collared Cléry in the Rue de Bretagne and after 'a great deal of blarney' had persuaded him to meet them that night at his wife's house.

*　*　*

As he shook Cléry's hand de Born felt it tremble in his.

"We too put our life in your hands," de Born said, understanding the man's all too evident fear.

"Yes, it's true, M'sieu. I am indeed scared," Cléry said. "A suitable reaction as I am only a servant, not a soldier or a hero. But it is my duty to help His Majesty - the Dauphin, I mean - even if my life is forfeit. Your friend here said that I may be able to help you. Please, M'sieu, I beg of you, tell me what you wish me to do," asked Cléry, trying but unable to hide his agitation.

"First," said de Born, "I need to know exactly where the Prince is being held. Second, how many guards there are, and how they are organised."

"Well, the first is simple enough," Cléry began. "The Dauphin is kept in what's called the Great Tower, which is approached by a covered gallery leading from the palace. It is surrounded by an 18-foot high wall with only one entrance door. This door has two locks, the keys for which are kept by two porters, who must use their keys in unison before the door will open. The tower itself is of stone, nine feet in thickness and about one hundred and fifty feet high, with a slate roof. There are four storeys. Each has four rooms. The ground floor is for the use of Municipal Officers, the first is used as a guard room; Louis-Charles is kept on the second and his sister, the Madame Royale, on the level above him."

"How is the second storey reached?" asked de Born.

"By a staircase which rises from the ground floor in the north turret," replied Cléry. "It's interrupted by guarded wickets at regular intervals and the way to the Dauphin's chamber is barred by two locked doors, one of nailed oak, the other of iron, both guarded and bolted from the inside."

"How many men do you estimate it would take to storm the turret staircase?" asked de Born.

Cléry smiled sadly. "M'sieu, the Dauphin would be dead long before your army reached the first wicket."

De Born paced up and down the room for a while, tapping his gun-stick on the floorboards. "By God, man," he said, confronting Cléry, "are you saying that it is utterly impossible to remove the Dauphin from the Temple?"

"By force, certainly, M'sieu. But I've thought hard about this problem and there is a way."

"Well?"

"Gold, M'sieu."

"Gold?"

"Yes. That's an army that might be able to carry out the task," replied Cléry. "Nevertheless, M'sieu, it would take a pile of gold louis as big as the Tower itself to take the trick."

"Perhaps not," de Born mused. "Who has unhindered access to the boy and also may leave the Temple grounds at any time?"

"No one, M'sieu," replied Cléry, "except, of course, for citizen Simon."

"Simon? Who's he?" asked de Born.

Cléry's face was sour. "They call him the Dauphin's 'guardian', but in fact he is simply Chaumette's creature, there to spy on the other Municipal Officers."

Chaumette again, thought de Born.

"Could he be bribed?" asked Ferris, who had been listening to Cléry with intense concentration.

Cléry made a face. "He's stupid, M'sieu, and a drunkard; but disloyal, no, I think probably not. In any event, he's terrified of Chaumette, as all the guards are."

"Where does he do his drinking?" asked Ferris.

"I'm not sure, M'sieu. I once saw him disgustingly drunk in the wine shop with the sign of the cat hanging outside. You might try there."

"View halloo, old cock," Ferris said in English to de Born. "Let's flush this fox from his den."

De Born shrugged. Clearly the valet didn't hold out much hope, yet he felt that before reporting total failure to Whitehall he must try all avenues. Stephens would expect nothing less.

De Born clasped Cléry's hand warmly in farewell. "You little know how much you serve your king in this," he said, patting the grateful valet's arm. "But you must not put yourself in any more danger for our sakes. If we meet again, say at the Temple ... " Cléry looked up hopefully. "... you must not know me or this man," he said, indicating

Ferris.

Dusk was falling as they walked back to *Le Chat Gris*. As they entered, de Born noticed several of the slaughterhouse men who had been the grateful recipients of his largesse.

"What, still after your lady friend?" one of them yelled over to de Born, who waved back and, going over to where they stood, ruefully admitted that 'the lady had been seduced by her husband and would entertain him no longer'.

After introducing Ferris as an old friend and buying a round of drinks, de Born asked his new friends if they knew a citizen Simon, as he had a packet for him.

"Simon, Simon, gent 'ere wants you," roared the leader of the group. As de Born looked round he saw a swarthy, thickset man in his late fifties approaching them from the other end of the bar. He was of middling height, dressed shabbily but with a brand-new liberty cap covering his lank hair.

"Well, what are you layabouts shouting about?" asked Simon in a surly voice. "Who wants me?"

De Born stepped forward and, taking a reluctant Simon's arm, smoothly manoeuvred him to an unoccupied table.

"Citizen, we seek your advice as a Municipal Officer and in your position as guardian to the boy Capet," said de Born.

Somewhat mollified by this, Simon assumed an air of self-importance. "Advice? Certainly, citizen, if it be in my power to give it."

"My friend and I," de Born nodded at Ferris, "wondered how we might go about obtaining the contract for supplying fuel to the Temple and, since you used to be the chief concierge before your promotion, we thought you might be able to, how shall I put it, steer us in the right direction."

"Nothing simpler, citizen," said Simon. "You must apply in writing to the Commune, setting forth your rates, price per brasse and so on."

"Yes, citizen, but we have no knowledge of dealing with such important members of the government of our glorious Republic," said de Born, "while you are a friend of the great Procureur Chaumette himself and would know the correct forms and etiquettes."

"It is true, citizens, that citizen Chaumette and I are on terms of intimacy," said Simon airily. "But you must not think that I would seek to influence him - even if I were to be recompensed for doing so," he added with a sly, greedy expression.

"I understand perfectly, citizen." De Born went on, "Yet your current duties are so burdensome that it would surely be wrong for the additional burden of providing us with information to go unrewarded."

Simon's expression changed quickly to one of suspicion. "What do you mean, information? About what, eh?"

"About how many persons inhabit the Temple, how many guards there are and so on," interposed Ferris.

Simon frowned and then, draining his glass, stood up. "You ask too much, citizen. This information could be useful to the enemies of our Republic. No, you ask too much," and stomped off.

"Damn," said de Born. "You went too far too fast, Dick."

"Nonsense," said Ferris. "They're all alike with their greasy palms. He'll be back."

No sooner had he said those words when his prediction came true. Simon had re-entered the wine shop and was pointing them out to two National Guard fusiliers.

"Let's get out of here while we've got the chance," said Ferris, moving rapidly to the door leading to the back of the premises. De Born, whose natural instinct was to brazen it out, had no choice but to follow. As Ferris hurried to the exit, he jogged the arm of one of the abattoir men, spilling some of his wine.

"Hey, you'll not leave until you've paid for another glass," said the aggrieved drinker.

Ferris looked uncertainly between the pursuing soldiers, now only feet away, and the man standing stolidly in his path. To de Born's dismay he saw Ferris expertly deliver a heavy punch to the slaughterman's head. As his victim reeled back, the landlord reached under the counter with a practised motion and brought out a club. There was nothing for it, thought de Born. He raised his gun-stick and, flicking out the trigger, aimed it at the landlord's chest.

As he steadied the gun in its upwards arc, something very hard crashed onto the back of his head. For a moment he staggered under the tremendous force of the blow. Then, overtaken by blackness, he fell senseless to the floor.

CHAPTER SIX

Quintidi, 15 Brumaire, Year II

As de Born regained his wits he realized that he must have been unconscious for some time, as the wine shop was now deserted save for Simon, the landlord and one of the fusiliers.

"Come on, let's be having you," said the soldier, not unkindly, helping de Born to his feet. Taking a length of cord from the landlord, he handed his rifle to Simon to hold and tied de Born's hands firmly behind his back.

"You must have a hard head, citizen," he said cheerfully. "You put a crack in the stock." Taking the rifle back from Simon, he showed a still-dazed de Born the damage.

"Right - everybody outside," said the fusilier. "You too, landlord. You may be needed by the Committee to give evidence."

As the little procession reached the door, de Born saw the other soldier standing over Ferris, who also had his hands tied. Both men were thrown into the back of a cart borrowed from the nearby livery stable. As de Born lay face down in the straw Ferris whispered to him,

"Let me do the talking. I'll get us out of this, never fear."

Although his confidence in Ferris was at a pretty low ebb, de Born decided that he was in no fit state to face interrogation and he whispered back his agreement.

After travelling about a quarter of a mile the cart stopped and they were deposited in the dusty anteroom of an imposing mansion. On the door opposite was a tattered notice: "Surveillance Committee of the Temple Section in session. No spitting". The doors opened and they were taken in.

The room was chaotically disarranged. At one end was a long table strewn with papers, pipes and bottles. Behind this sat the President, slumped half asleep in his chair, his sword of office lying before his place. Simon stood beside some of the Committee-men lounging together in a corner, smoking and chattering. The others lay on benches scattered about the room, dozing with fatigue or drunkenness. The soldiers pushed de Born forward roughly and he stumbled into the pool of light from an oil lamp hanging over the table.

"Name and profession?" asked the President in a bored voice.

De Born answered and Ferris gave his name as Guillaume le Bon, herbalist. No one in the room was paying them the slightest attention. Above the sounds of chattering and laughter, de Born thought he could hear someone drunkenly humming 'Ca ira'.

"Papers?" Sternly this time.

One of the soldiers took de Born's *carte de sûreté* from his hatband and fumbled inside Ferris' coat until he found his set of papers, before handing them both with a respectful gesture to the President.

"Citizen Cheftel," said the President as he finished noting their particulars in a large leather-bound register. "You are a notary and thus you are aware that it is a serious offence to attempt bribery of a Municipal Officer."

"Of course, citizen President," began de Born. "Nothing could have been further from my mind, I do assure you."

He could feel the cold sweat trickling down the ridge of his spine. His broken head throbbed.

"He lies, citizen," interrupted Simon. "He wanted information about the Temple and was willing to pay for it."

At the mention of the Temple the President leaned forward. In the full light of the lamp his look was harsh and stony.

"Why did you ask about that place?"

De Born explained about the fuel contract and noted the waves of hesitation and doubt on his interrogator's face as he looked between Simon and the prisoners, his suspicions of the former obviously gaining apace.

"The fact is, citizen," Ferris said in an injured tone, "he had the gall to ask us for money."

De Born groaned. Predictably, Simon was enraged.

"Lies, all lies!" he spluttered. "I demand in the name of my superior, citizen Chaumette, that these counter-revolutionary profiteers be charged under the Law of Suspects."

At this the President's face changed abruptly. Doubt was replaced by alarm. He made a decision.

"Citizens," he called out to the Committee-men. "The Republic one and indivisible demands your verdict against these suspects - so eloquently accused by citizen Simon," his voice rose slightly, "on behalf of the illustrious Chaumette, whose contributions to the well-being of the Republic are legion and legend. How say you, citizens?"

After a few muttered cries of "guilty", the Committee continued its chatter, turning their backs indifferently on the proceedings.

The President wrote something in his register, slammed it shut and uttered the words de Born had been dreading above all others.

"Take them to the Conciergerie."

As they left, de Born could hear the President congratulating Simon on his 'public diligence'.

*   *   *

As the cart carrying de Born and Ferris rumbled down the Rue St Martin and on to the Ile de la Cité, de Born thought of all the times he had stood outside the very same prison taking note of new arrivals for the Ambassador's despatches. He had even been inside this hell-hole once to see an Englishman arrested in error.

The Conciergerie was the oldest prison in Paris and, when the Revolutionary Tribunal was set up earlier that year in the Palais de Justice, the adjoining prison became the natural place to put suspects who were waiting to be tried. Security had been tightened considerably since de Born's time, especially since the September massacres, when the mob had burst in and hacked most of the five hundred prisoners to death. Of all the prisons in the Republic, the Conciergerie was the most feared, the most sinister. Parisians called it the 'ante-chamber to death' and women made the sign of the cross when they passed its gates.

Where prisoners ended up depended on their finances. Those with no money were sealed up in the underground cells, furnished only with straw soiled by their own excrement. The doors were opened once a day for their only meal, and to let in a pitiful amount of dank prison air. A private room like Marie Antoinette's could be had for 45 livres or, for half that amount, four could share. Most of the prisoners slept forty or fifty to a room in a series of cave-like vaults, four to a straw-covered bunk.

A corridor separated the sexes. Half way along the prison authorities had installed a metal grille through which the prisoners could converse.

The turnkeys took the two men down from the cart and one of them asked Ferris, whose hands he was untying, how much money he had.

"A few sou only, but I'm sure I could get more," said Ferris.

Unimpressed, the turnkey looked at de Born. "And you, have you any of the chinking stuff?"

Reluctantly de Born exposed the cache of gold louis hidden in his heel. He held out two.

"How many friends have these got?" asked the turnkey, grabbing the coins.

De Born opened his palm to reveal another three. The turnkey grabbed de Born's wrist with one hand and scooped up the remaining coins with the other.

"One month's rent for two people exactly, citizen," he said, laughing at de Born's expression of dismay. "Don't worry, citizen," he said roguishly. "You won't be in here for a month anyway," and winked at his mate, who - despite the many times he had witnessed this performance - never failed to find it hugely entertaining.

Whistling happily, the two thieves led de Born and Ferris to a low, narrow vault. It contained about a dozen beds set very close together, upon which sat or dozed four times that number of men. The squalor was appalling and the stench from the large tub in the middle of the room, mixed in with burning incense, was at first overpowering. De Born quickly brought his handkerchief up in a vain attempt to stop the odour seeping into his nose. Pointing to a bed in the corner occupied by a portly, florid man who was snoring loudly, the turnkeys locked the door and retreated down the corridor to the accompaniment of a satisfied chinking of de Born's gold.

De Born felt a crushing sense of failure and misery. As he sat down on the thin straw pallet he couldn't help repeatedly going over the train of events that had led him to this place. A bitter litany it was. One stupidity had followed another. The involvement of Cléry was not only foolhardy, but possibly fatal to the loyal valet. The witless attempt to bribe Simon into revealing the Temple's secrets, and then the panic in the wine-shop. Finally the goading of Simon at the Surveillance Committee. De Born felt nothing but shame and humiliation. His strength seemed to desert him all of a sudden and, badly depressed, he gave himself over to a fitful sleep.

At midnight he was awakened by the vicious barking of the turnkey's pair of mastiffs, accompanying their master on the nightly round. The original occupant of the bed also woke with a startled, "What, those foot-pads have gulled me, by God. I paid them to sleep alone. Who on earth are you, sir, and who, moreover, is this ... gentleman?" he asked irritably in a heavy English accent, poking the comatose Ferris. The sound of the turnkey's staves, as they beat a tattoo on the iron bars set into the doors, faded into the distance.

De Born hastily introduced himself and explained their 'purchase'.

"Five gold louis, eh," the Englishman said and gave a grim laugh. "Well you were gulled too, which I suppose evens the score. No hard feelings, Monsieur." He stuck out his hand to shake de Born's. "Name's Codrington, by the way. I ain't French, although I speak it tolerable well. I'm English, don't y'know."

De Born again apologised for the intrusion but was greeted only by another outburst of Anglo-Saxon snoring and soon he too, exhausted, fell into a deep, comforting sleep.

* * *

At ten o 'clock the next morning the turnkeys returned to open the door and carry out the tub, which by now was brimming over and fouling the cell floor. The men emerged into the corridor, coughing in an effort to relieve the terrible dryness of their throats and scratching at the bites which fleas and lice had left during the night. A breakfast of watery soup, stale herrings and bad, black bread had been provided and de Born was surprised to see the men eagerly press forward for their share. One or two had brandy flasks to wash the meal down, but the others made do with well water.

For a couple of hours the men either paced up and down the corridor, chatting arm in arm, or sat apathetically, staring into space. Then de Born heard a rustling noise from the other end of the corridor. The sound was caused by the silk dresses and lilting, twittering chatter of a group of women prisoners.

Most of the men gathered at the grille which separated the corridor from the women's court, where much bowing took place, accompanied by cheerful greetings and polite enquiries after the ladies' health.

Here and there lovers stole brief hand-shakes through the iron-work, which were witnessed by the older prisoners with tolerant approval and by their jailers with a leering prurience.

Still greatly depressed by the events of recent days, de Born slumped down beside Ferris and moodily began to remove the grime from under his finger nails with a small sliver of wood he had found on the floor.

"Cheer up, old cock," said Ferris. "We'll soon be out of here, never fear."

"And what," said de Born heavily, "leads you to form that conclusion?"

"You'll see," Ferris insisted. "Our master's long arms will reach in to this stinking hole and fish us out like trout tickled from a stream."

De Born reflected on what he knew and Ferris could not. Philip Stephens would conduct them to the steps of the scaffold personally it if meant protecting the Lord Commissioners of the Admiralty - nephew or no nephew. They were abandoned for certain.

Day followed tedious day. Night followed cold, miserable night.

Although de Born had become fond of Ferris, he found his unceasing, stupid optimism wearing. Sir William's conversation seemed to consist entirely of lengthy accounts of his past associations with the Prince of Wales, who by all accounts lived only to accompany Sir William in the hunting field and there marvel at his extraordinary exploits.

While at night everyone dreamed of food, their days were spent avoiding the '*moutons*', or prison informers; in listless gossip; or by the taking of the illicit opiates that circulated freely.

At first de Born was full of enthusiastic plans for escape, but could find no one to take him seriously. Only Ferris was cautiously interested.

"But even if you could get out, which seems bloody unlikely, where would you go?" he asked de Born. "You'd never make it to the coast."

"Oh, I'd go home, I suppose," said de Born.

"Why on earth would you go there, after what happened to your father?" asked Ferris.

"That's exactly why I want to go," said de Born.

After a while Ferris flatly refused to have anything to do with the notion and insisted that, as long as their identities were not discovered, they would get out somehow.

De Born did, however, make some friends. One in particular, a draper from Agen, became some solace to him as their friendship meant they could reminisce about their native region.

"What's your favourite time of year?" asked the draper one day.

"Oh, spring," replied de Born. "When the plum orchards are white with blossom and the geese are let out to crop the early grass, each sternly marching single-file behind their gander. And you?"

"The summertime, certainly," replied the little shopkeeper. "When the shop is closed and I can join my wife on her father's farm. We sit in the cool shade and watch that fierce, dry August heat hurl itself onto the red tiles of the dove cote."

"Yes," said de Born, "until one longs for the May morning mists, that linger until the midday bell."

And then both men would fall silent and think on happier days and smoke their pipes. In this fashion the men comforted themselves with talk of home, of family, loved ones and what they planned to do when they left prison. Each day brought, however, a reminder of their more likely fate as their companions were each taken in turn to the tumbrel. Every night the turnkeys would come and read the list of tomorrow's condemned. De Born became fascinated with how each man took the news. Some merely shrugged and went on with their game of cards, while others stared into space, unable to take in the news properly. Not a night passed that de Born didn't speculate how he would react to hearing his own name. One day it was the little draper's turn, and after that de Born made no more new friends.

*   *   *

He was not the only one interested in the study of humans under extreme stress. One day de Born noticed a turnkey, after referring to a large roll of paper in his hands, pointing out several prisoners to a visitor with a hideously disfigured face.

"Who's that ugly fellow with the sketchbook, Sir Codrington?"

"Oh, some artist-johnnie called Jack David," replied the

Englishman. "Used to see him creeping around Versailles in the old days, arse-licking to the court. Turned his coat in '89 and became a politician. Member of the Committee of General Security; that's why they let him in."

"But what's he doing?" asked de Born, puzzled. "Why does he pick some faces to sketch and reject others?"

"Because he only draws those who are on the condemned list," explained Codrington. "It was the same during the '92 prison massacres. He was pleased to employ himself drawing the agonies of the dying, God rot his soul."

De Born watched this jackal prowl the vaults looking for fresh victims. By and by, David passed in front of de Born as he leaned up against the corridor wall. The artist turned to the warder, who consulted his list and shook his head. As David began to move away, de Born spat calmly and expertly full into his face. While the warder intervened, pushing de Born back towards the wall, David stood motionless, the spittle dripping from his swollen, scarred cheek. After the initial shock had worn off, his shame and mortification were apparent in his eyes. The corridor rang with the sounds of prisoners clapping and shouting their approval. David was forced to retreat to the main door through the lines of jeering inmates, his head bowed in humiliation.

And this, thought de Born, is what everybody in Whitehall is so
scared of. If they could only see what weak, cowardly creatures they are.
He also had assumed that the Jacobins would go on governing because
they deserved to. They were, he had imagined, superior beings who had
defeated the Girondins, crushed the Vendée peasants and killed a king
because they were strong. Now he could see them for what they really
were: vicious, self-righteous bullies who murdered out of fear. As the
days passed, de Born became more and more interested in his country's
future, although fully aware of the irony of studying a subject which
personally he found was in very short supply. He talked to everyone
who would listen about the political situation, and asked endless
questions. Few of the aristocrats had any ideas other than the
restoration of the status quo. Others longed for an 'enlightened' utopia
of merry peasants and avuncular landlords. A tiny minority followed
Talleyrand's line of an alliance with England leading to the restoration
of the Bourbons, but under a constitutional monarchy. Most, like
Ferris, had given the matter no thought at all and were completely
uninterested. During his time in the Conciergerie the future of France
became de Born's overwhelming obsession. For the first time he
realized just how deeply he loved his country.

*   *   *

One evening de Born spied a new face at the grille. Up to now he had tended to avoid contact with the female inmates, despite several glances from that direction that might perhaps have encouraged another man, one less full of self-pity and poisonous recriminations. Briefly their eyes met, hers to pass on, his to stay locked on her face. Gradually something stirred in de Born's memory. A wedding in the country. That same face under a mulberry tree in a garden. Music and people dancing.

Still uncertain, and a little excited, de Born sought out his English friend.

"Sir Codrington," the deliberate solecism delivered in his atrocious provincial accent, "pray tell me if you can, who is that lady standing at the left of the grille?"

Codrington peered down the corridor. "That, lawyer Cheftel, is the damnably fetching marquise de Roquefère," he replied, looking amusedly at de Born's expression.

This face, not conventionally pretty by the fashion of the day, was nevertheless what his uncle would have called 'handsome'. De Born could see the great strength in that jaw and a fierce intelligence in those dark, glittering eyes. She was surrounded by gallants and, while her full-lipped mouth often twisted into a polite smile, she did not return any of the compliments and addresses paid to her, which seemed only to bore or irritate her.

"Won't you introduce me?" asked de Born, who could not hide the mounting agitation in his voice. Of course! Now he remembered. It must be seven years since he last saw her, when his father took him to a neighbouring château for the wedding of his cousin, Etienne de Roquefère. They had met briefly during the dancing after the ceremony, and then only to exchange a few traditional courtesies. Sophie, he now remembered; her name was Sophie.

As Codrington introduced them, de Born watched her face closely for any signs of recognition. He bowed, relieved at their absence, and began the usual conversation of the inmates.

"I trust, Madame, you find your quarters not too uncomfortable?" de Born asked.

"Then, Maitre Cheftel, you trust in error," she answered. Her voice was low, level, precise.

"At least, Madame, we all share the same misfortune," said de Born, taken aback.

"And why, Monsieur, do you suppose that your somewhat inaccurate supposition should make me feel better?" asked Sophie, who seemed a little bored.

De Born felt that he was in a deep hole and perhaps it would be better to stop digging.

"Still, no doubt your innocence will soon be proved," he said, hearing, even as the words left his mouth, the sound of shovel biting into heavy clay. "And you will then find life much improved."

"I very much doubt it, Monsieur," she said with the hint of a smile. "In the first place I am as guilty as sin and in the second, the Tribunal seem fully intent on cutting my head off at the earliest opportunity. I would not have thought parting with it will be any great improvement."

De Born was reduced at first to silence by this onslaught. Gamely he tried to respond.

"Perhaps, then, madame, you would gain solace from the ministrations of a priest? There are several here incognito who would, I'm sure, be glad to help you."

"Help me what?" demanded Sophie, her mood changing. "I don't believe in that hocus-pocus any more than I judge you do, and I certainly have no time for those creeping clerics or their bogus promises of a paradisiacal after-life."

At this, de Born roared with laughter for the first time since he had passed through the prison gates, while she grinned delightedly to see his reaction. What an extraordinary woman! It was more like talking to another man. Not a simper or a coy look. Not a fished compliment. None of the usual cooing and pouting. No repellent repertoire of sidelong glances. No pretence or artifice. Simply extraordinary.

The five o'clock bell interrupted this compilation of virtues and reluctantly he bade her goodnight.

The marquise rose from her curtsey and then came very close to the grille so their faces were only a few inches apart. He could smell her body. Then she did a most extraordinary thing. She winked.

"Goodnight, Jean-Baptiste," she said, using the form of his name by which he was known in the family. "Sweet dreams," and turned and walked quickly across the courtyard towards the women's quarters.

De Born's spirits soared. She did remember him after all. And somehow she had understood instinctively that his real name must not be revealed to others. He stared after her in admiration. Beauty, intelligence, courage, even a sense of humour. Suddenly he went cold. He remembered again where they had met and why she had been at Roquefère. He sought out Codrington.

"I suppose the marquis de Roquefère is taken also?" he asked Codrington idly, who was not such a fool as he sometimes appeared.

"Why do you wish to know, Cheftel?" he teased. "Would you prefer it if he were taken? Perhaps better still, already executed?"

De Born stood aghast at his own inexcusable thoughts.

Codrington had guessed exactly right. He had unbelievably been hoping the man was dead. Not consciously wishing perhaps, but certainly unconsciously hoping. As quickly as the fever of her presence had come upon him, it subsided.

As he saw de Born's face fall and noted his guilty silence, Codrington, taking pity on him and regretting at least a little his previous harshness, attempted to lift his spirits.

"Be of better cheer, Cheftel," he said, putting his arm around de Born's shoulders. "The marquis in fact lives, and prospers, I dare say, in Philadelphia."

De Born muttered his thanks mechanically and retreated into their cell. He lay down on the bunk and stared at the ceiling, ignoring Ferris' attempts to interest him in the latest gossip. Ferris looked past him at Codrington with mute enquiry. Shaking his head as if to say 'best leave him alone for a while', Codrington took his place and all settled down to sleep. That night only two succeeded.

On subsequent days de Born rarely ventured near the grille, preferring to stay at the other end of the corridor amongst a card school that had grown up around a new intake of young bloods. He hardly ever spoke to his companions, betting large sums he could not afford with savage indifference to the outcome. He took his losses in high bad humour and no pleasure in his successes.

Each morning Sophie would approach the grille and seek him out. She would stand for a few minutes, irresolutely, and then with a frown she would wander away again. After a while her visits to the grille ceased and she stayed in the ladies' courtyard, even though the air there was becoming chilly and damp.

*   *   *

On the day before what used to be called Christmas, de Born felt his neighbour at the card table nudge him and point to the entrance door. Two officers were talking to Ferris, who was in the act of pointing out de Born. Seeing he had his friend's attention, he motioned for him to join them.

"Hurry up, we haven't got all day," shouted one of the officers at de Born as he strolled over to them. "You're keeping the Tribunal waiting."

"Tribunal?" said de Born. "You're in jest, surely? On trial without a preliminary examination, as the law demands? I haven't even had the chance to engage counsel."

"What are you getting so worked up about?" asked the officer in charge. "You have nothing to worry about. If you are innocent, doubtless they'll set you free, and if you're guilty, well then, no amount of your lawyer's tricks will get you off."

As it turned out, the previous case was still being heard and this gave de Born a chance to look about him from their position in a box at the back of the Tribunal. He soon spotted Simon, glowering at him from near the witness stand, and beside him stood the landlord from the wine-shop, looking frightened and lost.

The great hall of the Palais de Justice was full to overflowing. Seated on a high bench were the five judges in their great plumed hats, two of whom seemed to be asleep. To the left was the jury box, where the twelve men lounged and whispered comments to each other. They at least seemed to be paying some attention. To the right, at a small table in front of the witness box, stood the Public Prosecutor in his sash of office, surrounded by his assistants. As de Born entered, the Prosecutor had just reached his peroration.

"This piece of dirt," he shouted, pointing dramatically to the accused, a homely-looking middle-aged woman who stared at him stoically, "unworthy of the sacred name of Frenchwoman, is guilty beyond all possible doubt of desiring the arrival of the Prussians, and hoarding provisions for their use. You have heard, citizens, from reliable witnesses, that she even engaged an opera box for the King of Prussia to enjoy after his hoped-for victory. What treachery, citizens.

No doubt," he said with a theatrical sneer, turning to the woman, "you wished the monster to take his ease after his exertions of the day slaughtering good patriots." The muted sounds of outrage from the jury-box evidently encouraging him, he continued in the same vein. "Perhaps you intended to share his entertainments and spread your legs for him, like the traitorous whore you undoubtedly are.

"Enough of this foul excrescence on the glorious name of France," he continued, with a gesture that suggested that her very existence disgusted him. "Citizens, I ask - nay demand - that in the name of the Republic, one and indivisible, you expunge this sub-human stain off the face of our great city." With this final flourish he sat down to receive the sycophantic plaudits of his assistants, mopping his brow and neck with a large spotted handkerchief.

The presiding judge then leaned over the piles of law volumes in front of him and peered at the jury.

"Citizens, do you find it necessary to retire in order that you may consider your verdict against this despicable wretch?" he asked with a meaningful glare at the foreman.

After a hasty consultation with his fellows, the foreman rose. "No, citizen President, there is no need. We find her guilty of treason against the Republic."

"Henriette Françoise de Marboeuf," the judge intoned, "widow of the ci-devant marquis de Marboeuf, having been found guilty of treason, you are condemned to death. Take her away."

As the condemned passed de Born on the steps below, she stumbled and de Born leaned down and put out his hand to prevent her from falling. The widow's face, which up to then had been expressionless, broke into a wan smile. "Our Saviour bless you and save you, Monsieur," she whispered before the warders hustled her on. She was, de Born reflected, about the age his mother would have been if she had survived his birth. He stared after the woman as she was led back to the cells. Then he looked down at the woman's garnet ring on his little finger, its blood-red stone gleaming out of the antique setting. He thought of his mother, her pain and her terror. His father had always refused to discuss what had happened that night. Once, in an effort to understand, he had gone to a lying-in hospital to observe a breech birth. The woman had looked to him more like an animal at bay. Eventually she died. It hadn't helped at all.

*   *   *

Ferris and de Born were brought forward to the well of the court, to a box ringed with iron spikes. One of the President's assistants presented the act of accusation to the jury and gave a lucid précis of the evidence against the suspects. De Born discovered only then that he had been charged under the Law of Suspects: First Category. "That he did by his conduct and remarks show himself a partisan of tyranny and an enemy of liberty." If convicted, he would be guillotined.

As he looked along the line of jurors, de Born's gaze met that of one of the slaughterhouse men from *Le Chat Gris*, who nodded and smiled happily at him. De Born then saw him dig his neighbour in the ribs and whisper some words into his ear. The other juryman looked at de Born and laughed out loud, much to the Prosecutor's annoyance. Evidently, thought de Born, his hopes rising a little, my career as a seducer of married women is being explained.

The Prosecutor then called Simon to the witness box.

"Name and profession?"

"Antoine Simon, formerly shoemaker, now Municipal Officer, Temple Section and," Simon left a significant pause, "guardian to Louis-Charles Capet." At the mention of the Dauphin's name a ripple of interest spread around the court.

"Relate to the court, citizen Simon, the events of 15 Brumaire last."

"Well, citizen Prosecutor," began Simon, "after a long and arduous day attending to my duties at the Temple, I decided to take my supper at a wine-shop in the Rue Béranger. I had not been there long when I heard my name mentioned, so I went to enquire who wanted me. Then those men ... "

"Which men, citizen?" asked the President.

"Those men there, the accused," explained Simon, pointing in de Born's direction.

The presiding judge scowled at the prisoners. "Pray continue, citizen."

"The accused then asked me if I would put in a good word for them with citizen Chaumette in the matter of a fuel contract," said Simon. "This was because they knew that I was intimately acquainted with citizen Chaumette," he added, inflated with self-importance.

"And what did you answer them?" asked the Prosecutor.

"I answered them," replied Simon, in the halting, mechanical way of the heavily coached, "that they should apply through the usual channels and take their chances like any other honest citizen."

"And then what happened?" asked the Prosecutor, in a tone that suggested that his patience was wearing thin.

"Oh yes, then they offered me money, knowing of my influence with citizen Chaumette." Again Simon looked at the jury. "But I refused and called them rascals and scoundrels.

"Then," Simon continued hastily, as he saw the look on the

Prosecutor's face, "they asked me about the Temple."

"And what precisely did they ask you about that most important and well-guarded place?" asked the Prosecutor.

For a moment Simon seemed at a loss. "I'm not sure I understand your question, citizen Prosecutor," Simon said, a puzzled frown on his swarthy face.

The Prosecutor sighed heavily.

"Is it not the case, citizen Simon, that these men asked you questions as to the displacement of the Commissioners and guards, information concerning the doors, staircases, gates and walls, facts that would be very valuable to the Republic's enemies?"

"Yes, that's right, citizen. They asked me all of that sort of thing," ended Simon lamely.

He was followed into the box by the landlord of the wine-shop, who seemed in his terror barely able to remember neither his name nor his profession.

"Please relate to the court that which transpired subsequent to the encounter between citizen Simon and the accused," asked the Prosecutor.

The landlord looked back at him blankly.

"Tell us what happened after their conversation," said the President sighing heavily.

"Ah, I see. Yes, well, the accused, that's them over there, they caused a commotion in my shop, which is always a quiet, orderly sort of place, My Lords, er, citizens, where no one ever raises their voice above a murmur or fights or even gets drunk, very much," said the landlord in a nervous rush.

"Did the accused le Bon strike any person?" asked the Prosecutor, indicating Ferris.

"Yes certainly, citizen, I saw it with my own eyes. He punched Martin la Gardonne, him we call Big Nose, because ... "

"Let me guess," said the Prosecutor acidly. "It's because his nose is very large".

"Why, yes," said the landlord, evidently surprised at the Prosecutor's uncannily intimate knowledge of his clientele.

"Anyway," he continued, "the big one with the beard punched Martin and I got my club from under the counter, which I keep there in case of trouble, not that there is ever any trouble in my shop," he added, glancing warily at the President, "and the other one, the one with the funny clothes, raised his cane as if he were going to hit me with it, me what hadn't done him any harm. Luckily the soldier hit him over the head with his musket, otherwise he could have killed me dead, probably."

De Born, having listened carefully to all this, decided that their only defence was attack. It was their word against Simon's about the bribery, and the assault on the other fellow was only a matter of a fine. If they could convince the jury that they had not mentioned the Temple guards they were out of danger.

"Where is your counsel, citizen?" the President asked de Born.

"I was not given enough time to engage one, citizen President," answered de Born in an injured tone.

"This is most improper," said the President, looking severely at the Prosecutor, who just shrugged and buried himself in his papers.

"With the court's permission," said de Born, "I would like to conduct my own defence and that of my associate, citizen le Bon."

"Although it is most irregular, especially as you are only a notary public," said the President grumpily, "I will allow it. Proceed with your deposition."

"The facts of the case are simple, citizens," said de Born, turning to the jury. "Citizen le Bon and I, two patriots whose only concern is to increase the Republic's prosperity by supplying cheap, high quality fuel to its citizens, asked this fellow Simon to advise us on how to approach the authorities with a view to gaining the contract to supply fuel to the Temple. He said he would advise us, but only on payment of 100 gold louis," de Born waited for the jury's gasps to die down, "and a significant fraction of our profits if we were successful in gaining the contract, which - he assured us - we would be. In his own words, citizens, 'Grease my palm and you'll have your contract'. Well, of course, we did what I'm confident you yourselves would have done: we refused. He then got very angry and called us rascals, us, citizens, whose only thought was to support the Republic in its time of martial strife. He threatened us with the law and said that he could have anyone arrested if he wanted to. Just like the aristos in the bad old days." De Born paused again while he let the significance of that remark sink into the jury's collective conscious. "We told him - forgive the language citizens, but we were outraged by his foul and unpatriotic behaviour - we told him to go to the devil. He, in a fury and, I might add, not entirely sober, rushed from the shop. As we were leaving by another door, one of the patrons of this disreputable place, no doubt one of Simon's accomplices, accosted my associate and barred his exit. I appeal to you, citizens, as free-born sons of France, wouldn't you have taken the same courageous course of action as citizen le Bon? Seeking only to defend my oldest friend, I was struck down from behind by a cowardly blow and lost my senses."

The reactions to his impassioned speech were various. The jury seemed impressed and not unsympathetic; Simon was beside himself with fury; the Prosecutor professionally admiring and the President deeply sceptical. Ferris, delighted by the reversal of their fortunes, kept clapping de Born on the back and whispering, "That's it, cockie, pound 'em and pound 'em again."

At that moment there was a flurry of activity at the entrance to the court. Sword drawn, a National Guard officer was clearing a way through the crowd. Having successfully completed this, he turned and raised his sword as a signal. To de Born's utter dismay, he saw the straw- coloured hair of Chaumette approach the bench, bow to the President and present him with a note.

When the President had finished reading the note, he called to an usher to bring forward the dossier from the hearing at the Surveillance Committee, which he opened and started to riffle through. De Born's heart sank as he remembered his uncle's warning about the forged documents. Eventually the judge pulled out what looked like a set of identity papers. Chaumette, after a brief word with the Prosecutor, went over to Simon and shook his hand warmly, all the time looking straight at de Born. The same look as he had given him in the restaurant, knowing and amused.

"Citizen Jurymen," said the President. "New evidence has come to light, for which we are eternally grateful to the diligence of citizen Chaumette. Citizen Cheftel's papers are clearly forgeries, indeed his name may not even be Cheftel. While forged papers are not of themselves evidence of treason, you may think as I do that only those with a great deal to hide go to such lengths. Have you anything to add, citizen Prosecutor?"

The Prosecutor rose with a lupine grin. "One could add nothing to such eloquence and clarity," he said, sitting back in his chair with a smug look at de Born.

"In that case, the jury may retire and consider its verdict," the President said.

As the jury filed out one or two were greeted warmly by Chaumette, while de Born's slaughterman friend looked at him reproachfully.

They were back within ten minutes. As each man stood in turn and answered "Guilty" to the clerk's question, de Born felt increasingly numb. Perhaps, he thought, there is a kind of rough justice about all of this. After all, we are spies, even if they don't know that. In any event, it is certainly better that we die in silence without either publicly embarrassing the Admiralty with our failure or handing a propaganda victory to an enemy government.

He hardly heard the judge's grim words of condemnation or saw Chaumette's look of triumph as they were led out of the court and back to the cells.

As usual, Ferris was impossible.

"Don't fret yourself, cockie, it could be worse."

De Born began to laugh, despite himself, and the sound of their merriment drifted back up the steps to the puzzlement of the judges.

As they reached the prison corridor he looked across at Ferris. "I'm truly sorry, Dick, for getting you mixed up in this mess."

Ferris gave him a slightly embarrassed smile. "Not your fault, old cock, risks of the trade - had to happen sometime, you know."

Despite its triteness, the sentiment cheered de Born up, so that when a worried Codrington appeared he was able to give the raised finger sign of death in a jocular fashion.

Looking down the corridor de Born saw Sophie waiting at the grille for news. He steeled himself to approach her.

"It seems, madame, that I am to discover before you whether the priests are right about an after-life," he said.

"I am truly sorry for it, Jean," she said with a tender look.

"Why so sad, Sophie?" de Born asked gently.

At the use of her name, Sophie looked up at him with a smile of pleasure. "Because the eyes do not lie, Jean, and yours are the eyes of a good man."

Suddenly, the strain of the trial and the tenderness of her sympathy became too much to bear. De Born was desperately afraid that he would break down entirely and for a while his eyes pricked with salt and he did not trust himself to speak.

"Do not be ashamed of your feelings, Jean. They come from the heart," said Sophie, reaching out her hand through the grille. De Born took it and held it between his. So used to wearing the mask, she was the first able to strip it away with just a few simple words. So clever at hiding his deepest feelings, she was the first able to expose the raw emotions below.

*   *   *

During the days following they were inseparable. First thing in the morning, both rushed to the grille, anxious not to waste a second. Last thing in the evening they stood, their hands clasped, until the turnkeys had to order them apart. Often they said nothing for long periods, finding peace and happiness solely from each other's proximity.

She told of her life, he of his. They never spoke of Etienne. They never spoke of the future. He found himself talking of things that he had never discussed with anyone before. She asked him questions that no one had ever dared to ask him. She contradicted him, normally something he could not tolerate, and he found that he did not mind. She teased him when he was pompous and self-important, and chided him when he was withdrawn and self-absorbed.

At night, de Born lay awake, astonished by his feelings for her.

When she was close, he was taut near to breaking. When apart, he thought constantly of having her, or even just holding her. He was alert to her every mood, transfixed by her every gesture. He felt overpowered. Losing control. Terrified.

CHAPTER SEVEN

Septidi, 17 Nivôse, Year II

It was the custom of the turnkeys to come each night to the cells after the clock tower had struck ten and read out what was commonly called 'the evening paper', a list of those condemned to die the next day. On the eve of the Epiphany, as it had been called under the old king, one of the older warders shuffled in and began calling out the names in a weak voice. De Born's was first.

As Ferris heard his own name he clapped de Born on the back. "At least we'll go together, old cock." To die together was, he felt, somehow not as bad as dying alone. De Born felt the same. He was also buoyed up by an obscure sense of satisfaction that the Republic did not even know who it was they were about to execute. In this at least he had outwitted them.

No one expressed sympathy. Every night was the same and they had grown used to the ritual. Each was secretly ashamed of the rush of relief when the list ended without their name being called. Most simply turned over in their bunks and quickly went to sleep. That night de

Born dreamt of Sophie. She was sitting under the mulberry tree at Roquefère, talking to someone with his back to de Born. The man turned toward him and he saw it was his father. Sophie beckoned him to join them. Try as he might he could not. The more urgently she beckoned, the more frantic his efforts to move his legs. Her face became ugly with fear and he summoned up all his strength, but it was no use.

He awoke sweating, his heart racing. The dawn light crept into the cell and he heard from below the sounds of the processional preparations. He woke Codrington and, taking a woman's garnet ring from his little finger, he gave it to him.

"What's this for, Cheftel?" Codrington asked sleepily.

"Please give it to Madame la marquise de Roquefère with my, my ... " De Born struggled for the right word, or at least an alternative to the word he had in mind.

"Compliments, old chap?" suggested Codrington.

"Yes, with my compliments," Said de Born. "Tell her please that it was my mother's and I wished her to have it."

"Certainly, old fellow. Glad to," said Codrington, putting the ring carefully into his waistcoat pocket.

*   *   *

As they assembled in the yard to have their hands tied, the prisoners studied each other in the grey light of early morning. A sorry lot we make, thought de Born. There were two cartloads, men and women mixed together, about a dozen all told. The carts were normally used to carry wood: three boards had been placed across them for seats, and on each board sat two prisoners. De Born had been the last to climb into his cart and only a little later did he realize that Ferris had been forced to get into the second.

Of the women, one was a common prostitute, who stared about her angrily and spat at any of the soldiers who got close enough. In front of her was a lady of almost regal bearing. She was wearing an immaculate English-style costume of white muslin trimmed with net and gathered by a velvet sash of broom-yellow. She had arranged her hair with great care and wore a simple but elegant bonnet. She took the liveliest interest in the proceedings, especially when the judge's carriage, which was to lead the procession, drew up. Beside her sat a much younger woman, whom de Born judged to be her daughter. She was plain, with a bad complexion and dowdily dressed, with a prim expression caused, it seemed, by the streetwalker's impressively obscene invective. As she sat she fidgeted with her rosary, but it did not look to de Born's eye as if she were praying.

The rest of de Born's companions were men. The first was old, perhaps seventy years of age, with chalk-white hair and a clerical air. He looked ill, rocking to and fro on his bench next to the whore, muttering unintelligibly and shaking his head. Sitting next to de Born was a comparatively young man, very ragged and dirty. He had an unhealthy yellowish pallor and shifty eyes that darted here and there, never at rest. His last companions, it seemed, were to be two aristos, a whore, a mad priest and a common thief. Good company for a spy, thought de Born.

A detachment of mounted gendarmes clattered up to the procession and took station at its head. At a signal from the officer, they moved off smartly towards the gate. The driver of the judge's carriage whipped up his team and bowled out of the courtyard in pursuit. The horses pulling de Born's tumbrel were hooded with canvas and blinkered, yet they were quick to follow what for them was obviously a familiar routine.

The jolting and swaying of the cart made it difficult for the prisoners to keep their seats, and the aristocratic daughter fell forward. After a few convulsive and unsuccessful attempts to rise, she gave up and lay slumped, half on her knees, half on her face, for the rest of the journey.

Beside the driver sat a very handsome, elegant man, occasionally looking at his watch. This was young Sanson, the executioner. One of his assistants sat beside the driver of the second cart, which was followed by a hackney carriage containing the *rapporteur* and his clerk, whose duty it was to witness the execution on behalf of the Prosecutor. The whole procession was guarded by single lines of pike-men, keeping step with the slow pace of the carthorses.

About now, de Born thought, Sophie will be waking and - pausing only to splash her face in the courtyard fountain - would come to the grille. Codrington would give her the ring and some words of sympathy. He was a little surprised to discover he could not predict her reaction, although he was quite certain she would not weep.

As they crossed from the island on to the Pont Neuf, de Born stopped his daydreaming and looked at the faces of the pedestrians. Very few seemed to be taking much notice of the procession, although de Born saw one man nudge his wife and point out Sanson, who affected not to notice.

At the far end of the bridge, he saw a figure who appeared from a distance to be writing on a board held on the bridge's stone parapet. As they got closer de Born realized the man was sketching rather than writing; indeed, his subject appeared to be the procession itself.

The cart halted momentarily nearly opposite the artist and de Born struggled to his feet.

"You bastard," he yelled, boiling with outrage and disgust. "You dirty bastard. Have you no shame? Leave us alone to die."

David paused in his work and looked up at de Born, shocked by the violence of the words. For a brief moment their eyes met, but the contempt and hatred in de Born's made David look away. As the cart jerked and moved on, forcing de Born to resume his seat, he looked back. David was looking towards him and sketching furiously.

De Born's outburst made him feel very much better. He had been uneasy about his reaction to imminent death. The preceding night had been filled with visions of cowardice, terror and ignominy. That he would be angry rather than scared had not occurred to him. Looking behind, he caught Ferris' eye, who winked at him. De Born grinned back gratefully.

*   *   *

As they turned into the Rue St Honoré, de Born saw that the street was full. Several of the crowd stopped to gawp at the procession, alerted to its presence by the noise of the cavalry troop. Others hurried along, not wishing to be late. One or two shouted abuse, which was met with a stream of obscenities and more spitting from the prostitute, until one of the pike-men pushed her back onto her seat. The noise and the shouting seemed to awaken the old man from his mutterings. As he caught sight of the Church of St Roch he stood up in the cart, swaying unsteadily with its motion, and looked around him as if seeing for the first time where he was.

"Father," he began in a desperate, pleading voice, raising his face to the sullen sky, "*de profundis clamavi*, let this chalice pass me by. I beg of you, send your legions of seraphs to my side." His gaunt, unshaven face worked frantically, his Adam's apple rippling up and down his scrawny neck. "*Agnus dei,* deliver me from this Golgotha, you who liveth and reigneth." He was now forced to shout above the growing jeers and catcalls of the passers-by. "*Kyrie eleison -*" His prayers were cut off abruptly in mid-stream by a well-aimed lump of horse shit, which struck him full on the cheek. For a moment he was stunned and stared at his tormentors in amazement. Then, head bowed, he began again, this time muttering sotto voce. He remained in this position until the carriage stopped at the scaffold.

As they entered the Place de la Révolution from the Rue Royale, de Born saw that a large crowd was waiting patiently for the procession to halt. A wintry ray of sun penetrated the early mist just for a moment. The scaffold, its beams and posts painted red, was on the left, on the Tuileries side, next to the plinth that had carried Louis XV's statue in the old days and now served as the base for a colossal statue of Liberty. Beside this was a large cart like a hay wagon, full of wicker baskets, also painted red. On the far side of the square the rented platforms were full of spectators scanning the proceedings through their opera-glasses. Around the right side of the scaffold and stretching to the centre of the square were seated the less monied but equally expectant crowd - looking for all the world, de Born thought, like the Drury Lane pit. Most were women, this being a working day, although some men stood about on the fringes. They chattered and peeled fruit and cracked walnuts. A fat, cheerful-looking man stood on the far side selling roast chestnuts from a brazier and giving a running commentary.

"Ah, here's Sanson. We've got the young 'un today, citizens. He's much quicker than his old dad," he shouted in a leather-lunged roar.

"Give a cheer for our brave soldiers too," he urged, and the crowd duly obliged, happy to be getting into the swing of things.

"So, who have we got today?" he asked rhetorically. He spotted the daughter staring around her wildly and looking on the point of hysteria. "Number One's a screamer, depend on it."

As if on cue, catching sight of the blade silhouetted high above her, the girl let out a series of staccato yelps. The two executioner's valets looked at each other and rolled their eyes. Swiftly and efficiently they cut her hair with a pair of shears, dragged her up the steep steps, secured the straps on the board to her arms and legs, slammed the neck clamp down, levelled the board and gave it a hefty shove so that it ran on the grooves until it came to rest directly under the blade. Each step was smoothly carried out at great speed and punctuated by the now piercing screams. Then Sanson pulled the lever and, just for a split second only, the screams stopped as the girl saw the plummeting acceleration of the triangular blade. Fourteen feet covered quicker than the eye could see. There was a brief silence, then the audience applauded, though not with any great enthusiasm.

With practised movements, the assistants threw the body into one basket, the head into another. Above the crowd's chattering came the voice of the chestnut seller.

"What did I tell you citizens? A screamer. I knew it," he said, pleased to be proved right. "Now comes her mum. She looks a tough old boot. That's what I like to see," he said, with much satisfaction, "a real aristo getting the chopper. There'll be a bit of an interval now, so you've time to get a lovely bag of my hot, sweet chestnuts. Chestnuts, 2 sou a bag, only 2 sou; best chestnuts," he shouted, waving his wares high into the air.

The interval was caused by the lady's bonnet. It had been fixed firmly to her hair by a large pin, the existence of which the assistant was unaware. As he yanked at the bonnet the pain inflicted on the prisoner made her give out with a loud objection. This led to something of an argument amongst the audience.

"Hey, that's not right," cried one of the tricoteuses. "Don't yank it like that, take it off properly."

"What are you moaning about?" shouted the chestnut-seller. "Do you think she wouldn't treat you just the same, or even worse, if the boot were on the other foot?" This convincing thesis produced a general murmur of agreement amongst the onlookers, helped, it must be said, by the look on the aristocrat's face, wherein contempt and a certain vengeful glint could be perceived. She looked, in short, exactly like one who, if the positions were reversed, would indeed have the cobbles running with the audience's blood.

The valet's shears having roughly chopped her greying tresses into a ragged fringe, the woman calmly mounted the stairs, shrugging off the helping arm of the valet. As she reached the platform, she surveyed the crowd imperiously.

Then, with a dismissive sniff she settled herself on the board and let herself be tied down. Her end was greeted with a cheer and a generous round of applause: the crowd had not liked that sniff one little bit.

When he spied the prostitute, the chestnut-seller let out a low whistle. "What, have the Committee of Public Safety made even that illegal now?" he joked waggishly, in tones of mock horror. "Citizens, if doing that is against the law now, we're all for the chop." For the first time that morning something of a smile was on the third victim's face. The crowd's attentions, which she took to be sympathetic, cheered her a little and she tripped lightly up the stairs and, on reaching the top, executed an awkward but creditable curtsey for one whose hands were tied. She turned to face the crowd.

"Fuck the Republic and long live the King," she shouted. "And now you can chop my fucking head off."

Her mood changed on the instant, however, when Sanson, nettled by the crowd's reaction, handled her roughly. She spat in his face and lashed out with her foot against his shins. As his assistants leapt forward to hold her struggling body down on the plank, her pornographic insults were drowned out by the outraged crowd's booing. They hadn't minded her royalist sentiments, but no one attacked their dashing hero Sanson and was allowed to get away with it. Boos turned to cheers when the foul stream was cut off in mid-insult and Sanson held up her head by the hair for the crowd's edification.

"Heaven help us, what have we got here?" said the chestnut-seller, as the old man climbed the stairs singing the twenty-second psalm in a wavering tenor.

"Number Four's as cracked as a nut. Listen to him, old loony.

Better off out of it, if you ask me." The blade ended the priest's song abruptly, but the crowd had grown a little bored and were already looking at de Born with interested anticipation.

By the damp, dark stain on his trousers and the pungent smell, it was obvious to everyone that the shabby thief had lost all control of his bodily functions. He was so overwhelmed by his terror that he had to be dragged up the steps, his eyes firmly fixed upwards, mesmerized by the sight of the blade. For some reason, his state excited the crowd and de Born could feel their visceral, animal reaction to the thief's frantic struggles. They were completely silent now, engrossed by his single-minded resistance. His end drew the largest cheer of all so far, the enthusiastic applause being engorged by pure pleasure.

"Dear me, look at Number Six's coat," said the irrepressible chestnut-seller, to roars of laughter. "My wife made a pair of cushion covers just like that last year. Mind you, by rights it should really be his tailor up there," he added, producing yet another appreciative giggle from the crowd, still excited and fidgety after the thief's death.

All de Born could think of was Sophie. It seemed to him bizarre that, only a few weeks before, he had no idea such feelings could exist. Now they were gone for ever. For some reason - no reason, really - Sophie had been convinced that she would die before de Born. He could hear her voice now as she repeatedly asked the same question: "Will you remember me?" Over and over again. "Will you remember me?"

The valet cut through de Born's stock and ripped apart the top of his shirt, baring his neck and breast. As de Born was spun round to face the scaffold he thought he caught a flash of straw-blond hair. He looked part-way over his shoulder and saw Chaumette, standing only a few feet away, holding a small dog in his arms. The bitch was excited by the smell of the blood and Chaumette was having difficulty restraining her. Finally he relented and watched as the animal set off eagerly to lick at the drips falling onto the ground from the edge of the scaffold.

The valet was about to shove de Born towards the foot of the stairs when Chaumette signalled a halt. He came very close to de Born and raised his hand to the prisoner's chest. He fingered the amulet lying there, turning it over so that he could read the inscription on the reverse. Then he leant forward and shouted into de Born's ear above the noise of the crowd, who were growing impatient.

"Do you have a word for me, de Born?" Oddly, he seemed to be giggling.

De Born, shocked by the use of his real name, stared back at Chaumette without replying.

"Do you have a word for me?" Chaumette asked again, still smiling.

De Born's mind was a blank. Then he remembered that

conversation on Horse Guards. He remembered the torches and the mist. His uncle whispering a peculiar-sounding word in his ear. The clamour of the crowd for his death was now overwhelming.

"*Mahabone,*" he remembered with a sudden shout.

CHAPTER EIGHT

Octidi, 18 Nivôse, Year II

As Chaumette's men hustled him off to a waiting carriage, de Born's eyes met those of his friend. For a brief moment Ferris merely stared at de Born, and then he nodded slowly in farewell.

As the carriage drew away de Born thought he heard behind him the blade's muffled thud. For some time after, he was to hear that sound and see that farewell nod in his dreams. It came to symbolize the desertion of his friend at the hour of his death. Sometimes, much later, when he dreamed of that day, it was his father's head he saw in the basket.

De Born had no way of knowing where he was being taken, tied and now blindfold as he was. The men either side of him neither spoke to him nor to each other, but sat alert with their arms linked tightly through his. He guessed they had travelled about a mile when the carriage came to a halt, so he knew they were still within the city walls, but in which direction he couldn't even guess. He felt no relief at having escaped death by a hair's breadth, but only bewilderment and confusion. The same questions kept repeating themselves. Who had

betrayed him? How had Chaumette discovered his real name? He must

know what de Born was, as well as who, so why didn't he reveal this at

the trial? If he had only just discovered the truth, why did he stop the

execution? Did Chaumette merely want him re-tried, this time as a spy?

He decided that the last was the only conclusion that fitted the facts.

He descended awkwardly from the carriage and was led through a

door, which was closed and locked behind him. The blindfold was

removed and he saw that he was in a windowless room, lit only by a

lamp hanging from the ceiling. By its light he could just make out a

large golden 'G', which hung from a chain attached to a ceiling hook.

The floor was a mosaic of a curious design. A single eye radiating light,

like the one on the amulet, was set in an equilateral triangle, both being

bounded by a square of tiles coloured blue, purple and scarlet.

Surrounding this were garlands of flowers and wheat sheaves.

One of the guards went ahead and opened a door in the far wall

and the other guided de Born into the adjoining room. This was much

larger, with black and white tiles for a floor. The ceiling had been

painted to resemble a celestial planisphere. The room was lit by candles

set on four torchères placed at each corner. At one end was a large

throne-like chair of an Oriental design. Above it was a baldachin of

white silk covered in skull and bones motifs. At the other end was a plinth on which stood what looked like a stone cube, although its sides had not been fully dressed. On the walls were fixed various ornaments and curios. De Born noticed in particular a sword with a twisted, almost spiral, blade, a gavel, a trowel and other objects the purpose of which de Born could not discern. It felt as if he were in a church or temple of some sort that had become disused and neglected.

In the middle of the floor lay an iron ring. The guard pulled hard at it and a square section of the floor swung up to reveal a set of steps going down into a cellar. The same guard returned to de Born, cut the cords that bound his wrists and pushed him down the stairs into the blackness. He felt his way with his hands outstretched before him until he came to a wall and then he sat down on the bare earth floor. After a while he heard the sounds of the guards retreating over the tiles and the closing of the outer door.

*   *   *

De Born was awakened by movement in the room above. He had no notion how long he had been asleep, except that he was very hungry and his throat was very dry. Suddenly he was dazzled by light pouring into the cellar as the trapdoor opened. A voice called his name and he stumbled up the steps to face the oriental chair. On it sat Chaumette.

"I trust you slept well, Monsieur le marquis?" he asked with his peculiar, sibilant lisp.

De Born stared back, but said nothing. One of the guards stepped over to him and, without warning, struck de Born hard on the face with his open palm. De Born staggered but did not fall and his eyes returned to meet Chaumette's unwavering gaze.

"I trust you slept well, Monsieur le marquis?" Chaumette repeated, in exactly the same tone of voice, just as if nothing had happened.

After a moment's silence, and after a barely perceptible nod from Chaumette, the guard struck him again, this time with his fist. De Born fell and had to be helped to his feet.

"As a matter of fact, I did," he said, wiping the blood away from his split lip and tasting more blood inside his mouth. It was pointless to resist, he decided, and incur further beating.

"If you're interested, I'm also hungry and thirsty," he added.

"And did your sojourn in the cellar give you time to work out what I know and how I know it?" Chaumette said, ignoring de Born's answer.

De Born shook his head.

"Or why I rescued you from the scaffold, or, most important of all, what I want now?" gloated Chaumette.

Again de Born shook his head, feeling decidedly unequal to the interrogation.

"So how do you like our Lodge of the Nine Muses?" asked Chaumette, gesturing to the room around him.

De Born was puzzled. What did he mean by 'Lodge'?" Nine Muses sounded more like a museum than a temple.

Now it was Chaumette's turn to be puzzled. "You are not of the Craft?" he asked sharply.

"I haven't the faintest notion what you're talking about," said de Born.

"Then where did you obtain that amulet, and how did you know the Master's word?" asked Chaumette, in disbelief.

De Born's explanation seemed to satisfy him, and his sly smile returned.

"Of course, Mr Secretary Stephens. Did you know he came here before the Revolution, here to this very Lodge, to become a member? The Nine Muses was the centre of the Craft in those days," he said, looking around the room. "Voltaire, Franklin, your Prince of the Welsh, Abbé Sieyes, they were all members, as later was the Lord High Sans-Culotte himself - Danton. I keep it up out of my own pocket, but since the old Grand Master Philippe Egalité was chopped, no one comes any more - they're all too scared.

"Incidentally, how is your dear uncle's health? I hear he underwent an operation in the summer for the stone. They say that the knife probed for seven minutes and he never uttered a sound. This in a man in his sixties; truly remarkable."

De Born was astounded by the extent of Chaumette's knowledge. If he knew such details, what else did he know? What most secret things? His informant must be in a very senior position to know so much. De Born made up his mind at that moment that, in the unlikely event that he ever got out of this mess alive, he would return to London, find the traitor and kill him.

"The answer to the question forming in your seemingly limited intellect," said Chaumette, "is that I know all I need to; certainly more than Pitt or Grenville deigned to tell you."

This time he laughed out loud to see de Born's obvious bewilderment.

"Yes, I know all about the meeting in Downing Street with 'Colonel Cornwall'. I know why you were sent here. We tracked you all the way to Portsmouth and then picked your trail up again at Chartres. We lost it temporarily in Paris, but soon picked it up again. By the by, the trick with the torn-up paper - very effective. I congratulate you." He gave a little bow.

"If you knew so much, why didn't you expose me at the trial?"

asked de Born.

"Because I did not wish others to learn what I know," answered Chaumette.

"And why did you go through the charade of snatching me from the guillotine, if you had no intention of letting me die?" asked de Born, genuinely curious now.

"Because I wanted you to have a taste of what is in store for you if you do not do what I ask. The fear of imminent death cannot be imagined, it must be experienced," replied Chaumette.

"And what is in store for me, if I don't do what you ask?" asked de Born.

"All in good time, Monsieur le marquis, all in good time," said Chaumette, evidently enjoying playing cat to de Born's helpless mouse.

"I could of course have impressed on you the seriousness of your situation by showing the corpse of your colleague John Page as evidence of my intentions, but unfortunately my over-zealous officers misinterpreted my instructions to shoot him. Instead of merely putting him up against the nearest, most convenient wall, they tied him to a nearby cannon and blew his body into a thousand pieces. Does Mr Secretary Stephens have the same trouble with underlings, I wonder?" Chaumette asked peevishly.

De Born's mind flashed back to the last time he saw Jack Page's rubicund face as he sat at signora Carloni's kitchen table, drinking that ghastly black porter he was so fond of and teasing a scandalized landlady. Suddenly he felt very angry.

"Go to hell, Chaumette. There's nothing you could say or do that would ever make me agree to any plan of yours," he shouted, taking a step forward before the guards restrained him.

"No?" asked Chaumette. "Perhaps it's a case not of something, but somebody."

With that he took a small, shiny object out of his pocket and tossed it on the floor in front of de Born. It was a woman's garnet ring.

All the fight went out of de Born at the sight of it glinting on the tiles. Chaumette evidently not only knew about his feelings for Sophie, he was hinting that her fate rested directly on de Born's co-operation. Chaumette watched the shoulders slump, the head fall and motioned the guards to stand clear again.

"I have indulged you long enough, de Born," he said, the mask of mocking politeness vanishing. "Now shut your aristo mouth and listen.

"Are you acquainted with the contents of the Law of 14 Frimaire?" he asked.

De Born shrugged. He had heard tell of it from someone in the prison but was hazy as to the details.

"Well I won't bore you with tedious minutiae, but effectively the

Commune's power, my power, over the National Guard and the Surveillance Committees has been destroyed. The Committee of Public Safety is now the great power in the land and your humble servant is not the force he once was. I have tried every avenue to regain that power, even trying to bribe Robespierre, but to no avail.

"Perhaps you can guess the result of this unhappy chain of events?" asked Chaumette.

"You'll go the same way as the enragés and the Girondins?" hazarded de Born.

"Quite so," said Chaumette, as if praising an unusually attentive student. "Robespierre will get rid of Danton and then me. Presumably he will then guillotine Sanson and be left the only survivor," he said with grim humour.

De Born's training in information-gathering asserted itself. "How do you intend to survive?" he asked.

"I intend to steal a jewel and barter it for my life," answered Chaumette cryptically.

"What jewel is worth so much and with whom do you intend to trade?" asked de Born.

"As to the latter, I have guaranteed my safety by forming a mutually profitable association with one Lewis Capet. He is perhaps better known to you as His Royal Highness, Louis Stanislaus Xavier,

Son of France and Regent, formerly known as the comte de Provence,"
Chaumette said, enjoying de Born's reaction.

"But what jewel could be so attractive to 'Monsieur' that he would
imperil his position as Regent?" asked de Born incredulously, scarcely
believing that the boy's uncle would stoop to dealing with a man like
Chaumette.

"Far from this imperilling his position, this particular gem will
make him king," Chaumette replied. "You see, de Born, you and I are
after exactly the same thing or, should I say, person. We both want the
Dauphin."

"I can see that such a prize might save your neck," said de Born,
thinking fast now after the initial shock. "But why do you need me?
After all, you could kidnap the Dauphin almost at will."

"Because 'Monsieur's' offer was an indifferent one and I think Mr
Pitt's will be far superior," said Chaumette.

"What on earth is so unattractive about Monsieur's offer?" asked
de Born, still unable to quite grasp the enormity of what Chaumette was
saying.

Chaumette replied in a tone of voice that carried a note of
petulance. "He wanted me to take the boy and then kill him. But with
the boy dead, how do I know he will keep his end of the bargain? No, I
now have a far better stratagem than putting my trust in princes. I will

give you the boy to take to England and you will see that Mr Pitt keeps his word."

"And what makes you so sure I will do what you say?" asked de Born.

"If you do not," said Chaumette, stepping down off the chair and standing close to de Born, "I will kill Madame la marquise de Roquefère. Not on the guillotine, you understand, but alone, slowly, after many days of pain and - how shall I put it? - bodily humiliation." He stared into de Born's eyes to make sure he was believed. He was.

"I'm still puzzled, though," de Born admitted, thrusting thoughts of Sophie from his mind. "Why didn't you let Ferris and me steal the boy first and then execute your plan?"

"At the beginning of your little odyssey," said Chaumette, "I had intended to do just that. But when I saw what a pair of bumbling imbeciles you and your late friend were, blundering around Paris like a couple of buffoons, alerting all and sundry and putting all my plans in jeopardy, I decided to have you arrested and put out of harm's way in the Conciergerie.

"Do you know," he went on, in the same humiliating tone, "what the sole result of your cretinous reconnaissance was?"

He waited until de Born was forced to shake his head.

"The Dauphin," Chaumette said with withering scorn, "is now

guarded more efficiently than ever before."

"If I'm such a buffoon, why choose me?" asked de Born.

"I had you watched very closely in London, until I was sure you were the right type," answered Chaumette.

"And what type is that?" asked de Born.

"Oh, hard, resourceful, courageous."

De Born bowed slightly in acknowledgement.

"And overweeningly ambitious," Chaumette added.

"May I enquire why that particular attribute is necessary for your purpose?" asked de Born.

"Because I needed a man who would do anything for recognition, applause, glory. That, de Born, is your weakness. That, together with the fact that you have all the silly notions concerning 'honour' of your class, which means your word can be relied upon."

"Even to do something dishonourable?"

"But what I want from you is not dishonourable, as you put it," answered Chaumette. "In fact you are going to do exactly what Mr Pitt asked you to do: rescue the Dauphin. The only change is that I am going to ensure your success and subsequent glory by helping you do it."

"Your price?"

"Well, certainly not recognition, and something a little bit more tangible than applause. To wit, a ship to America and one million gold louis - cheap for a king, I would have thought."

"And if I do what you say," ventured de Born, "how do I benefit?"

"You mean, of course, in your delicate aristo way," answered Chaumette spitefully, "that as everybody else has their nose in the trough, when do I feed?" Again he waited until de Born had been forced into reluctant agreement.

"First you will not be beaten to death by my men and buried in that cellar," answered Chaumette crisply, pointing to the floor.

"Secondly, you achieve the everlasting glory you seek as the man who rescued the Dauphin. Is that not enough?"

"No, it is not," said de Born. "I too have my price, and that is the life and liberty of the marquise."

"My dear fellow," said Chaumette with a sinister amiability. "Have her by all means. As soon as I'm on ship, sitting on the lid of a locked iron trunk containing one million louis, you may cuckold the marquis de Roquefère as much as you care to, with my envious benediction."

"Payment in advance," said de Born. "Release her and we'll talk."

"My terms are not for negotiation with messenger boys," Chaumette snapped. "Deliver the Dauphin and I give you my word that she will be released."

De Born's answer was a short, dismissive laugh.

"Very well, I will give you one hour to change your mind," Chaumette said, turning to leave. "Perhaps some food and wine might make you see some sense," he said, signalling to one of the guards. "But remember this, de Born: refuse me and not only will you die, but the boy and, after him, the marquise you are so hot for, will follow."

As he watched Chaumette's retreating back, de Born began to review his position as coldly and calmly as if he were his uncle outlining policy options for the First Lord. He did not wish to die, painfully or otherwise. In any event, his death would achieve exactly nothing. He wished to save Sophie from death and that was only possible if he agreed to Chaumette's demands. It was his duty to carry out his mission, if at all possible, and save the Dauphin from death. That too was only possible if he fell in with Chaumette's plans. Yet if he gave in to Chaumette and agreed to the offer guaranteeing Sophie's freedom, Chaumette could kill her at any time or use her as the lever to obtain further prizes. If Sophie died he knew that his life would effectively be over. He had to take the risk and stand firm. If he was wrong, both he and Sophie would be together - at least in death. True, from what he had just been told, the boy would probably die too, but that was as likely at Robespierre's hand as it would be at Chaumette's. He was decided. He wolfed down his dish of cassoulet and sat in his cellar prison waiting for Chaumette to return.

*   *   *

It was, he guessed, more like three hours later when he heard the noise of footsteps above. As soon as he saw Chaumette he sensed danger. His persecutor was in a towering rage, his face fit to burst its blood vessels, his eyes staring in a peculiar, unfocussed way with the pupils dilated to the point where the iris had all but disappeared.

"Well?" he demanded.

"You already know my terms," said de Born, careful to keep any emotion from colouring his tone, cautious as he was of Chaumette's mood. "They are unchanged."

"Take him downstairs and kill him," said Chaumette without hesitation, turning to leave.

"Do that and you will never survive to the end of this month," said de Born desperately, his gamble having failed utterly.

Chaumette turned back and considered de Born for a moment. "Why?" he asked.

"Because in that crowd at the guillotine this morning," said de Born, "there were two of my uncle's agents, Pingo and McPheat. They know you have me. Kill me and he will certainly kill you. Your position is no armour against his assassins, I assure you."

Chaumette went to the chair and slumped down into it, looking exhausted. De Born noticed that his skin shone with minute droplets of sweat, even though the room was cool.

For several minutes, Chaumette considered de Born's notion and then he jumped up. "Very well, but I warn you, if you so much as think a treacherous thought, the woman will be killed."

"You have my word of honour," de Born said, having no thought of ever keeping it.

Only somewhat mollified, Chaumette's anger turned to its real source.

"Why am I put in such a position, bartering for my life with imbecile aristocrats?" he shouted. "Robespierre - that holier-than-thou, bloodless eunuch. Always Robespierre, at every twist and turn." He gripped de Born by the lapels of his coat, shook his unresisting body and screamed into his face, "He is closing in. I feel his fingers at my throat. He intends to hunt me down, corner me, kill me."

For a moment de Born thought some fever or even a fit of madness had taken hold of Chaumette. Then he caught the pungent sickly-sweet smell that surrounded his captor. Ether, he thought: he's been taking ether.

A look of cunning came over Chaumette's face and he wiped the slobber from his chin. "What we need is blood, more blood, more and more blood until it overwhelms the monster himself, until he's drowned in an ocean of it." Chaumette's voice rose again to a shriek as he fell to his knees. "All the terror in the world is not enough; we must murder wholesale. We must punish the indifferent, the malcontents, the hoarders, the culottes-dorés, the whores, the rich peasants and the speculators. We must destroy the revolutionaries, the counter-revolutionaries, the aristocrats and the bureaucrats. We will kill all the priests, emigrés, lawyers and journalists. Eliminate the Federalists, royalists, Brissotins, Jacobins, montagnards, anabaptists, Jews and yes, even the Masons." He was shaking and gasping with the effort needed to remain conscious. There were rivulets of sweat on his cheeks, running freely like rain down a pane of glass. "When only the innocent remain, they will cry out for a leader and we will give them a leader. And that leader will have their power, real power that only comes from the people. And I shall be behind that leader. I shall be always in his shadow. And then, and only then - SHALL-I-BE-SAFE!"

Chaumette ended his speech with a huge shout, then his eyes rolled up into their sockets until only the whites showed and he dropped to the floor, his body twitching intermittently. As one of his men rushed to help him, the others hustled de Born back to his cellar. In the slight confusion he picked up and pocketed the garnet ring that was still lying on the floor where Chaumette had tossed it.

*   *   *

De Born was not to know it, but it was fully three days before
Chaumette would return. Interrupted only by his twice-daily meal of
soup and bread and the emptying of his pail, he thought with great care
and concentration of his next moves.

His first priority was to get a message through to his uncle at the
Admiralty, but to do that he would have to be free to go back to his room
in the Rue Béranger, retrieve his portmanteau and use the bottle of
Jay's agent. For a moment he considered writing a coded letter to his
Aunt Anne, but he soon dropped the idea. Chaumette was no fool, even
if he was drug-crazed. He would never allow any letter to go to
England. The best course, de Born decided, was to write a letter to
Sophie, which Chaumette could read and approve, and then fill up the
spaces between the lines with the invisible ink. But how could he get
Sophie to understand that her letter contained another, and that it
should be conveyed to Whitehall? He puzzled over this for a long time
but no answer came, so he left the problem to itself for a while, a
technique that had served him very well in the past, often producing

from nowhere a simple answer to the most intractable of problems.

His second task was self-evident. To devise a plan for extracting the Dauphin from a heavily-guarded prison and getting him to England without being captured on the journey. This took him a day to complete and it was, he congratulated himself cheerfully, flawless.

The third and last plan was the most pleasurable of all on which to work. It concerned the exact method he would employ to double-cross Chaumette.

CHAPTER NINE

Primidi, 21 Nivôse, Year II

When de Born was finally hauled out of the cellar it took some time for his eyes to adjust to the light. Chaumette was lolling in the chair as before, petting his lap-dog, but de Born saw that this time he was clear-eyed and calm. He guessed that Chaumette would not even remember his grotesque performance the last time they met.

"Well, de Born," Chaumette said. "Even you must have been able to come up with a decent plan given three days, eh?"

"I have indeed," de Born said. "But I'm going to need a great deal of equipment."

"Your every heart's desire shall be granted," said Chaumette expansively, stroking the dog.

"To begin with ... " de Born started.

"Wait," Chaumette interrupted, holding up his hand and ordering one of the lurking entourage to get paper and pen.

"Firstly," dictated de Born after the scribe had settled himself in readiness. "I need all the equipment I left in my rooms in Rue

Béranger, and the stick that I dropped in the wine-shop.

"Second, I need detailed plans of the Temple buildings and the surrounding area, including all sewers, drains and cess-pools.

"Next I need two new sets of papers. One should be of a doctor, born in Ballinasloe, County Galway, Ireland, with the name of John Callanan." He paused to spell the unusual name out to the scribe. "The other should be a retired army major named Pierre Delahousse, born in Cahors.

"To accompany those I want three sets of clothes for myself. Those of the doctor, including a medical bag containing some sort of salve, preferably evil-smelling, and a length of heavy gauze. Next, clothes that a retired officer might use for travelling, including riding boots and a heavy cloak or oilskin. In addition I want some old, worn clothes, such as a fishmonger's wife might wear; the dirtier the better. I also want a large cart and horse, loaded with barrels of oysters that have gone bad.

"For the boy I will need two sets of clothes, one of a common street girl, the others those that might belong to the son of a fairly prosperous retired army officer."

"Anything else?" asked a fascinated Chaumette.

"Yes," replied de Born. "We will need to establish a headquarters somewhere close to the Temple, preferably a house or at worst a large set of rooms."

Chaumette nodded his acquiescence.

"The last request may be difficult to come by," warned de Born.

"If it exists in France," replied Chaumette, "you shall have it."

"I need a boy the same size as the Dauphin. The hair and face are immaterial, but his shape and size must be identical, so we'll need to know the Dauphin's measurements. And most importantly, no one must know that this boy has disappeared from his home."

"The clothes are all disguises, evidently," said Chaumette. "But why the boy?"

"Because," replied de Born, "we are not going to kidnap the Dauphin and try to outrun the inevitable hue and cry. Instead we are going to substitute him with another, who, to all intents and purposes, is the Dauphin."

"Excellent," said Chaumette. "You know, de Born, I think I may have underestimated you."

Despite his hatred for Chaumette, de Born listened to this praise with pleasure. Little by little his professional self-confidence was returning.

"That just leaves the matter of Madame la marquise de Roquefère," said de Born. Chaumette's smile turned to a scowl.

"I have already given you my word that she shall be released,"

Chaumette said with a note of warning in his voice. On his lap the bitch looked up enquiringly at her master and whined softly.

"These are my terms," said de Born, ignoring Chaumette's reply. "I must see her in a public place, talk with her and give her a letter. You will, of course, want to read the letter and listen to our conversation, but I would prefer that you did that privily. She must arrive with her pardon signed and be free to go anywhere she desires."

"Very well," said Chaumette grudgingly. "But she may not leave the country, as all passports have been cancelled and no new ones will be issued until the war comes to an end. Agreed?"

"That seems reasonable," conceded de Born. "And the meeting?"

"Oh, as to that," said Chaumette, smiling mysteriously at some hidden joke, "I know the very place."

His expression changed with its customary swiftness. "Remember, de Born, what I said about trickery. The slightest attempt to renege on your promises and the Admiralty's External Department will find itself with a vacancy. Cross to England without me and I'll find that woman wherever she hides and kill her."

De Born nodded, careful to keep his face expressionless. Like many essentially shy men, he was an excellent actor, adept at assuming an impenetrable mask. Chaumette, who only ever judged others by his own degenerate standards, was convinced that he had de Born under his thumb. Which was exactly what de Born wanted.

*   *   *

Chaumette gave instructions for de Born to be taken back to his rooms on Rue Béranger to shave, bathe and change, and then to be brought to the Palais Royal, or Maison Egalité, to give it its new name. Meanwhile the headquarters would be set up, the maps and equipment obtained and a search initiated for the clothes.

By the clamminess of the air de Born, whose blindfold had been re-tied, could tell it was night outside. Since he had disappeared into the cellar, the weather had changed for the worse and he felt slush underfoot.

It was not long before the blindfold was being removed and de Born saw that they were approaching his lodgings in Rue Béranger. Watched closely by two of Chaumette's men, he cleaned himself up, shaved, leaving only the heavy moustache stubble, and changed into a fresh set of clothes. Amazingly, the gold was still in the bag, though the assignats had disappeared. Palming the bottle of Jay's agent, he walked over to the table, cut a fresh point for the pen, and scribbled out a short note addressed to Sophie. Taking advantage of a momentary lapse of concentration on the part of his guards, he poured some agent into the spare inkwell and wrote out a note to his uncle between the lines of the original, simply saying that he would bring the boy to the inn at Chartres and for him to arrange agents of *La Correspondance* to contact them there and take them back along the safe house route to St Malo. He sanded the letter, folded but did not seal it, and handed it to one of the guards. He returned the bottle of Jay's to the portmanteau, palming the knuckleduster as he did so, and announced that he was ready to leave.

When the carriage arrived at the Palais Royal one of Chaumette's toughs was on hand to guide de Born past the cafés, with their bright windows and sounds of happy carousing, through the arcades where the whores paraded (some of whom he noticed were children as young as ten) and on to the door of what appeared to be private apartments.

Going up a narrow staircase, they emerged at a landing where his guard knocked on a set of double doors. They opened slightly. The unseen inhabitants satisfied themselves of their visitors' identities. They were bade to enter. De Born found himself in a splendid salon strewn with thick Persian rugs and stuffed with delicate boulle furniture, including a magnificent Riesener roll-top desk worth a king's ransom, above which hung a succulent Fragonard showing an overwrought nobleman peeking up the dress of a pert young woman on a swing.

De Born was shown by the maid through into another long room furnished with altogether more masculine taste, where a substantial log fire was burning. The arrangement of the furniture, however, seemed to de Born to be quite extraordinary. An immense horse-hair sofa faced away from the fire instead of toward it and, what was even more strange, had been placed no more than a yard from the opposite wall, which was blank except for a series of oval portraits set in a row, only about three feet from the floor.

Chaumette was sitting in a tub bergère by the fire, his bitch on the floor by his side. Instead of asking de Born to take the other chair, he got up, moved to the sofa and silently pointed to his visitor to sit beside him.

No sooner had both men settled when the guard returned and nodded to Chaumette, who leant forward towards the wall, swung one of the medallions aside and applied his eye to a tiny spy hole. He then motioned de Born to do the same, cautioning him by a finger held at his lips not to speak.

De Born pushed aside the medallion opposite him. His hole allowed him to see clearly into the adjoining room. To the right was an empty chair. To the left was a large wooden frame in the shape of an H supported at a 70° angle by a strut, which was fixed firmly to a square of wood bolted to the floor. The frame was padded with stuffed leather, except for the cross-bar, which was covered in red velvet. The uprights had straps and buckles fixed to them top and bottom. As de Born puzzled as to its use, he saw hanging on the wall behind the frame a rack containing whips of varying types and lengths. Amongst the ordinary horse-whips and long lunge-rein schooling whips, de Born could also see bundles of large twigs gathered like brooms, various thin canes and a vicious-looking cat, whose tails were tipped with metal.

De Born drew back from the wall as if suddenly stung. He was looking at a room in a house of flagellation. He glanced towards Chaumette, to find the latter studying him with a mocking smile, obviously amused by de Born's reaction. He motioned de Born to look again through his hole, which he did reluctantly. He saw a door on the far wall open and Sophie walked in, accompanied by a hard-looking woman of middle-age who, de Born guessed, was the brothel keeper. She pointed to the chair near the whipping frame and he heard her tell Sophie to wait.

He watched as Sophie took in her surroundings, the puzzled frown at the frame, and then the uncomprehending glance at the wall to the rack of whips. She appeared very tired and unhappy to de Born. Her face was thin and she had dark smudges under her eyes. She sat listlessly in the chair, staring dully into space. The door opened again and the woman returned and handed her de Born's letter, which she took without any curiosity. As she opened it, the garnet ring de Born had folded into it fell out onto the floor. Sophie gave a cry as she recognized it and fell to her hands and knees in order to retrieve it. Standing up, she placed it on her finger and eagerly tore open the letter and scanned its contents. When she saw the signature she kissed the letter and read it once again, her face transformed with joy.

De Born could stand it no longer and, without waiting for Chaumette's permission, he opened the door next to the sofa and walked in to the room where she sat. As he entered, Sophie was stuffing the letter into her bosom for safe keeping. She looked up at the noise of the door opening and, seeing de Born, ran to his arms.

After only a brief moment, no more than a quick, tumescent stab of desire, de Born pushed Sophie very gently away. All of a sudden he felt self-conscious, partly because of the overwhelming effect the softness of her body had on him, partly because he was disagreeably aware that Chaumette was watching.

It took quite some time for either of them to compose themselves sufficiently to talk, and then Sophie's questions flooded out. How did he escape? Who arranged her pardon? Why had she been brought to this strange place?

Sitting her back down in the chair, de Born knelt by her side and did his best to answer her. He had come to an honourable arrangement with one who had great power, not willingly but because duty demanded it of him. This man had arranged her pardon and would arrange her freedom also. He could not tell when they would meet again, perhaps never, but whatever happened he would always remember her.

"Keep this letter as a memento of our brief time together," de Born said, clasping her hand and moving his body until he judged that he had obscured Chaumette's view of Sophie. As he talked he sketched the letters 'P.S.' on her palm with his finger. Sophie frowned, puzzled why he would not say the name out loud, until de Born saw her dawning realization that they were overheard. She nodded in understanding and quietly promised to do as he said.

Their parting was mercifully quick. As he kissed her hand, the hard-faced woman entered the room and took Sophie by the elbow and steered her towards the door. It was only afterwards that de Born realized that he had not told her what he felt for her. He had never used that word to a woman. Now, he thought, I probably never will. He stared after her in an agony of doubt. Was he deserting her as he had deserted Dick Ferris? He sat in the chair, examining his conscience, until he became aware of Chaumette's gaze through the peep-hole. For one mad moment thoughts came of rescue and flight. He fingered the brass knuckles in his pocket, imagining them crunching bloodily into Chaumette's face, seizing Sophie and escaping into the night. It only lasted a moment before cold reality set in and he resolved there and then to carry out his deal with Chaumette with no more distractions. No more thoughts of Sophie and freedom. From now on he would be bound only by the iron fetters of his duty.

"Touching, truly touching," said Chaumette as he entered. "Unfortunately I haven't got the time nor the inclination to watch you lust after some silly little aristo slut. We have work to do."

De Born silently shrugged off the coarse words. He was beginning to understand Chaumette's Machiavellian workings, the deliberate provocations to reveal true feelings, the sudden reversals to keep an opponent off balance and unsettled. The man was a clever devil, certainly, but for the moment at least he needed de Born and that was a weakness.

*   *   *

The headquarters Chaumette had arranged were in a house on the Rue Charlot, the street that formed the eastern limit of the Temple. On the ground floor was the kitchen, a scullery and a large room containing an ebonized pine table covered with maps and plans. On the first floor was a spacious withdrawing-room, comfortably furnished, with a dining room and a study. The second and attic floors contained bedrooms, all of which were empty save for three, in which narrow camp beds had been placed, together with a supply of sheets, bolsters and coverlets. The house was damp, suggesting the owner's lengthy absence, but fires had been lit in the main rooms and it was drying out rapidly.

Access to the courtyard at the back was by an arched coach entrance cut into the facade of the building. De Born could see a pump beside an old well in the middle of the stone-flagged yard. After a thorough inspection, de Born chose one of the bedrooms which had a wash-stand and, without taking off his clothes or snuffing the candle, fell instantly asleep.

The next morning de Born looked out of the barred bedroom window to see that the roofs of the neighbouring houses sported a thick layer of snow. Breaking the ice in the wash-jug, he poured the freezing water into the bowl and splashed his face until he was completely awake. Hearing sounds of life downstairs, he went to the door and, finding it bolted, banged on its panels until one of the guards opened it up.

De Born brushed past him without a word and went downstairs to the kitchen, where he found a cook preparing breakfast. As he ate, one of the guards stood by the door to the courtyard. The maid served him in a state of great nervousness. All in the house had been briefed that he was a dangerous criminal and, as the domestics had interpreted this to mean that he might become violent if crossed, the service was designed to please.

Having finished his bread and hot sugared milk, de Born went to the large room facing the street, which was still shuttered. On asking the surly guard why this was, he received only a brusque one-word reply of "orders" and a finger pointing to the candlestick on the table. Lighting this with a wax taper from the fire, de Born looked about him and saw that his portmanteau and trunk had been brought from his lodgings. The lock on the trunk had been smashed open and, judging from the higgledy-piggledy state of its contents, both it and the portmanteau had been searched thoroughly. De Born noticed with delight that Whitehead's stick was standing next to the trunk and seemed undamaged, although de Born was reluctant to examine it, for fear the guard would divine its purpose.

Gathering up all the maps, he went upstairs to the drawing room and, clearing a large space in front of the fire, laid out all the building plans to one side and the street maps to the other. His careful study of the sewer system was interrupted after only a few minutes by Chaumette. He looked debauched and pallid. His eyes were red-rimmed with lack of sleep and his gait was a trifle unsteady. De Born caught a faint sickly whiff of the now familiar narcotic as he stood beside him looking down at the maps. He had stayed behind at the Palais Royal after de Born left and was still wearing the same clothes as he had on the day before.

"Found something?" he asked, his voice a little thicker than usual.

"Maybe," said de Born, "but I'm going to need the advice of someone who knows the Temple well."

"Get Simon and bring him here at once," shouted Chaumette at one of the guards, without even looking up from the plans.

"What are these lines here?" he asked de Born, stabbing the paper with an ivory handled riding crop. De Born couldn't help wondering whether the whip had been in use the night before. And if so, on whom and by whom?

"Sewers and drainage tunnels," said de Born, starting to explain his interest, but Chaumette was bored and restless.

"Got everything you need?" he asked, walking about the room aimlessly.

"No, I have neither the clothes nor the papers I asked for," replied de Born, pleased at the dismay that this answer produced on Chaumette's face.

Dismay turned to black anger. He wheeled around to face one of the guards.

"Where are they?" he roared.

"There was so little time," stuttered the guard, whom de Born recognized as the scribe from the Lodge.

"No time? No time?" shrieked Chaumette, working himself up into a rage. "I'll give you no time." His crop slapped viciously against the guard's cheek, who clapped his hand to the open wound and stumbled from the room before the whip could land a second blow.

Chaumette stood for a moment in the middle of the room, breathing hard and still clutching the crop with whitened knuckles, until the frenzy passed and he sank into a chair by the window and stared out of it towards the Temple towers. Presently de Born, who had meantime returned to his study of the Temple's drainage systems, heard snoring and, looking over to the window, saw that Chaumette was asleep, mouth open. The crop had fallen from his hand to the floor beside his chair.

His slumbers were interrupted less than an hour later by the arrival of Simon, who looked shabbier than ever. His reaction to de Born's presence was an essay in incredulity. He stood gaping in amazement, with the beginnings of a suspicion that his usual diet of alcoholic hallucinations had taken a decided turn for the worse.

"No, he's not a ghost," said a vastly amused Chaumette, prodding de Born with the crop by way of proof.

"But he's dead," said Simon, appealing to Chaumette for confirmation.

"Not only is he not dead," said Chaumette, "but you have never met this gentleman before."

"Never met - ? Why, he's that ... " Simon began truculently, glaring at de Born, until Chaumette's voice lashed out.

"Are you going deaf, old man?" Chaumette shouted.

Simon, who up to this time had been staring stupidly at de Born and only half listening to Chaumette, reacted quickly to his master's anger.

"If you say so, citizen, it must be so," he said quickly, eyeing the crop. He had seen the damage it had caused on his way up and had also been told of Chaumette's dangerous mood. "I must have been mistaken."

"You are indeed mistaken, you old fool," said Chaumette. "This is Dr Callanan, a noted Irish surgeon."

Now thoroughly bewildered, Simon bowed and muttered some greeting, still glaring at de Born, but in such a way so as to prevent Chaumette seeing from his angle.

"Now tell the good doctor what he wants to know," Chaumette said, as if encouraging a servant of limited intelligence to humour an honoured house-guest.

"Look carefully at this map," ordered de Born, "and tell me what that building is," pointing to a rectangle marked on the plan next to the Great Tower.

Simon shuffled over, pulling out a rusty pair of spectacles as he did so, and peered at the spot de Born was pointing to.

"That's the old stable-block."

"'Citizen Doctor'," Chaumette prompted, the crop twitching in his hand.

"Citizen Doctor," Simon repeated hastily, bobbing his head.

"And what," asked de Born, "does this line here, leading from the stables to the Rue Charlot, signify?" pointing again to the plan.

"There? Why that's the main stable drain," answered Simon. "It leads from the mews to the main street sewer under Rue Charlot."

Chaumette walked over to the map and looked thoughtfully down at it.

"Could someone enter the drain at the stables and emerge in the street on the other side of the wall?" he asked with sudden enthusiasm.

"Yes indeed, citizen," said Simon. "I inspected those drains only last autumn. A man must stoop a little, but as long as there's not been a storm, water is at most ankle high."

"Where does the drain enter the main sewer?" asked de Born, his excitement growing.

"Here," said Simon, pointing to a spot not ten yards from the house in which they stood. "There's a set of iron ladders leading up to the Rue Charlot, with a heavy grille at the top."

"So," mused Chaumette, catching de Born's eye. "A man might walk from the turret door, cross the yard to the stables, disappear into the drain and emerge only moments later in the street."

"Yes, citizen, quite possible," said Simon, looking between the two men and desperately trying to figure out what was going on.

"Good, very good," Chaumette's crop cracked against his boots, making Simon jump. "Now get back to the Temple and tell the guards to expect the citizen doctor and myself sometime today to inspect the boy's health on behalf of the Commune."

"Yes, certainly, citizen, at your service, citizen," Simon toadied, eager to leave the room. "Yours too, of course, citizen Doctor," he remembered, just in time, before scuttling off.

As he left, the guard with the mark of Chaumette's ungovernable temper on his face entered.

"If it please you, citizen," he said, slightly out of breath, keeping well out of crop-swinging range, "the papers have arrived for your signature; also the clothes that were ordered."

While Chaumette signed the papers, de Born went downstairs and checked through the clothes. He found the set of doctor's clothes a tolerable fit, but they smelled badly of stale sweat and spilt wine. He then checked the leather bag, which contained a pot of greenish salve with a disgusting aroma and a roll of gauze but not, de Born noticed, any sharp instruments.

As he re-entered the room he murmured to the guard that the boy's clothes were still missing. There was no harm, he decided, in making a friend and he did not want to see a repeat of Chaumette's tantrum.

Chaumette swung round from the desk. "What are you two whispering about?"

"I was just congratulating your fellow on finding clothes of such a good fit in such a short time," de Born said, receiving a grateful look from the guard.

Chaumette merely grunted and returned to his writing.

"Here you are, citizen Doctor whatever-your-name-is," Chaumette said when he had finished, tossing a set of identity papers at de Born. "Unlike those pathetic forgeries the Admiralty produced for you, these will get you anywhere you want to go."

"Citizen Doctor C-A-L-L-A-N-A-N," spelt out de Born. "Do try and remember the name. You would look foolish indeed if you were to forget it in front of the Temple guards."

For a moment de Born thought Chaumette might strike him, but instead he strode out of the room and, with a stream of vile-sounding oaths, called for his carriage to be brought round. With a slight smile and a shrug the guard motioned de Born to follow.

*   *   *

The carriage pulled up outside a grim, white-washed building not far from the Bicêtre prison in the Rue de la Roquette. Outside on the gatepost was a roughly lettered sign announcing 'The St Maur Orphan Asylum For Boys', underneath which there was a scurrilously obscene graffito in a childish hand referring to the beadle's sexual proclivities. The object of this libel stood at the main entrance, one hand nervously washing the other. On his plump face there played an uncertain smile of welcome. Ignoring the proffered hand, Chaumette swept through the door and began to inspect the large dormitory beyond. De Born introduced himself and followed the uneasy beadle into the room. Although a little down at heel, the dormitory was surprisingly clean, the floor swept and sanded, the windows spotless and the linen patched but serviceable.

In all, de Born guessed, there were about fifty boys, each one standing stiffly by his bed eyeing the strangers curiously. Most were very young, between four and six years old, but a few were as old as twelve. All had been shaved.

"Measurements," Chaumette bawled at one of his men, who brought him a piece of paper. "Chalk," he barked, which started off a panic amongst the guards and orphanage notables until a piece was obtained from the schoolroom. Chaumette went to the end wall, where there was a brick column, and marked off two lines.

"Beadle, you will march the boys past these lines. All boys whose height is between the lines will remain in the dormitory; the rest can amuse themselves elsewhere."

"May I ask, citizen, what - ?" began one of the notables hesitantly.

"No, you may not ask," said Chaumette nastily. "You may leave, that's what you may do." Taking the hint, the massed notables hurried out before some fate worse than sarcasm befell them.

As it turned out only two boys were exactly the right height and shape. One was a good looking lad with a bold, bright slightly feverish eye, the other was a sickly-looking individual with a sunken head and rounded shoulders.

Indicating the weaker of the two, Chaumette asked, "What's the matter with this one? Aren't you feeding him?"

"This boy is suffering from a scrofula disease, citizen," said the beadle. He had whispered, to spare the child's feelings, but the boy gave no sign that he was aware he was the subject of their deliberations. Throughout, he slouched with bovine indifference to the examination, only occasionally moving to wipe his nose on his cuff.

The other stared around him at the visitors with frank curiosity. In his hand was a ragged scrap of paper. When De Born leaned over and asked to look at the paper he flinched and then seeing the man's kindly expression he shyly proffered it. De Born saw that it was of all things a portrait of Marie Antoinette, an engraving made in the early days. Not the lesbian harpy, or Madame Veto, or the Austrian whore of more recent vintage, but a print from the Vigée le Brun portrait. It was shocking to remember those times.

"What is this woman to you boy?" asked De Born.

Suddenly the boy's features came alive, he motioned to De Born to bend down so that he could whisper in his ear. "She is my angel" he replied in a minute voice, "my guardian angel. She will come for me soon, God willing".

De Born studied him carefully, it was impossible to discern whether the boy really believed it, or was just clinging to some hope that one day someone would come and take him away from his orphanage prison. Clearly however the boy had no idea who the woman was -or had been.

Chaumette turned the boy this way and that. "What's your name, boy?" he asked.

Instead of replying, the orphan merely turned his sad eyes to gaze up at Chaumette and remained mute. The resemblance to the prisoner in the Temple was close, de Born thought, perhaps not close enough to fool anyone who knew the dauphin well, still at a distance it just might work.

"What!" exclaimed Chaumette. "Doesn't he speak?"

"We think he can speak, citizen," replied the beadle tentatively, "but he refuses to. That is, since he came here he has not spoken - except once to ask for food in a whisper. You see, citizen, he was in the Bicêtre when the massacres of the boys took place and since then, well, you see for yourself. His name is Louis Raffin"

"Summary executions of known juvenile enemies of the Republic," Chaumette corrected him automatically, but without his usual rancour, being too interested in the orphan to get worked up by the beadle's faux pas.

"Just so, citizen," called out one of the notables. Since their dismissal they had hung about in the doorway, not daring to come in but feeling it was their duty to attend.

"Louis eh? "said Chaumette leering at De Born. "We'll take him," said Chaumette to the beadle abruptly, as if he were choosing a suckling pig.

"Of course, citizen Chaumette," said the bewildered beadle. "But what for?"

"What for? What for?" repeated Chaumette, for once flummoxed by the question. He caught sight of de Born's smirk. "The doctor will explain."

"Citizen Chaumette is conducting a scientific experiment," said de Born in a confidential tone to the beadle. "This Raffin boy is to be educated together with the son of an aristocrat. Citizen Chaumette wishes to prove that a true son of the sans-culotterie can, given equal opportunities of diet, study and exercise, indubitably prove superior to the epicene progeny of that degraded caste."

The beadle, not understanding half de Born's words but getting the general drift, beamed with pleasure.

"A scientific experiment, eh?" he said in wonder. "Just fancy, one of my boys selected for such an honour. Just wait until I get home and tell the wife. Bless my soul, a scientific experiment."

"However, beadle," said de Born, "you are not to mention this abroad. It will only make the other beadles unnecessarily jealous. After all," he continued with a winning smile, "we chose your orphanage as it was reputed to be the best-run in all Paris."

In the carriage afterwards, Chaumette looked at de Born speculatively. "Quick-thinking, aren't you, aristo?" he said. "A clever tongue, too. Ever thought of coming to work for me?"

"I am working for you," said de Born, "and I don't care for it."

"Care to tell me why you went through that charade?"

"What charade?" asked Chaumette asked warily.

"A moron could see that you came for that boy and no other".

Chaumette's scowl suddenly broke into a broad grin.

"That fool of a beadle had no idea who he is, or was rather".

Then he tapped his nose slyly. De Born listened as Chaumette told him how he had found out. A huge bribe from a grand seigneur about to die for Chaumette to look after his mistress and bastard. The bribe pocketed, the mistress promptly executed and the boy secreted in the orphanage until the day he could be of use. "You won't guess whose child he is in a thousand years" he said triumphantly to De Born.

De Born could not resist the challenge. "If I guess will you let me go?" Suspicious, Chaumette shook his head. Then he shrugged, "But I might not kill you".

"Orleans Egalité" said De Born with a conjuror's flourish. It was hardly a miracle. He had immediately noticed when the boy was brought in that the orphan's ear was misshapen, the right lobe being much longer than it's companion. The last time De Born had seen an ear like that it's owner was in Pitt's private closet in Downing Street. As unlikely as it seemed Louis-Philippe and this sad little boy were half brothers.

Chaumette went as white as his hair and then swore loudly and at some length.

"Bad loser" smirked De Born.

This merely raised another scowl from Chaumette and a sulky silence which lasted until they reached the main Temple gates in the Rue de Bretagne. There, de Born noticed that the sentries were all veterans, big men with luxurious black moustachios and weather-beaten faces. In spite of the fact that they quite clearly knew who Chaumette was, they still examined his papers minutely, even if the effect was somewhat spoilt by the sergeant holding them upside down.

The coachman wheeled the carriage around in front of the old princely palace, where two Municipal Commissioners waited, in their sashes of office, while Simon lurked in the background. Chaumette was all politician with the Commissioners, shaking hands and talking bluff and hearty, asking them solicitously whether their meals were acceptable and whether the wine he had sent them had arrived. These were, after all, the foundation of his power. Without the support of the leaders of the working class sections, his fall would be quick and final.

He introduced de Born as an Irishman loyal to the Republic's glorious cause, hater of the English (who daily trampled and violated his country), and expert in the healing arts. He explained that while their guardianship of the boy Capet was above reproach, he was dissatisfied (and here he cast a black look at Simon) with the boy's health and the good citizen Doctor was present so that he might examine the boy thoroughly and recommend a course of treatment.

The commissioners welcomed de Born enthusiastically. Any colleague of citizen Chaumette was indeed very welcome, and so on. Commiserations were expressed as to the foul treatment his country was suffering at the bloody hands of the perfidious English, who, since Cromwell etc. etc. They too, it transpired, had coincidentally been disturbed by the boy's state of health (more looks askance at Simon) and welcomed this opportunity of availing themselves of the distinguished services of citizen Doctor 'Calnan'.

So, bar one, it was a happy band of brothers who walked along the covered walkway towards the Great Tower, which loomed up one hundred and fifty feet above them. Looking to his right, de Born saw the stable block on the other side of the cobbled yard, perhaps one hundred yards distant.

As they ascended the narrow staircase in the north turret, the guards presented arms and the wickets were opened with alacrity. When they reached the second floor the guard outside the oaken door announced them and they heard the sounds of three bolts being drawn. As they stood in front of the second door, this one of iron, the same operation was repeated and then de Born found himself in some sort of ante-chamber dominated by a great stove. A man was feeding its enormous bulk with a faggot of ash sticks. Hearing their entry he turned and de Born saw, with a slight jump of his heart, that it was Cléry. His anxiety, however, proved groundless as Cléry merely bowed to the company and continued with his work.

From the room opposite came the sounds of a game of tric-trac being played and a child's treble mixed with a tuneless contralto. Following Chaumette, de Born entered the room. On one side of a table sat a fat, matronly type of woman, singing a verse of the *Ça ira*, tapping out the rhythm on the stone flags with her clogs. On the other, bawling out the chorus lustily, was a small boy, a red liberty cap askew on his long chestnut curls, dressed neatly in a slate-grey coat with brass buttons and fawn breeches. For a moment he ignored the newcomers as he threw his dice from a leather cup onto the table, but, spying a stranger present, he looked up at de Born with frank curiosity. De Born stared back into his mischievous blue eyes, into the merry, red-cheeked face of His Most Christian Majesty, Louis, King of France and Navarre.

CHAPTER TEN

Duodi, 22 Nivôse, Year II

"Well, Capet, where's your manners? Here's Dr Calnan come to visit you," chided Chaumette. The boy flushed and got down from his chair and came over to de Born, making him a little bow before holding out his hand.

"I am enchanted to make your acquaintance, citizen Doctor," the boy said. His voice was oddly slurred. De Born felt the unusual warmth of the child's hand and put a palm up under his fringe as La Signora did sometimes when he felt a cold coming on. That was warm, too; very warm. At de Born's touch the boy staggered back a pace, unsteady on his feet. Swiftly de Born bent down and sniffed at the boy's breath. Incredibly, it smelled of brandy. The boy was drunk.

"Who's been giving this child spirits?" demanded de Born, outraged at his discovery. All eyes swivelled towards Simon, who shuffled from foot to foot uneasily.

"The soldiers will give it to him," he whined. "I've asked them to stop but they will do it."

"I'll deal with you later," snapped Chaumette, glaring at the hapless Simon. "Meanwhile, gentlemen," he smiled graciously, "we must leave the doctor to examine the boy in peace. Come, I have an excellent bottle of St Emilion to punish next door. I would be grateful if you would honour me with your opinion of its qualities."

"Help the boy off with his clothes," de Born ordered the matron, who turned out to be Simon's wife. As she did so, he could see by the way the boy giggled ticklishly that they got on well. Equally, it was obvious from his anxious glances at Simon that he feared a beating after the doctor had left, for putting his guardian in such an awkward spot over the brandy.

The boy seemed painfully thin to de Born, but he dimly remembered that he too was skinny at that age. As well as the vaccination marks, he also had a large yellowing bruise on his left forearm and several smaller ones on the back of his legs.

"How did these happen to you?" he asked the boy gently.

"I fell over," Louis replied in a small voice, but could not resist another swift look at Simon.

De Born turned to the old man. "How did they happen?" he asked, not so gently.

Simon went through a pretence of fumbling for his spectacles. He peered at the boy for a few moments. "How did what happen?"

De Born's hand shot out and grabbed Simon by his throat and dragged him down onto his knees. His face was now only a couple of inches from the boy's arm.

"How did that happen?" repeated de Born.

Shocked and frightened, Simon muttered something about the boy always falling down and hurting himself.

De Born dragged him upright until their faces were close enough for him to smell the man's foul breath. "Touch the boy again," he said in a chilling whisper, "and I'll beat you to death with my own hands," before flinging him against the wall.

"Now get out and stay out until I call for you," he said, watching Simon shuffle off on his gouty feet, still clutching at his throat. "And you citizeness," as the terrified old woman made to follow her husband, "will stay until I tell you may leave."

The effect on the boy of this scene was singular. He looked up at de Born in awe. No one had ever treated citizen Simon in this manner before, not even the great citizen Procureur Chaumette, who had cut papa king's head off and was thus the most important person in the whole world. He was deeply impressed, excited, and not a little scared.

*   *   *

De Born took the boy's head in his hands and lifted up the hair covering his right ear. There again was the misshapen extended lobe the boy's cousin Egalité *fils* had spoken of in Downing Street. That all now seemed like a lifetime ago to de Born, which indeed for Louis-Philippe's father it was. The Prince of Wales' ardent wish for his fate had been granted, for he had been guillotined while de Born was in prison awaiting trial.

The boy's clothes having been replaced by Madame Simon, de Born curtly gave her permission to leave and settled down at the table to interrogate the boy.

"Who are you?"

"Louis-Charles Capet," said the boy without hesitation. He coughed sharply like a fox barking.

"Who did you used to be?"

"The Dauphin of France and before that the Duke of Normandy," replied the boy after a pause. Again the coughing.

"Where is your father?"

"Gone to see God, citizen, because he was a traitor to the people," said the boy as if remembering his lessons. He leant forward over the table towards de Born. "May I whisper in your ear, Monsieur?" he asked. After receiving de Born's nod he got off his chair, trotted round to de Born's side of the table and stood on tiptoe to reach his ear.

"But he was a good man for all that and I loved him," he whispered solemnly before marching back to his chair.

De Born smiled to encourage the boy.

"Where is your mother?"

"Upstairs with my sister Marie," Louis said simply, pointing to the ceiling.

For a moment de Born misunderstood the gesture, thinking the boy was indicating heavenwards, but suddenly he realized that the boy genuinely had no knowledge of the Queen's execution or even that she had been taken from the Temple to the Conciergerie months earlier.

The boy yawned sleepily and de Born decided to let him rest. Patting him on the head he told him that he would see him again very soon.

The boy's face brightened. "Thank you for coming to see me, citizen Doctor," he said. "It's nice to talk to a new friend, as I'm not allowed out of this place and don't meet new people any more."

De Born waved his goodbye at the door and went back through the ante-chamber to the dining room on the other side, where the noise of toasts being drunk and pipe smoke filled the air.

"Well, citizen, what news of the boy?" asked Chaumette, his face flushed with wine and conviviality.

"Grave tidings," said de Born, adopting the sepulchral tone favoured by the most expensive quacks. "The boy is ill and needs immediate treatment."

General consternation greeted this news. "How ill is he? What illness does he have? What will the Committee say?" all came out in a breathless rush.

"Now, citizens," de Born said, holding out his arms to calm them. "The treatment is simple and, providing we take care, we need not worry about a relapse."

"Well I never," Chaumette said to the Commissioners, overacting and enjoying himself hugely. "It's a damn good thing for you I brought the doctor. He'll see you all right, never fear."

"The boy's head must be shaved to release the foul humours in his brain," said de Born, "and a special salve must be applied to the face. I'll leave a pot for the old woman. It will itch a little, so to stop the boy picking at it, a gauze mask must be tied below the eyes."

"I'm sure, doctor, we can leave these dedicated representatives of the people to see that your instructions are carried out to the letter," Chaumette said to the two nodding Commissioners, their anxiety dissipating under the force of de Born's cool competence.

"However," said de Born, "a thorough examination must be made of the Temple's sewers and drains. This condition is often the result of foulness carried on the damp air."

"Perhaps, doctor, as you are a noted practitioner in this subject, you could honour us by making an inspection in person?" asked Chaumette with a suppliant air.

After de Born had graciously agreed and Simon having been sent for, the two of them went off to look at the stables. As the old man limped after de Born he cast anxious glances at the younger man, dreading a re-occurrence of de Born's sudden violence, and brooded over Chaumette's as yet unfulfilled threat. As they reached the stable block de Born could now see that in reality it was two buildings joined together. On the right was an untenanted, two-storey cottage with a steep slate roof. The left side was divided into a series of individual boxes, ending in a roofed-over section open to the yard. It was to this part that Simon directed him and de Born saw, in the middle of the sloping floor, a circular grille the size of a cartwheel. Spotting a pair of groom's overalls hanging on one of the stalls, de Born put them on and helped Simon swing the grille off the hole and lay it on some nearby straw.

He climbed down slowly, testing each rung under his weight. The brickwork was firm, but the mortar was damp, albeit in reasonable condition. He stepped off the last rung gingerly and felt his boot sink about an inch into the sewers' contents, which were the consistency of a thick peasant soup. The sewer stretched behind him in the direction of the old palace and in front of him in the distance he could just make out a shaft of light from the manhole in the Rue Charlot. As he walked towards it he could hear the alarmed squeaks of the rats as they scampered ahead of him. He could not stand upright under the brick arch of the sewer and, to steady himself, he had to use his hands on the sides, but the going was not particularly difficult. He became aware of a strange rumbling noise, which seemed to be getting closer. He stopped for a moment, moving his head this way and that to discover the direction of the noise, before eventually realizing that it was the sound of carts rumbling along the cobbles of the street above him. The rungs of the manhole ladder were rusty but the brickwork held his weight without any sign of strain. He gave the manhole cover a cautious shove, not wanting to open it completely. Although much smaller than the one in the stables, it was much thicker and so just as heavy. He judged two men would be needed to lift it.

Retracing his footsteps, he climbed up the ladder to see Simon sitting on a pile of damp straw smoking his pipe, evidently pondering what de Born was up to but not daring to ask. De Born took off the overalls and washed his hands and boots in the trough before returning to the Great Tower. Obviously, he thought, that was the ideal way out, but how to get the boy from his room, past the guards and across the yard to the stable drain? And even more tricky, how was he to get the duplicate Dauphin from the orphanage into the boy's room without detection? Just at that moment an ostler appeared leading a superb percheron along by a rope. De Born stopped to admire the huge horse, with its winter coat hanging long and glossy. And then all in a rush it occurred to him how to solve the problem. The solution tickled him so much that he laughed out loud and, seeing the surprise on the ostler's face, he laughed out loud a second time and jubilantly tipped the astonished man 10 sou.

*   *   *

Chaumette was waiting for him under the covered walkway.

"Well?" he asked, all his pretended insobriety and false conviviality having vanished.

"If the level inside the sewer doesn't rise, it's very nearly perfect as an escape route," said de Born. "But the manhole cover in the Rue Charlot needs two men to lift it."

"My men can do that on the night," Chaumette countered, brushing aside the problem. "They'll signal the oyster cart to draw up to the manhole to screen you from any onlookers as you emerge."

As they strolled back to the palace forecourt they acknowledged the salutes of the sentries and they took the carriage the short ride to the house in Rue Charlot. As they did so de Born casually asked Chaumette just how *au courant* he was with the works of Virgil. Chaumette, stung by the implication in the question, challenged him to cite his reference.

"Our biggest problem," said de Born, "is to smuggle the duplicate boy into the Tower undetected. Agreed?"

Chaumette assented reluctantly, unhappy that he was being led by the nose but unwilling to ask his destination.

"We will do as the ancient Greeks did," continued de Born, "and leave the Trojans a present: a large, wooden rocking horse."

Chaumette struggled silently with this preposterous idea for a few moments before losing patience.

"In God's name, man, what are you babbling about?"

De Born explained. "In about a week's time - say 30 Nivôse, that's not a working day - Simon and wife will take their leave of the boy and move into the stable house with their belongings."

"Why on earth should Simon do that?" asked Chaumette.

"Because you will sack him and give him a week's notice; or, better still, find some reason why he must resign. Use of the house can be explained as a sop to his feelings. The boy will be hidden in amongst their chattels."

"Yes, I see," said Chaumette, still struggling with Greeks and horses. "But how does the duplicate get - ?" Here he broke off and looked at de Born in delight. "Of course!" he yelled. "The story of the Trojan horse, the horse with the Greeks inside it. You intend to put the duplicate inside the horse."

"Exactly," said de Born, his eyes shining with excitement. "And the Simons will give it to the Dauphin as a goodbye gift. All the guards will see is a horse going in and staying in. If they look inside the room all they will see is a shaven-headed boy whose face is as usual covered by a gauze mask, playing happily with his new toy."

They had arrived at the house and Chaumette bounded up the staircase to the salon and rang the bell. When one of the guards answered the summons, he told him to find a carpenter who made rocking-horses - large ones. He then paced up and down the room, occasionally chuckling to himself at the plan's daring and originality. Suddenly he stopped in the centre of the room and clapped his hands.

"I've got it!" he shouted, pleased that he too could come up with ideas. "The new regulations forbid any person from holding two public offices at the same time. Simon will give this as a reason when he resigns, and return to his tasks as a Municipal Officer in the Temple section." He then pulled the rope again and ordered up a Lucullan dinner for two, after which he went off and left de Born to his sleep and to his uneasy dreams.

This time Sophie lay face down under the mulberry tree. She was not moving. When de Born turned her over he saw that she was dead and, like Thisbe, her blood had stained the fruit bright red.

*   *   *

The next few days were spent organising the manufacture of the horse and arranging Simon's transfer. A carpenter who specialised in supplying the toy shop on the Rue Richelieu was found and brought to the house. He watched carefully while de Born sketched out his requirements: 'a gift for his nephew', it was explained. The size was not a difficulty, the carpenter explained proudly; he had made an even bigger one once for a real duke, but he had never made one that was hollow. When de Born insisted that the front and rear sections should be capable of separation, the carpenter patiently explained that when the child sat on the saddle above the join it was liable to break in two. But, seeing that the gentlemen were set in their ways and fearing that he might lose the job to another, he went off promising to do his best.

Simon took the news of his 'resignation' philosophically as he had been terrified by Chaumette's threats and this fate was far better than all the hideous ones his imagination had dreamt up. Chaumette and de Born had agreed that he should only be told about the escape at the last moment, as his drunkenness made him talkative and unreliable.

De Born spent most of his time overseeing the detailed planning and in visiting the boy. He went every evening, passing the time of day with the Commissioners and carrying twists of tobacco for the sentries. Before very long he was being let in with just a wave and a chat about the weather or the terrible price of bread.

He chatted to the boy while he changed the dressing, to gain his confidence, and never failed to arrive with some trifle; a toy or some bonbons. Although Louis would never refer to any event that took place before his imprisonment, he seemed happy enough to talk about his life in the Temple.

"What do you like doing best, Louis?" de Born asked him one evening.

"Playing fetch with Moufflet," replied Louis, referring to his lively cocker spaniel.

"What else?" asked de Born.

"Talking to Cléry," Louis said. "He tells me about the places he goes and the people he meets when he goes out. I like that, because it's a bit like I'm meeting them too."

"Perhaps one day you'll be able to go out and meet all those people yourself," ventured de Born. "Would you like that?"

"Oh, yes," said the boy wistfully. "That would be best of all." His face fell. "Sometimes I ask when I may leave, but the citizen Commissioners," he stumbled over the long word, "never answer."

"What would you do if you could leave?" asked de Born.

"Oh, that's an easy one," said Louis, cheering up instantly. "I'd go and see Cléry's granddad. He's ninety-two and still got all his own teeth," he said in awe.

De Born stuffed his hands behind his back and then placed his fists on the table.

"Which hand?" he asked, playing the guessing game that usually signalled his departure and made it less of a burden for the lonely boy.

Louis was in an agony of indecision, hopping from one foot to the other. For three nights in a row he had successfully chosen left and didn't want to break his winning streak.

"Left," he shouted finally in an ecstasy of anticipation. Slowly de Born unravelled his fist. Louis gave a triumphant yell which brought Cléry into the room. The boy waved the candied fruit above his head in his excitement and then impulsively ran to hug de Born and kiss him goodbye.

The first time this had happened de Born had been taken aback.

He was not used to children, and their animal joy and spontaneous show of feeling surprised and embarrassed him. Little by little he got used to the boy's need for physical affection and found himself responding. After so many weeks of thinking of Louis more in terms of an object, a problem to be solved, an opportunity for glory, the discovery that he was human had come as something of a shock. He had begun to feel protective about the boy, which made him a little uneasy. His world was changing so fast he really could not take it all in. Only a few months ago he would have scoffed at the idea that a mere woman could come to mean so much to him, or that some brat of a boy could arouse in him the instincts of a father. He felt changed, but he was unsure where the change was leading.

The unease was made all the greater because none of this fitted with the way he thought about himself. A rational, serious man, who despised romanticism and domesticity. A man of action and destiny, not to be tied down by a bourgeois hearth or uxorious apron-strings. These ideals now seemed somehow less important to him and he feared this meant that he was surrendering to some sort of weakness in himself. He gave thanks that his father was not around to see it. Imagine what he would have said. "Duty, honour, truth," he used to say, thumping his stick on the floor for emphasis. "That's all a man needs to dwell on." Ever reluctant to accept that his father may have been even slightly mistaken in any of his opinions, de Born felt guilty that he should enjoy these new pleasures of the spirit.

As Cléry watched his charge's happiness overflow, he smiled in contentment.

"God bless you, M'sieu," he whispered to de Born, and led the boy, still flushed and -excited by his triumph-coughing convulsively, off to his bed.

*   *   *

On the morning of the 30th Nivôse, de Born woke and hurried to his window. To his dismay the yard was awash with rain, streaming down the roof of the house opposite and soaking the oyster cart that had been left on the cobbles overnight.

Looking at his Breguet hanging on the door handle he saw that he had overslept and, when he went down to the kitchen, he found that Chaumette had already arrived.

"Good afternoon," said Chaumette while de Born busied himself with his bowl of coffee to hide his embarrassment.

"Has the horse arrived?" he asked Chaumette, whose expression changed to one of irritation. Despite endless discussions with the carpenter, the version they had seen two days before was hopeless, being both too small and too clumsy in its system of joining the halves together.

"It had better," said Chaumette, "or I'm going to guillotine that carpenter myself."

At the sound of a commotion at the front door, both men rose and investigated. It turned out to be the errant carpenter and his two muscular assistants, manhandling the huge horse up the stairs to the salon.

"There you are, citizens," the carpenter said with a flourish. "Works perfectly. Even sat on it myself. Nary a shudder nor a creak. Best elm, that is, last for years."

De Born unbuckled the two catches on either side underneath the girdle. The carpenter had solved the problem neatly by putting a horizontal lip-joint onto the body so that the top and bottom divided into two. The halves separated smoothly when the head was pulled and then slid back together easily. So fine was the craftsmanship that only a faint line was visible, and then only if the harness and saddle were removed.

The carpenter and his team were paid off handsomely and, as they departed, whistling and grinning at their good fortune, Chaumette called for the boy. He had been brought from the orphanage the previous evening and had slept in the room next to de Born's. During the night de Born had been awakened by some sort of noise, which he thought may have come from the boy, but on hearing nothing further he decided to let him sleep on. The orphan was the only part of the operation de Born was uneasy about. On the one hand, he rationalized to himself, being taken from an orphanage, from the poor diet and routine brutality of the older boys and given the life of a prince wasn't the worst fate one could imagine. Yet, somehow, when he looked at that face, it was hard to hide the fact from himself that sooner or later the authorities would discover the swap. They would then almost certainly kill the boy, if only to cover up their embarrassment, and then announce he had died from natural causes. That would also have the beneficial effect from their point of view of casting doubt on the identity of the Dauphin when Pitt paraded him as King. It was no use saying to himself that it was for the greater good, or he would die anyway in the orphanage, or any of the hundred and one excuses he had created in his mind. The boy was on his conscience and he knew he always would be.

The object of all this soul-searching shuffled into the room. He had been taken from that horrible place where the boys all beat him and made fun of him. He had come in a carriage, the kind rich people travelled in, been given meat and wine and allowed to sleep in his own bed in a nice warm room. Everywhere in this place there were wood fires and candles, warmth and the smells of food cooking. No one beat him. He dimly remembered another house like this, a place with soft women and people laughing, but it was a very long time ago and he was not sure that it wasn't something he hadn't dreamt rather than actually experienced. The men were speaking to him but he couldn't make out what they were saying. He felt hungry so he put out his hand for food and soon he was led away and given some breakfast.

"This was all your idea," fumed Chaumette, panicked by the boy's glassy eyes and obvious failure to understand their promptings. "I knew from the start that the whole thing was too complicated. We should have just removed the Capet boy and made a dash for the Channel."

"Stop your whining," de Born said contemptuously. "We'll just sedate the boy by putting something in his food and put him in the horse ourselves. That way he won't make a noise when we carry him in and he can sleep it off in the Dauphin's bed. Even if he does speak eventually and gives the game away, I'll be in Dieppe awaiting your arrival."

Chaumette calmed down immediately, reassured by de Born's air of certainty.

"Perhaps we should give him something to make him sleep for ever," Chaumette said with a sly expression.

"If the boy dies," de Born said, "what good will the real Dauphin be to us? Robespierre will say he's an imposter and Pitt will hang you for wasting his time."

A shadow of fear flitted over Chaumette's face. "Yes, you're right," he muttered. "Just my little joke. No need to mention hanging."

The rest of the day was spent rehearsing every move. Simon and his wife had been pleased with the idea of the escape after they got over their initial shock about their part in it. They saw it both as a way of getting back into Chaumette's good books, and an opportunity to blackmail him later on. Either way, they received their instructions cheerfully and went off to arrange matters at the Temple.

Simon told the Commissioners that the couple would move out to the stable block on the dot of midnight with all their possessions. He then procured two hand-carts, one for linen, which would carry Louis, the other for their meagre collection of furniture and other effects.

The Commissioners had also been told that de Born would come that night in order to sign the certificate for Simon attesting that the boy left his care healthy. By early evening there was little to do except watch the rain falling and wait. At ten o'clock, Chaumette - as he did every night - took himself off to the Palais Royal 'to get the latest political news' -or so he said.

As he heard Chaumette's footsteps going down the front steps to his carriage de Born seized his chance. He scribbled a note to Simon advancing the entire operation one hour, carefully copying Chaumette's signature from a letter he had found in the salon desk a few days earlier. Calling one of the guards, he asked if Chaumette had left and, on being told that he had, exclaimed in annoyance.

"But he's forgotten to send his note to Simon," said de Born in dismay. "You'd better go over to the Temple and make sure he gets it. It's obviously important." By now the guards were used to taking orders from de Born, who was clearly in league with their master in this strange affair. The man took the note without a word and left hurriedly. De Born watched him trot down the street towards the main entrance of the Temple in Rue de Bretagne, pulling his cape over his shoulders to prevent a soaking from the still falling rain. He waited impatiently for the messenger's return, using the time to prime the gun's reservoir. After ten minutes or so, he saw him jogging back along Rue Charlot and then he heard the front door slam.

"Citizen Simon says he will be ready," the man repeated his message, shaking the water off his sodden cape onto the floor. De Born appeared not to have heard; he was studying a letter and giving out with a string of oaths.

"God's blood," shouted de Born. "Quick. There's no time to lose. Citizen Chaumette has put the venture ahead by one hour."

Reacting to the urgency in de Born's voice the guard immediately left to get the boy from his room, while de Born threw the blank piece of paper he had been reading into the fire. He then rushed down to the kitchen, where the rest of the guards were waiting, drinking coffee and smoking. He shouted out Chaumette's instructions and the men jumped to their feet, swallowing the last of their bowls and knocking out their pipes.

"Get the oyster cart round to the manhole in the Rue Charlot, and make sure my portmanteau and the spare clothes are under cover," de Born yelled. "If anyone asks, tell them its wheel is broken and you're waiting for a replacement.

"You two," he shouted at the largest of the guards. "Follow me. At the double, dammit!"

The boy, sleeping peacefully after his drugged meal, was lowered gently into the horse, his arms fitting neatly into the forelegs and his legs into the hindquarters. The pupils of the horse's eyes had been pierced and a slit put into the mouth to enable the boy to breathe. The men struggled with the horse down the steps and loaded it onto a flat bed cart waiting outside. De Born climbed up beside the driver and the other two men stayed on the back, holding the horse steady.

De Born looked at his watch. Twenty to eleven. Chaumette was due to meet him in exactly one hour and five minutes' time at the Temple gates. After they had loaded Louis into the linen cart,

Chaumette was supposed to wait one hour and then leave, telling the sentries that de Born had decided to stay the night as the boy was very ill. The next watch came on duty at dawn and the chances were that the outgoing shift would forget to tell their comrades that the Irish doctor had been in the Temple at all. None of this would matter, thought de Born, if Chaumette stuck to the timetable. He imagined his reactions. The initial puzzlement as he was told that the Irish doctor had already entered, along with a bloody great rocking horse; the anxiety as he raced up to the second floor; the full-blown panic when he removed the mask of the sleeping boy; the furious rush to the stables; an explosion of rage at a bewildered Simon and, finally, the depressing certainty that he had been out-manoeuvred.

De Born's pleasantly vengeful reverie was brought up short by the sentries' challenge.

"Citizen Doctor Calnan, come to see the Capet boy," called out the driver into the darkness.

"Pass, doctor," said the voice, which de Born recognized as the illiterate sergeant's.

"Wait!" the sergeant's voice suddenly rang out and one of the sentries grabbed the horse's bridle. "What the bloody hell is that thing?" he shouted, holding his lantern up to the horse.

"Present for the boy from the Simons on their leaving," said the driver.

"Well I've not been told about it," said the sergeant huffily. "You'll have to leave it out here until the officer gets back from his supper."

"What - in the rain?" yelled out the driver into the downpour. "It'll be ruined."

"I can't help that," said the sergeant. "You're not taking that thing in without permission."

"Well, I'm needed inside," interrupted de Born, handing his bag down to one of the sentries as he stepped off the cart. "So I'll leave you to it. Besides, I don't want to be here when friend Chaumette arrives and sees what's happened."

"Eh? What's that about Chaumette?" asked the sergeant.

"That's right, sarge," said the driver. "I'm delivering the horse on citizen Chaumette's direct orders. So on your head be it."

"Perhaps in all fairness you should write the driver a receipt and he can leave in good conscience, his duty done," said de Born to the hovering soldier.

"That's it," said the driver. "Give me a receipt and I'll be off - and leave you to do the explaining."

"There's no need for that," said the sergeant. "I've got my orders, same as you. Oh well, you better take it up."

As the cart rumbled up to the turret door, de Born felt his heart pounding and a harsh dryness in his throat. Could he rely on Chaumette's timekeeping? Perhaps, in his anxiety, he would come earlier? Impatiently de Born hurried the men as they carried the horse up the stone staircase, swearing at them as they bumped the rocker on the narrow, twisting walls, frightened that the Commissioners might emerge from their supper to investigate. Far from obstructing them, the sentries - happy about the break in their dull routine - put down their muskets and helped carry the horse up and into the dining room, anxious to get a good look at this marvel.

De Born went into the Dauphin's room, where the boy was playing with his dog, watched by Cléry. After greeting Louis, he took the valet aside and whispered the plan into his ear.

"What can I do to help, Monsieur?" asked Cléry, his face suffused with hope.

"Go up to the Simons' rooms and help them to bring the linen cart down here," said de Born, holding out his hand in gratitude. "Then bring me some hot water and soap."

As de Born removed the salve from the boy's face he prepared him for the journey.

"Tonight you get your wish, Louis," said de Born. "I'm going to take you out of this place.

"Never to come back?" asked the boy, wide-eyed.

"Never."

"But what about Maman and Marie - are they coming too?"

"Perhaps later; we'll see," said de Born, trying to sound reassuring.

"Come on Moufflet, we're going to visit Cléry's granddad," chirped the boy, picking up the dog.

"I'm afraid Moufflet has to stay behind," said de Born.

"But why? He's no trouble," said the boy, aghast at this news.

"Because I say so," snapped de Born, his nerves getting the better of him.

"Well, if he stays, I stay," said Louis, clutching the dog to his breast.

For a moment de Born was stumped by this unexpected rebellion. Then inspiration came.

"If we take Moufflet, Marie will be lonely, left all alone with no one to play with," said de Born. "We must be fair and think of her."

Reluctantly, unable to counter this, the boy set the dog down and began lecturing it on its future behaviour in a sorrowful whisper.

De Born looked at his watch yet again. Five minutes to eleven. Chaumette was due in exactly fifty minutes. He took scissors and a razor from his bag and started to shave off the moustache he had grown while at the Rue Charlot. Going into the dining room he ordered

Chaumette's men to open the horse and lift the orphan boy out. De Born examined him as he emerged and all seemed well; he was breathing normally and his pulse was strong. As he was brought in and placed on the Dauphin's bed, Louis was full of curiosity.

As he put the salve and face mask on the boy, de Born explained to Louis that they must leave without the soldiers knowing, and this boy would help to fool the guards into thinking he was safely asleep. Louis seemed to accept this readily, and after drinking the vial that de Born gave him went on collecting up his toys, sleepily intent on taking them with him - as they were obviously of no use to his sister. De Born gently but firmly took them away as fast as they were picked up, finally being forced to promise to send them on 'very soon'.

Simon arrived with the linen cart. De Born carefully lowered the sleeping boy to the bottom and the dirty linen was piled loosely on top of him. De Born left the room to say a swift farewell to Cléry waiting outside, telling the two guards to wait for Chaumette and to let no one in the dauphin's room until he came. Holding his handkerchief to his mouth, as if for protection against the night air, de Born sauntered down the staircase, saying his goodnights to the sentries as usual, the linen cart bumping down after him.

As he reached the foot of the staircase, one of the Commissioners emerged with a lantern to begin his rounds. Seeing de Born, he invited him back in for a glass of wine.

"Not tonight, thank you, citizen," replied de Born. "I have a slight chill, brought on by all this rain. I'm away to my bed.

"Physician heal thyself, eh?" the Commissioner laughed, and wished him a good night. De Born slipped into the shadows on the other side of the turret wall. Just as the Simons were leaving the Tower, he pushing the cart with the furniture, she with the linen cart, de Born heard the Commissioner's voice again.

"Leaving us early, Simon?" he asked.

"Yes, citizen Commissioner," replied Simon, his hands working nervously. "We've so much to do in our new home."

"Well, I hope you're not taking anything that doesn't belong to you," said the Commissioner, coming over to where they stood, and starting to poke about the carts.

"Certainly not, citizen," said Simon, sweating visibly now, although the night air was chilling.

The sharp eyes of the Commissioner, noting Simon's anxiety, prompted him to take a closer look. Holding his lantern up to the furniture, he checked every item. Then he moved to the linen cart and tossed the clothes on the top to and fro. De Born, standing not ten feet away, pressed back against the wall, feeling sure that anyone passing must be able to hear the loud pounding of his heart.

"Hello," said the Commissioner, his hand rummaging amongst the linen. "What's this?"

CHAPTER ELEVEN

Decadi, 30 Nivôse, Year II

De Born flicked out the trigger on the cane and, raising it to his shoulder, took aim at the Commissioner's head.

"That, citizen, is one of my undergarments," bristled Madame Simon in the authentically outraged tones of a decent woman whose lingerie is being poked about for no good purpose by a man not her husband.

"Really? They're so big I thought they might be a set of curtains, stolen from upstairs," said the Commissioner, roaring with laughter at his own joke. His laugh faded into the distance as he beat a tactical retreat.

De Born realized that he was still rigidly aiming the gun, so he relaxed his grip, uncocked the trigger and returned it to his side. The stable yard was lit by the half moon, but the light drizzle still falling helped to obscure the trio as they made their way to the stables, where a lantern glimmered in the distance.

As soon as they reached the light, de Born whipped out his watch and saw he had only twenty minutes until Chaumette's arrival. He lifted the boy out of the linen and went over to a corner of the stable, where the clean straw was piled high. Thrusting his hand inside, he felt about until he found the bundle of old clothes that had been put there the day before. While Madame Simon helped dress the still drowsy escapee with the girl's clothes, he himself put on a traditional fishwife's stiff linen bonnet and a shabby brown dress of some coarse material, sticking the cane into its sash.

After helping Simon to remove the grille set in the floor De Born stepped down into the drain. He instantly felt the freezing water against his boot. The constant rain had altered the level in the drain until now it reached to his waist.

Simon handed the boy down and de Born held him in his arms while Simon replaced the grille. They were now in almost complete darkness. Louis flinched at the sound of the rats screaming in their panic to escape the flood. De Born waded gingerly down the drain, surprised at how heavy the boy was. Once he nearly overbalanced, when Louis -fully conscious now in the chilly damp of the drain - fidgeted uneasily in his arms. Finally he felt a rush of cold, fresh air from the grille above him in the Rue Charlot. He pushed Louis onto the ladder and followed him up. At the top he stood behind the boy and whistled for Chaumette's men to remove the grille. Although he could see the edge of a cartwheel illuminated in the moonlight, no one answered. He tried again, this time a little louder. Still nothing.

Chaumette must have reached the Temple gates by now. He would simply have to try to lift the grille on his own. Telling Louis to take the cane and go back down to the bottom rung of the ladder, he braced himself and pushed with all his might. The grille lifted about an inch and then slammed back down again. After a brief rest, de Born tried again, with the same result. He paused and forced himself to calm down. Should he go back down the ladder and then go further into the sewer system and seek another exit? He looked up at the cartwheel, so tantalizingly close. He must get to the cart: that was the only way he was going to pass through the Porte St Martin. Besides, the way the water was rising in the tunnel, they would probably drown before they found a suitable manhole.

He climbed up two more rungs, until he was bent almost double under the grille, and braced his shoulders against it. Despite the chill in the tunnel, he was sweating freely. Using the power of his thigh muscles, he gradually straightened up, pushing at the grille with his shoulders. He felt it lifting and, in a burst of manic energy, he gave a fierce final thrust and the grille toppled over, clanging noisily onto the cobbles.

Cautiously he poked his head out of the manhole. The street seemed completely deserted. Presumably the guards had been panicked by a passing patrol and had taken to their heels. The horse, more interested in its nose-bag and weighed down by the heavy cart on its shafts, had fortunately decided to stay where it had been left.

Stealthily, de Born climbed out of the hole and crawled over the entrance, calling Louis softly to climb up the ladder. As soon as the boy reached the top, de Born swung him up onto the front board and then removed the horse's bag and flung it, with the cane, into the back of the cart, where he could see the outline of his portmanteau and the bundle of spare clothes hidden under a tarpaulin.

He jumped up onto the board, released the brake and, seizing the whip from its holder, urged the horse into a trot. He had not got far along Rue Charlot when, looking down, he noticed his boots sticking out from under his dress, as were the boy's expensive pumps. Leaning back, he grabbed a piece of old sacking and wrapped it around their feet to hide them. As he turned left into Rue Béranger he saw the National Guard patrol that had scared off the guards marching back towards the Temple. Although one soldier in the last rank turned his head to discover the source of the noise, he soon lost interest in the cart as it sped up the street. After a couple of turns, de Born could see ahead of him the lights of the Porte St Martin gleaming out of the rain, which had been getting steadily heavier since they left the sewer.

As they slowed down to a walk to approach the gate, he calculated that Chaumette would by now have discovered his ruse and be making for the stables to talk to Simon. It would only be a matter of a few minutes before he would hurry back down the covered walkway and into the palace forecourt to his carriage. If he guessed de Born's intentions correctly, and did not stop for help at the Rue Charlot headquarters, he would be coming round the corner of Rue Réaumur into the Rue St Martin in a matter of moments. From there he would be able to see the cart in front of him at the end of the street.

Assuming a cracked falsetto, de Born wished the guard sergeant a good night, hawked bronchially and spat onto the cobbles.

"Good morning, you mean," corrected the sergeant. "It's gone midnight you know."

De Born's stomach turned over. He must have lost all track of time in the sewer. Chaumette must now be right behind him. He listened for horses hooves, but heard only the rain lashing down onto the cobbles.

"Papers," demanded the sergeant, eyeing the barrels. "What you got in the back?" he asked, thumbing through the papers mechanically, hardly glancing at them.

"Best oysters," replied de Born. "At least, I calls them 'best'. Those stupid bastards (here he spat again for emphasis) at the fish market said they were tainted."

"Oh yes?" said the sergeant sceptically, as he climbed up onto the cart and started to lift one of the lids.

De Born fought down his rising anxiety.

"I ask you, sergeant," he whined, "how's a poor widow woman to make a decent living if these interfering inspectors, who are probably all royalists anyway, won't let you sell your honest wares? Miasmic plague indeed." He spat again disgustedly. "What's that supposed to mean, eh? Some sort of disease, they said. Rubbish, I said. They're just a bit green round the edge - if you cut round the outside and fry them, they're as good as anyone's."

At the mention of the dread word, the sergeant's hand froze in the barrel and then he withdrew it hastily, wiping it carefully on his trouser-leg.

"What's that you say about plague?" he asked anxiously, handing back her papers, which he held by two fingers at arm's length.

"That's what they say," de Born said darkly. "But I think it's just a plot by that thieving whore on the next stall to put me out of business. And on top of that, the National Guard just stopped me twice, making me late. Me that's got to get back to Dieppe quick and get a doctor for my little Lizzie, what's been take ill all of a sudden."

"Why did they stop you?" asked the guard, casting a nervous glance towards Louis and instinctively stepping back a couple of paces from the deadly cargo, which smelt to him of drains.

"Haven't you heard?" asked de Born, as if amazed that he was ignorant of such momentous news. "An émigré traitor disguised as citizen Chaumette tried to grab the Capet child out of the Temple not an hour since. Some patriots discovered his scheme in the nick of time, but he got away in a carriage."

"Well he better not try and come through this gate," said the sergeant, "or it'll be the last thing he ever does."

"Ah, if only there were more strong, patriotic men like you, sergeant, France would be delivered from her enemies," de Born said with a winsome smile.

"Open the gates," the sergeant ordered his men in a gruff voice, to cover his bashful pleasure at this handsome compliment.

"On your way, citizeness, and a pleasant journey to you," he called out after them.

As they passed through the gates, de Born thought he heard behind him in the distance the noise of a carriage being driven at high speed. He dared not look back for fear the guards' lanterns would illuminate his face, which up to now he had kept carefully hidden in the shadow of the large bonnet. It was with huge relief that he heard the heavy town gates

shut behind him and the clang of the massive iron bar being slammed
back down into its slot.

*   *   *

As he whipped up the horse he looked down at Louis beside him
and winked happily in relief and exhilaration. Louis grinned back at him
shyly and linked his arm through de Born's. Drowsiness eventually
overcame the boy's curiosity about the length of their journey, the name
of the horse, and the names of the crops growing in the fields on either
side of the road. He put his head down onto de Born's lap, arranged
himself comfortably and, sucking his thumb contentedly, fell fast asleep.

As the boy slept, de Born thought hard about Chaumette's next
moves. He remembered the wise words of his uncle: 'Always ask
yourself, John, what would your enemy like you to do next - and then do
the opposite.'

Chaumette's instructions had been to go straight to St Denis and
wait for him there, having jettisoned the cart and both sets of female
clothing on the way. That meant Chaumette had men in the town, so de
Born must turn off long before he got to it. Chaumette had undoubtedly
also placed men at Dieppe, if only to arrange their passage. De Born

could try for another port, but without the help of La Correspondance, he stood every chance of being discovered. Best, he thought, to stick to the plan he had outlined in his letter to Philip Stephens, and so he turned the horse southwards towards Chartres.

As dawn's first light broke, de Born, exhausted by the nervous tension of the escape as much as by lack of sleep, decided to pull off the road onto a cart track running alongside a tall hedge. There he halted the cart in a place hidden from the road, put the brake on and hobbled the horse. Taking the tarpaulin out of the back, he laid it under the cart and, lifting the still sleeping boy off the seat, put him on the tarpaulin so he was protected from the rain. He stowed the portmanteau and stick-gun next to Louis. Finally he slipped off the dress and bonnet and, pulling his travelling cloak over both of them, snuggled up to the boy for warmth.

He was awoken by the boy's stirrings and automatically he reached for his watch. Ten o'clock. He had slept for four hours. Chaumette must be in St Denis by now, being told by his men that no cart had been spotted on the road, nor any military man and his son travelling together.

"I'm hungry," said Louis.

"Climb up onto the seat and look in the driver's box, maybe there's some breakfast in there," suggested de Born, kicking himself for not thinking of the need of food for the journey.

Evidently someone in the Rue Charlot house was more efficient than he, as Louis came bounding back with a leather satchel containing bread, roast chicken and a flask of wine, together with two wizened apples, obviously meant for the horse.

De Born rummaged around in the portmanteau for his dirk to cut the chicken, but it apparently had been removed by Chaumette's men. Curious to see what else was missing, he tipped out the entire contents onto the tarpaulin. Suddenly he froze, and then frantically began a thorough search through the pile, item by item. At last he halted. It was no use looking any longer. He simply could not find the two bottles of Jay's anywhere. Then he thought of the letter he had given Sophie. After applying the re-agent it would be the work of only minutes to crack the crude code. Perhaps Chaumette was already in Chartres waiting for them. Perhaps he had known all along that de Born aimed to double-cross him and had arranged matters so that as soon as the boy was clear of the Temple, or better still the city gates, they would be followed and taken. The combination of de Born's ruse of advancing the hour and the desertion of the guards holding the cart in the Rue Charlot must have ruined his whole scheme. Chaumette would have also known, however, that his reserve stratagem was foolproof: he need only wait at Chartres for de Born to turn up and fall right into his lap.

Sending Louis off to a nearby dew pond to refill the flask, which he had been unconsciously emptying while he worked out his plans, de Born changed into the retired major's clothes, taking care to see that the relevant papers were in his coat pocket. He then helped Louis into his new suit and buried both sets of female clothing under the hedgerow, tearing the set of papers that belonged to them into tiny pieces and grinding them into the mud with his heel. He then folded the Irish doctor's clothes into a bundle with the boy's old set and put them into the portmanteau. He took the horse out of the shafts and let it finish its nose-bag, while he lifted the barrels off the cart and poured their contents into the dew-pond. He and Louis then pushed and pulled the empty cart behind an old rick, before mounting the horse bareback, with only a rope attached to its bridle for reins, the portmanteau being held awkwardly between him and the boy's back.

He could not go to the coast, nor could he risk going to Chartres for help. His thoughts went back to that conversation with Ferris in prison. He had never seen his father's grave, nor paid his killers a visit. Time to settle a debt. He and the boy could hide amongst friends for a while, until the hue and cry died down. He was decided. He would imitate the fox scurrying from the hounds - he would go to earth. He would go home.

*   *   *

He made first for the nearest market town, there to trade in the valuable carthorse for a more spirited nag for himself and a lively pony for the boy. He was tempted to travel only at night, but the risk of a fall was too great and the threat of thieves and deserters ever-present. The rain had now stopped and they made good time, reaching the town in the early afternoon. On the way, de Born took the opportunity of telling the boy who he really was.

"So you're not a doctor?" asked the boy, struggling to understand.

"No, I am employed by the English Admiralty and I was sent by them to find you and bring you to England," said de Born.

"England!" Louis exclaimed, twisting around on the horse's back to look at de Born. "But they're our enemies."

"No, that's only what you have been told by the Jacobins. The English desire only that you be free," said de Born.

"The English eat babies," said Louis doubtfully. "Nonsense" said De Born explaining that they mostly ate beef and potatoes. To pass the time and to reassure the boy he began to describe life in London. "You'll be happy there" he said,"the English make wonderful toys and love all sorts of games"

Louis took some time to digest all of this, breaking his silence only to repeat mournfully his firm belief that "all English men eat babies."

"But what shall I call you now?" he asked.

"Well, we now have papers that say I am a Major Delahousse. You can't call me 'major', so you had better call me 'father'," said de Born.

"Couldn't I call you papa?" asked Louis.

"Yes, of course, if you wish it," said de Born.

"Then I've found a new papa," laughed the boy. "Hello papa," he shouted, and gave de Born a big smacking kiss on his cheek.

De Born just laughed and told the boy not to fidget so much on a horse which was not used to having small boys running about all over its back.

Louis stroked the horse's mane thoughtfully.

"And shall you be my new papa for ever now?"

De Born hesitated. It was both wrong to deceive the boy and unfair to raise his expectations.

"I shall look after you until we get to England."

"And then?" Louis persisted.

"And then, we'll see."

This seemed to satisfy the boy and he gave a great 'hooray', loud enough to put two magpies to flight, and kissed his new papa 'hello' for a second time.

De Born dug his heels into the horse's flanks and persuaded the mare into a stately trot. By now they could see the town's church spire. The stable was hard by the inn and it was only a matter of moments to conclude a satisfactory agreement with the owner, who offered de Born a fine chestnut cob and a frisky pony in exchange for the mare and some of de Born's stock of gold louis. De Born asked if the liveryman could recommend an inn for the night, and was told that the Oak Apple at Rambouillet came highly recommended, a benediction the man claimed was quite unconnected from the fact that it was run by his cousin.

De Born and Louis trotted off to the outskirts of the town and then, where the ground was softer, they spurred their horses into an invigorating canter. They were still about five miles out from their destination when de Born called out to Louis, who was ahead of him, to halt his pony. They were to rest the horses and let them drink at a pond by the side of the track. Just as Louis was bringing his mount out of the trot, a heron erupted from the reeds that bordered the pond with a loud flapping of its huge wings. The pony reared in fright and, before de Born could grab him, Louis had tumbled backwards over the horse's haunches. He fell awkwardly to the ground, striking the back of his head on a massive stone embedded in the turf. The pony, still in a panic, galloped off and was soon lost to sight.

De Born leapt off his horse and, tying it to a willow, went over to the boy. He was lying on his back, arms outstretched, so still that for one terrible moment de Born thought he was dead. Getting closer he saw the chest gently rising and falling and heard Louis utter a faint moan. Carefully, de Born lifted the boy's head from the ground and inspected the damage. The stone had left a bloody, jagged gash at the curve of the skull.

CHAPTER TWELVE

Primidi, 1 Pluviôse, Year II

Looking about him, de Born saw smoke rising from the crooked chimney of a stone farmhouse about a quarter of a mile off. He picked Louis up in his arms, carried him up the muddy track to the house and kicked at the nail-studded door to attract attention. After a brief silence he heard sounds of the inhabitants moving about and then above his head he saw the barrel of an ancient musket poking out from a narrow slit in the wall on the first floor and a voice asked him to "stand off and be identified."

He moved back from the door a few paces so that the man at the meutrière could see him clearly. Apparently his military rank and bearing and the limpness of the boy's body were persuasion enough, because the bolts were quickly drawn back and the door was opened by an old man in a blue smock, who beckoned them inside.

The room he entered evidently served both as kitchen and bedroom, in the usual fashion of those parts. De Born laid the boy down on the bed and turned to study the elderly couple in front of him.

Both in their late seventies, with white hair, they had the brick-red complexions and hunched stance of people who had worked all their lives in the fields.

"Have you water to bathe the boy's wound and bandages to wrap his head?" he asked the old woman. Without a word, she went to a dresser and took out some worn linen, cut up from sheets, and, ladling some water from the copper into a basin, she went over to the child.

De Born watched as she carefully lifted the boy's head and saw her frown as she saw the extent of the wound. She felt over his chest, arms and legs.

"Some of his ribs are broken, but they'll mend soon enough if they are bound up tight," she told him. "The crown may have been cracked, though. If it has, I'm no use to him - he needs a proper doctor's care."

"Nonsense, woman," said the old man. "She's just being modest, M'sieu. She can cure any living animal. Cured Dufaud's goat last autumn of the breathing sickness," he confided.

"Shut up, you old fool," said the woman, but not unkindly. "I tell you, this boy needs a doctor or the blood will thicken in his head and then he'll die."

"My horse is still by the pond where the boy fell," de Born said. "If you give me directions I'll fetch the doctor myself."

The couple looked at each other. "It's five miles to the town and getting dark. But mind, the doctor will not come out until morning," said the old farmer.

"Go on, tell him," urged his wife.

"No," said the old man gruffly. "It's not our affair. Let it wait until morning."

"Tell me what?" asked de Born.

"Well, M'sieu," the old woman said, "there is a doctor Ricard close by, but people don't go to him any more. He was the brother of our lord who is now in prison in Paris. No one visits him or speaks to him for fear that their land might be taken by the Jacobins."

"Where does he live?" asked de Born.

"Oh, not far," replied the woman. "Through the oak wood and then to the church. His house is the one that stands apart, with two towers, one set either end. Lugagnac, it's called."

De Born turned to go and then a thought suddenly struck him.

"Will this doctor coming to your house put you in any danger?"

The old couple looked yet again at each other, then the old man looked down and busied himself with his pipe.

"Who knows, in these times, M'sieu?" said the woman with a shrug. "All I do know is that the boy is some mother's son and if he were mine I would like him cared for properly."

Lugagnac was sited on the summit of a short rise, really no more than a sweep of the land, with a side path lined with lilac bushes leading to the church and a carriage drive coming up to the front of the house from the road below. Finding the drive barred by a rusty pair of locked gates, de Born led his horse up the path.

The place had a neglected, shabby air. The render on its walls had fallen off in large chunks, exposing the crumbling stones underneath. The grey paint on the shutters had long since given up the unequal struggle against the sun's rays and was cracked and peeling. Someone had taken a hammer to the coat of arms above the door and smashed it so badly it was unrecognizable. He called out for the doctor. A window on the first floor opened and a middle-aged man stuck his head out. He had a lean, close-shaven, ascetic face framed by a somewhat moth-eaten, tie wig in the old-fashioned style.

"What the hell do you want?"

"My son has hurt himself after falling from his horse," answered de Born, after introducing himself.

"Where?" asked the man abruptly.

"Over by the pond near the cottage with the crooked chimney," said de Born.

"No, man," said the doctor, even more irritably than before. "Where on his body has he hurt himself?"

"Oh, I see. I'm sorry," said de Born, slightly flustered at the misunderstanding. "It's a bad wound on his head."

"His head?" replied the doctor. "Wait there and I'll be down directly."

After a short while he emerged from a side door carrying a bag and limped past de Born without even looking at him, although he condescended to throw the solitary word, "Ricard," over his shoulder at his visitor.

De Born followed on, leading his horse by the rein and endeavouring to catch up.

"My profound apologies for this interruption," said de Born as he drew level.

"You are not sorry, nor should you be, so why do you say you are?" Ricard asked.

"Merely good manners, sir, as I was taught," answered de Born, more than a little irritated at the man's rudeness.

"Good manners, he says. Good manners, Monsieur, or citizen, as I am supposed to call you now we are all 'equal'," the doctor added with heavy sarcasm. "Good manners died the day the mob stormed the Bastille."

"You do not, I take it, have a very good opinion of the People's Revolution?" asked de Born, struck by the man's complete absence of restraint. Sentiments much less violent than these had been the death of many a man in the last four years.

"The people, as you are pleased to call them, are a lot of pusillanimous, grasping, brutal, drunken, ignorant, superstitious imbeciles who are thrilled by blood and cruelty," said Ricard. "And talking of superstition, I suppose Ma Dubois tried to put a spider's web on the wound or tickled his feet with holly leaves or some such nonsense?"

Taking 'Ma Dubois' to be the old peasant woman, de Born answered that au contraire it was she who had impressed upon him the seriousness of the wound and the urgent need for professional aid.

"Humph," was all Ricard would say, and remained silent until they reached the cottage, despite de Born's occasional attempts to restart the conversation.

As he entered, the farmer stood up respectfully and 'Ma' Dubois dropped a curtsey, old habits apparently dying hard. He ignored both these marks of respect, making straight for the bed to examine the boy with his narrow, elegant hands.

"He's damaged his rib-cage, which should be bound up," he told de Born briskly. "The skull-bone is not fractured, though he has suffered a very grave wound. Undress the boy, Ma, and you, Dubois, bring your hay-cart round to the front door. You'll have to do without your mattress for a while - we'll need it to carry him up to the house."

"Wouldn't it be safer to leave him here?" asked de Born anxiously.

"Hah! Yet another doctor, I see," Richard said, with a look at 'Ma' who, well aware of its import, prudently ignored it. "Well, 'doctor'," he said, this time addressing de Born, "and where pray did you pursue your studies? The Sorbonne perhaps? Or if one may deduce by the occasional oddity of phrasing, perhaps London?"

Alarmed at the last comment and struck dumb by this frontal assault on his lack of medical qualifications, de Born decided to adopt Ma Dubois' policy of keeping his opinions to himself.

After he had bound Louis' skull and ribs, Ricard motioned de Born to help him lift the mattress off the bed and out onto the cart. Then, without a word to anyone, he marched off back to Lugagnac. Dubois followed, leading his carthorse. De Born, after thanking the old woman, stood by the boy on the back of the cart.

"Why do you think Dr Ricard is in such a foul temper?" asked de Born.

"Always is," Dubois replied, still puffing on his pipe. "Same when he were a boy. No harm in it, mind. It's just his way," he added tolerantly.

*   *   *

Having put Louis to bed in a room bare save for a worm-eaten day bed and a thick layer of dust, de Born settled himself down for the night to watch over the boy. Although Louis was unnaturally pale, his breathing was deep and regular, at least as far as his tightly bandaged chest allowed.

Around midnight, de Born was awoken from his dozing by the doctor's candlelight.

"How is he?"

"It would greatly assist his recovery if I were allowed to treat the boy without being asked damn-fool questions," retorted Ricard. "But, since I know from bitter experience that parental concern is not to be denied, I say in answer to you that the boy is in a state known in the medical profession as unconsciousness."

"And when, doctor, if I may make so bold as to ask, will he be in a state we ordinary mortals might describe as awake?" asked de Born acidly, suddenly tired of this incessant display of ill-humour.

Ricard looked up at him and grinned. "Do you play chess?"

"Yes," stammered de Born, disconcerted by this abrupt change of subject. "In my youth the curé was a keen player and taught me well."

"Excellent," enthused the doctor, rubbing his hands together energetically. "I've no one to partner me now my brother is absent. The merchants of the town are too dull to appreciate the game's subtleties and the peasants, although quite devious enough, reserve that quality for their land-dealings."

"You still haven't replied to my question," said de Born.

"The boy will most likely wake up tomorrow morning with an acute headache," Ricard said, returning to his usual, businesslike manner. "He cannot be moved from his bed for at least three days if the ribs are to mend properly. He may not ride until a week has passed."

De Born pondered this while Ricard checked the boy's strapping and re-bandaged his head. Lugagnac was out of the way, and Ricard was probably royalist by inclination. At least, he would have no love for the Jacobins who held his brother. Moreover, by staying here a while, the trail would go cold for Chaumette and his men.

"I am most grateful for your hospitality," said de Born.

"There's no need to be, Major," said Ricard, again displaying his wolfish grin. "I intend to wager you one gold louis per contest and at that rate in a week you will have paid off your debt handsomely."

And so it proved. Louis duly woke up the next morning and complained, as predicted, of a 'little smith in his head, who would not stop banging on his anvil'. He was moved to a truckle bed placed in the library, where he could watch their daily chess game, promising de Born that he would 'huzzah papa' when victory came. It never did. Ricard was a deadly opponent, full of guile and complicated traps.

*   *   *

The days passed pleasantly enough, although Louis chafed at the enforced inactivity. In the mornings, the doctor, who was engaged in writing a medical treatise, would retire to his study, while de Born would read to the boy from La Fontaine or they would just sit together talking. After dinner the contest would commence, rarely lasting until dusk.

On the third day Louis was to be allowed out of bed. As de Born helped him on with his coat, the slate-grey one the dauphin had been wearing that first day in the Temple, one of its brass buttons flew off. Retrieving it from under the bed, de Born noticed that it was inscribed. Around an engraving of a liberty tree the words 'Live Free or Die' were written. No hope of that, de Born thought, poor little bastard. Given his parentage he'll never be free of fear, and if either Robespierre or the Comte de Provence have anything to do with it, an early death seems a reasonable prognosis.

When the weather was fine they generally spent their mornings walking in the meadows that surrounded the house. De Born's affection for the boy grew daily, and so too did his admiration. In his eight years Louis had seen and suffered much more than the average adult could conceive of experiencing.

And yet he remained, to de Born's eyes, a happy, easily amused, willing, friendly and seemingly normal little boy. Only his nightmares gave any clue to his short unhappy life. Try as he might, de Born could never discover their content. Life had taught Louis an indelible lesson: that he should never under any circumstances talk to anyone about the events of the last four years, not even to his new 'papa'.

*   *   *

A week having passed, de Born's thoughts turned to leaving Ricard's house and making their way home. He had made up his mind to discuss this with the doctor that very morning so, when he heard the sound of his host returning from a visit to the town, he went to meet him at the stables.

As soon as he caught sight of de Born coming out of the house, Ricard's expression became harsh and forbidding.

"What, sir, is the meaning of this?" he demanded, thrusting a poster into de Born's hand. Headed by the word REWARD in large type, the bill offered 'a handsome reward to any patriot who apprehends alive one CHEFTEL masquerading under the alias Major DELAHOUSSE, who is wanted for WAR PROFITEERING in that he looted the bodies of soldiers in our glorious army as they lay upon the field of battle and sold this blood-stained booty to our Austrian Foes'.

There followed a brief physical description of de Born as 'dark-haired, very blue eyes, sneering aristo look to face, strong build and above medium height', and added 'may be travelling with eight-year-old son'. The reward was given as two hundred gold louis and the proclamation was signed by Pierre-Gaspard Chaumette, *ci-devant* Procureur Syndic of the Paris Commune.

De Born smiled. A typical Chaumette effort, he thought; a little overdone, perhaps, but guaranteed to make a people at war, fed on stories of enemy atrocities, into a vengeful mob intent on ferreting out this despicable traitor from his rat-hole and tearing him to pieces. Frustrated by his own lack of success in tracking down de Born, Chaumette had conceived the ingenious idea of enlisting the entire French nation into his private army.

"What do you mean by smiling, sir?" asked Ricard in a rage, shocked by de Born's reaction.

"I smile, doctor, only at the ingenuity of my enemy," de Born said, handing the bill back to Ricard, "the Chaumette who has signed this bill. That is, upon my honour, a farrago of lies and I am a little surprised, doctor, that it fooled a man of your perspicacity."

Ricard's anger turned to dismay. He had seen Chaumette's men posting the bills on the walls near the market square and had taken one out of curiosity. His first reaction on reading it was disbelief. He prided himself on his judgement of men. He had observed de Born closely and had noticed the strain in the eyes, the small evasions and attempts to change the subject when certain areas were touched upon. The man's honour was, however, above question. It was inconceivable that he could be involved in such a heinous crime.

Nevertheless, on the ride back to Lugagnac, somehow the doubts began to crowd in. This was an official proclamation, after all. What did he actually know about this fellow Delahousse? Slowly the doubts became certainties. He had been tricked by this grave-robbing swindler, who was laughing at him behind his back. How could he have been so stupid? Perhaps he should turn back and get help to arrest him? No, he would confront him with the bill and, when the fellow broke down and confessed, he would hand him over to the authorities.

Now he realized that, instead of sticking to his first instinctive judgement, he had been duped by the expert manipulation of the very government he professed to regard as fools and knaves.

Impulsively he gave de Born his hand. "I am deeply sorry if my foolishness in believing these calumnies has offended you. Would you do me the honour of accepting my apology?" he asked humbly.

"No apology is necessary, I assure you," said de Born, shaking the proffered hand. "You saw an official government notice and believed its contents. What could be more reasonable? Besides, by bringing it to me you have saved my life. Tomorrow I would have entered that town entirely ignorant of the fact that my nom de guerre is now a deadly threat."

Relieved at de Born's graciousness, Ricard suggested they go in to dinner, where de Born explained his predicament.

"The facts are these," said de Born. "I have offended a powerful man and he is out for revenge. I cannot tell you how, or even why, but on my word of honour, you would have acted as I did if you had been in my place. I was travelling with the boy to my ancestral home to hide away from my enemy's wrath amongst friends who will protect me. I had planned to tell you this morning that we were to leave your house tomorrow. The poster simply means that our departure is imperative to protect your position."

"How can I help?" asked Ricard, desperate to make up for his foolishness.

"You can only help us by putting yourself in grave danger," replied de Born.

"Oh, as for that," said Ricard dismissively. "Since they came and took my brother, I have been sitting in this gloomy pile just waiting for them to come for me."

"May I ask why they have not?" asked de Born, who had often been curious about this point but had not liked to trespass on his host's privacy.

"Because the chief Jacobin bandit in the area owes me a great favour," replied Ricard. "It was I who saved the life of his daughter after the town quacks had given her up for dead. One day, though, he'll fall - as they all do in the end - and me with him."

"Well, there is a way you could do me a great service," said de Born, still a little hesitant about involving someone that had done so much for him and the boy already, but unwilling to let an opportunity go by to solve the problem that had been nagging at him since they left Paris.

"There is one unavoidable barrier between me and my goal - the Loire," de Born said. "It cannot be got round and the local militia is sure to have placed men on every bridge."

"Mmm," mused Ricard. "This is a two-bottle problem, I think," and he rang for the aged servant who, along with his wife, the cook, and the coachman-cum-gardener, was all that was left of the score or so servants that had lived at Lugagnac in the old king's day.

He sipped his sweet wine, smoked his pipe and frowned in concentration for nigh on twenty minutes. At last he spoke.

"Can you drive a coach?" he asked.

"Certainly," replied de Born.

"Then you are hired," said Ricard with a smile.

"As what?" laughed de Born.

"As my coachman, of course," replied Ricard. "You are going to drive me and the boy over the bridge at Orléans in broad daylight. You will be well wrapped up against the cold with scarves and handkerchief protecting your face against the wind."

"That's fine," said de Born, "but they'll recognize the boy."

Ricard looked at him sharply. "Recognize him? What do you mean?"

De Born inwardly cursed his stupidity at making such a gross blunder. "I just meant that they know I am travelling with my son and when they see Louis they may put two and two together."

"Oh, I see," said Ricard. "For a moment I thought ... well, never mind, I have a solution to that also, just you wait and see."

*　*　*

The next day was spent cleaning and repairing Ricard's carriage, which had become dusty and down-at-heel through disuse. The coat of arms on the door was, as the new law demanded, given a layer of black paint and the horses were curried until their coats gleamed.

Just before dinner, Dr Ricard came out into the stable-yard. When he reached de Born, standing by the now immaculate equipage, he turned and shouted for Louis to come out.

"May I introduce my nephew, Louis Ricard," he said with a flourish. "Who, due to his carelessness, has been badly burnt by a kettle full of scalding water."

De Born saw that the boy's head was almost completely encased in bandages, leaving only two clear strips across the eyes and mouth.

"Well done, doctor," de Born said. "His own - he'll never be recognized by anyone in that disguise," stopping himself just in time from saying that Louis' own mother wouldn't recognize him.

Ricard basked in de Born's admiring remarks, for he divined in the latter a professionalism when it came to stratagems and disguises and had become convinced that de Born was some sort of royalist agent.

"Ah, but you have not yet seen my deus ex machina," said Ricard mysteriously, taking a paper from his pocket and handing it to de Born.

Unfolding it, de Born saw it was a *laissez-passer* signed by the Regional Commissioner, allowing citizen Doctor Ricard unlimited travel within that area and forbidding any hindrance being put in his way.

"Don't you see?" Ricard said excitedly. "No local militiamen can stop me from crossing the river."

De Born was privately dubious, knowing full well that the local militia were quite capable of making the good doctor eat his own *passe partout* before throwing him into the Loire, his pockets stuffed with stones. Yet it would not do to tell Ricard this, de Born thought. Armed with his precious document he would feel, and therefore look, invulnerable.

"Where did you get such a marvel?" he asked.

"That Jacobin, whose little girl's life I saved, gave it to me after I complained that his solders' searches were making me late answering his summonses," Ricard replied. "He simply forgot to cancel it after she recovered. I had thought to use it if I ever got forewarning of my own arrest, but this is a much more appropriate opportunity."

De Born looked at him with gratitude.

"You know that I cannot tell you all the circumstances of our escape, or even who our masters are," he told the doctor, "but believe me, Monsieur, when I tell you that if the old king were alive he would bless you with all his heart for what you are doing for us."

Ricard nodded solemnly, his conclusions as to de Born's identity seemingly confirmed, and arm in arm they went in to their last dinner together.

When the servants had left and they could talk more freely, de

Born asked Ricard about the origin of his limp.

"After the Jacobins took over, a deputation came to see my brother," Ricard said. "They wanted him to give up his land and hand it over to them in the name of the people. They got pretty short shrift, as you can imagine, so they returned at night a few days later with papers for his arrest as a royalist."

"And was he?" asked de Born. "A royalist, that is?"

"Not in the sense they meant the word," answered the doctor. "My brother was an enlightened man. His view was that no reasonable person could support a regime based on the forced labour of the corvée or draconian game laws, never mind press censorship and *lettres de cachet*. He thought that King Louis should become a constitutional monarch along English lines, as did I. Anyway, there was a fight, I was wounded in the leg and my brother dragged off to Paris to await trial."

"And what happened to him?" asked de Born.

"He rots there still," said Ricard. "They can't get their hands on the estate until he signs those papers and he continues to refuse. If he dies without a trial, I will inherit and they know I'm an even harder nut to crack."

"So it's a stalemate," said de Born.

"Yes," Ricard hesitated. "Unless the revolutionary government were to fall, or better still be pushed."

"And be replaced by what?" asked de Born.

"By a regency made up of well-meaning, honest men, committed to bringing up the Dauphin to recognize that his subjects had certain inalienable rights," replied Ricard.

This vision of the future intrigued de Born. Instead of being used as a device to turn the clock back to the despotism before 1789, perhaps Louis could become part of a new France.

"But what's to stop this boy king becoming as despotic as his ancestors?" asked de Born.

"What's to stop King George?" countered Ricard. "We could have our own Magna Carta, our own Bill of Rights or even a Constitution like the Americans have. The detail isn't important. What is important is to get rid of these murderous tyrants who abuse their power. You see," said Ricard, warming to his theme, "the idea of a monarchy is still a good one, for kings have, but do not use, the ultimate power of a tyrant. By having it, they deprive tyrants from having and using it. D'you see?"

"You talk of the English system, doctor," de Born said. "Perhaps then it would be best if the Dauphin were to be delivered into their hands?"

"Good God, no!" replied Ricard. "Do you think Pitt could resist the temptation to control France through the boy and his two ghastly uncles? No, we would soon be a vassal territory, ruled by the English.

We must never allow that to happen. The Dauphin must be brought up by free Frenchmen to rule a free France."

"And where, may one ask, would such men be found?" asked de Born with a meaningful smile.

Ricard grinned back at him slyly. "Who can say, Major? Who can say?"

They talked long into the night about the future of their country, while above their heads the future slept peacefully.

*   *   *

De Born kept the horses at a steady trot along the Orléans road, hardened by the winter frost. One hand was on the reins, the other on the life-preserver his predecessor as coachman had given him 'to protect the doctor from those Jacobins'. A foot long, it was made of heavy canvas filled with damp sand and, although it would reputedly stave a man's skull in with a single blow, de Born took no comfort from its presence. If the militiamen recognized him from the poster's description they would shoot him long before he had got close enough to use it. His stick gun lay hidden with the portmanteau under the doctor's seat, it too being useful only for close quarter killing.

He had so far acquitted himself well on the journey in his new occupation, although he had caused much hilarity at the inn where they had stopped to change the horses. Seeing the mess he was making of the harness, a kindly old ostler took pity on him and, gently moving him aside, re-arranged his efforts, thus preventing both horses from being instantly strangled the moment the carriage moved off.

Dr Ricard was nearly as excited as Louis by the journey. After months of inactivity, the danger enlivened his spirit and he felt better about himself by striking this blow for the cause he and his brother held so dear.

Louis himself had to be restrained both from incessantly leaning out of the carriage window exhorting his papa to go faster and his constant attempts to scratch the itches under his bandages by unwrapping them.

De Born reined in the team to a walk when they entered the outskirts of Orléans. As they neared the cathedral the traffic slowed to a crawl. De Born stood up on his box to see over the numerous wagons and coaches that barred his way. At the foot of the bridge a group of soldiers had surrounded a diligence whose passengers had disembarked and were standing on the pavement. For an hour the queue crept forward. From time to time the officer, accompanied by a civilian in a black coat, would move off to a carriage drawn up by the road-side, evidently seeking further orders or handing over some papers to be examined by the occupant of the carriage. Too late to turn back without attracting the attention of the soldiers, de Born sat patiently on his box with a professionally contemptuous air toward the pedestrians who pointed out the gleaming equipage to each other, a comparatively rare sight in those egalitarian times, when the fearful bourgeois hid their family coachwork in their coach-house and hired common hackneys.

The soldiers waved through the brewer's wagon immediately ahead of de Born without inspecting it, and then ordered him to halt his team a few yards from the bridge approaches. He had earlier found a battered pipe a tobacco pouch in the pocket of his greatcoat and now he took these out as nonchalantly as he could and proceeded to smoke the foul mixture, taking great care not to inhale.

Ignoring him, the officer, a grizzled veteran who looked like he had received field promotion, approached and, after staring hard at Dr Ricard, ordered him and the boy out of the carriage.

"What's the matter with the boy?" asked the officer, looking at Louis.

"My nephew has been severely scalded in an accident, citizen, and I am taking him to Vierzon for further urgent treatment," Ricard said in an authoritative manner, with just a touch of impatience.

"Tell your man to take the carriage back to the main square while your papers are examined further," ordered the officer, looking slowly from Ricard to the boy as if making up his mind about something.

"But why?" asked Ricard with some asperity. "We have done nothing wrong and it is outrageous that this boy's treatment should be interfered with in this way. If I am held up any longer I shall complain to the authorities. Hippolyte," he added to de Born, "do not move from this spot until you have my express permission to do so."

"You can complain to Robespierre himself for all I care," said the officer, "and as for you, Hippolyte, if you don't move this broken-down old heap off my bridge in the next five seconds, one of my men will do it for you, while you try and see if you can swim the Loire fully-clothed."

"This," Ricard said loftily, thrusting his *laissez-passer* into the soldier's hand, "is the authority to whom I shall complain."

On seeing the signature the officer stiffened and muttered, "Wait here." He went over to the waiting carriage and handed the note through the window to its mysterious occupant.

"What does the man look like?" asked a voice from inside, and de Born froze. There was no mistaking that sibilant hiss. Chaumette.

CHAPTER THIRTEEN

Primidi, 11 Pluviôse, Year II

De Born dared not turn his head towards Chaumette's carriage, but his hand tightened instinctively on the butt of the life preserver as he listened to the officer describe Ricard.

"Arrest them both," Chaumette ordered.

"I'm afraid, citizen, I cannot do that," said the soldier. "If I did, I would be a Private again by nightfall - if I'm lucky."

"All right," Chaumette said. "For God's sake stop your whining. Go back and check the colour of the eyes. Those can never be disguised. The man I seek has very unusual, clear blue eyes, nearly turquoise."

As the officer went to carry out his instructions, de Born, only feet away, could hear Chaumette's impatient tapping of his crop on the carriage door. De Born was profoundly perplexed. How on earth could Chaumette have guessed he would be heading for home? Only two people had ever known he harboured thoughts of avenging his father's death. One had been guillotined, and as for the other, his uncle was hardly likely to have shared the secret with Chaumette. Yet Chaumette seemed to know everything - the master's word, the meeting in Downing Street, the rendezvous at *Le Chat Gris* - everything.

For the life of him, de Born could not remember the colour of Ricard's eyes. He tried visualising his friend hunched over the chess-board, but he simply could not remember the eyes. The suspense was broken by the officer's return.

"Brown, citizen Chaumette, and getting angrier by the minute," he said.

"Let them go," Chaumette said with evident disappointment. "But next time don't wait to ask. If a man with blue eyes travels with a boy, arrest them on the spot, no matter who's signed their papers."

The officer saluted and returned to the doctor.

"A thousand apologies, citizen Doctor," he said with considerable oiliness. "You are of course free to proceed at your convenience."

"I shall tell my old friend of your devotion to duty," Ricard called back out of the window, managing to make it sound more like a threat than a promise.

No sooner had de Born got the horses started on the short climb up to the bridge when he heard behind him a voice shout, "Halt!" The officer came running after them, repeating the order. For a brief moment de Born considered whipping the team into a gallop, but resignedly he tugged at the reins and put the brake on to stop the horses being dragged back down the slope of the bridge.

"What now?" asked Ricard irritably as the officer reached the carriage. "Really, this is too much."

"Apologies yet again, citizen Doctor," said the officer, breathing hard and handing something in through the window. "But you forgot your *laissez-passer*."

"Ah yes," Ricard said, somewhat mollified. "Thank you, and a final, I hope, goodbye to you. Hippolyte, what are you dawdling for? Get a move on, you lazy good-for-nothing." And with that unfair epithet ringing in his ears, de Born manoeuvred the team over onto the far bank and set off at a brisk canter towards Vierzon.

As they parted, de Born found it difficult to express his deep gratitude to the doctor. Fortunately, Ricard - faced with the possibility of embarrassing emotions being exhibited - reverted to the gruffness he manifested at their first meeting, muttered something about it being his 'duty to help', patted Louis on the head and, before de Born knew it, was gone.

The memory of the recent accident prompted de Born to purchase only the one horse and, loading Louis, portmanteau and himself onto it, set off southwards for home.

*   *   *

Two weeks passed. Two cold weeks of taking shelter from winter storms under hedgerows on lonely tracks. Two anxious weeks of skirting around towns of any size and staying in a variety of farmhouses, inns of pilgrimage, barns, stables and even, on one memorable night, an enormous hollowed oak. Two long weeks of avoiding all unnecessary contact with their fellow humans, darting off the road at the sound of carriages behind them and averting their faces from the curious glances of the carriers and pack-horse trains.

Louis, however, proved a marvellous companion, enlivening the journey considerably, ever curious about all the strange new sights he saw on the road and everything about his new 'papa'. De Born found himself telling Louis stories that he had nearly forgotten about his boyhood home, his family and his schooling. At night he would tell Louis the ghost stories that he had been told by Pierre Niolle, his father's game-keeper. Tales of *tornas*, 'they who return', and the hob goblins, the *luti*, who loved playing practical jokes on the peasants. Tales of the *leberou* or werewolf, who, when tired, would jump on the backs of unwary travellers to be carried home. Of the evil fairies in their 'fades' or magic circles and, most fearsome of all, the black satanic *Aversier*, who waited at crossroads for his victims and could only be killed by a strong dose of holy water.

It was Louis' invariable custom to say his prayers every night, no matter how tired he was. One night de Born was astonished to hear him ask God's forgiveness for the men who hunted him. He questioned the boy, only to be told that the Jesus would not like him to ask for vengeance. De Born himself never joined Louis in his prayers and the boy was curious about de Born's attitude to religion. He sensed somehow that his guardian held different views but, being too polite or too shy to ask, the mystery remained unexplained. One day, when they were eating their frugal midday meal under a hornbeam hedge by a sluggish bourn, they heard the sound of a tinkling bell in the distance. Looking towards the field opposite, where a few peasants were clearing stones from the furrows, de Born was surprised to see the women suddenly kneel and the men remove their hats. The priest that had caused this reverence soon came into view, holding the host in its golden monstrance before him as he walked the track accompanied by a boy in his blood-red cassock shaking the warning bell.

Louis knelt and crossed himself as the duo passed and then looked up at de Born with surprise.

"You do not bow before Our Saviour, papa?" he asked, amazed at de Born's action in remaining sitting, with his hat firmly stuck to his head. "Perhaps you are a Protestant or a Mussulman?" he asked hopefully, seeking a reason to forgive de Born's wicked behaviour.

"No," said de Born, "I am neither."

"What then?" asked the bewildered boy.

"I am what the priests call a pagan, or an unbeliever," answered de Born.

This reply continued to trouble the boy for the rest of the journey. He promptly inserted special pleas for de Born's salvation into his nightly prayers. This nettled de Born as, truth to tell, he was jealous of the boy's simple faith, his certainty of God's love and life everlasting. He wanted to believe, but could not. Indeed he had never, since he was capable of mature reflection, believed in anything outside of himself, not even the cause of his adopted country. In his thoughtless self-absorption, he had narrowed his world down until it rested on the single support of his beliefs about himself.

Sophie's hand had guided him towards a different world altogether, one where self was unimportant, where others were pre-eminent. De Born saw this world as if through a piece of smoked glass. It seemed to him very far off. The only person in it he perceived at all clearly was Sophie, although as the days passed, he recognized that Louis had also become another of its inhabitants.

The boy continued to worry about the idea of his becoming an Englishman. One night de Born was awakened by a strange sound coming from the other side of the farmhouse bedroom. It was the boy crying. He went over and sat on his bed.

"What's the matter, Louis?"

"I had a horrible dream, and I was surrounded by soldiers and other men but they didn't have the faces of men but wolves and tigers and wild animals and they wanted to eat me," answered Louis in a rush.

"But that's silly Louis. When one is free, no one is able to hurt you," said de Born.

" But you are free and if they catch you they will kill you?" observed the boy sadly.

Having no more words to comfort him, de Born returned to his bed.

*   *   *

At the end of this fortnight, on a damp, raw day, guardian and boy found themselves on the muddy road between Issigeac and Villeréal, the nearest town to Château Born. It was Saturday, market-day in the bastide and, although de Born would have preferred to give the town a wide berth, not only did his horse need the attentions of a farrier but he himself needed to find the only man in France he trusted. Jamming his hat down over one eye, he advanced up the street that led from the river to the main square with its covered market and surrounding arcades. He knew that the man he sought would be standing by the pump on the church side of the square. He left Louis by the convent on the opposite side and walked under the oak-beamed *halles*, through the peasants yelling their wares, to where Bernard Laparre stood.

Laparre, or to give him his proper title, the Sieur de Hautevignes, was a huge, fat man of about sixty years of age with a magnificent set of false teeth made from walrus ivory. He was almost completely bald, as one could see when he doffed his hat, with only a fringe of creamy white hair around the ears. Like most fat men, he had a jolly air to him, which was entirely bogus. He was easily the most ruthless and dangerous man de Born had ever known. He was also the most honest.

Apart from his teeth and his word, which had never been broken, the Sieur was famous locally for his paunch. This was a staggering, monumental construction of Rabelaisian proportions. The product of endless jugs of local wine, *magret* fat and coarse garlic sausage his belly had come to resemble the great oak casks from which the wine came. Even in Bordeaux they had heard of the Sieur's paunch, and all the locals were proud of the fact. On market-day he invariably stood by the town pump to accept petitions, redress grievances, receive rents or just listen to the gossip. Some parents brought their children just to see the paunch of legend, and he would always present them with a juicy dried Agen plum from a seemingly bottomless pocket in his greatcoat. He had been the oldest and closest friend of de Born's father and the old marquis had trusted him with his life.

De Born worked his way carefully through the crowd until he stood directly behind Laparre. Then, leaning forward, he whispered into the old man's good ear.

"Do you know whose voice this is?"

"Saw you enter the halles ten minutes ago from the convent side," said Laparre. "How are you, son?"

"Well enough," replied de Born, "but I need your help."

"Wait by the side door of the convent until the Angelus rings. I'll join you then," said his friend, still smiling and nodding to the line of peasants paying their respects as they passed his waiting place.

As he returned to the convent de Born saw that Louis was playing ball near to a veteran sitting on the convent steps and reading a yellowing copy of a revolutionary newspaper. Louis' wayward aim had succeeded in bouncing his ball off the old man's shattered legs and he looked up petulantly from his reading.

"Go play with your ball further down the street, child," he said, waving his hand at Louis in an effort to move him on.

Unabashed, Louis stood firm.

"Not until you have returned my property," he said imperiously, pointing to the ball which lay beside the old man's crutches.

"You speak like a lord, little one," said the veteran, amused despite himself by the boy's manner.

"My father had a carriage like a lord's, white and gold," Louis confided shyly, advancing until he stood before the veteran.

"Ah, doubtless you have inherited his ability to command," said the old man, winking at de Born.

Louis cast a sideways look at de Born and hastily changed the subject. It had been drilled into him time and time again on the journey that he must never ever talk about his life in Paris.

"Who's that?" he asked, pointing to the newspaper.

"Eh? Who's what?" The old man turned the journal around so that he could see what Louis was pointing at.

"Oh, her!" he said when he saw the illustration of Sanson showing a woman's head to the crowd. "Why, that's the Austrian whore Marie Antoinette herself getting her just desserts," he replied, spitting both for emphasis and sheer relish.

At the mention of the woman's name, Louis went very pale and looked intently at the crude wood-cut, and then, before de Born could properly react, he took to his heels, running wildly down the street, half-blinded by his tears.

De Born, who had only been half-listening to their conversation until he heard the victim's name mentioned, leapt up to follow, but, becoming entangled in the bewildered old man's crutches, momentarily lost sight of the boy.

When he had recovered his balance, he ran furiously down the street after Louis, looking along each of the narrow alleyways that intersected it as he did so. Panting, he came to rest at the end of the long, empty street and looked frantically all about him, but the boy was nowhere to be seen. He had completely disappeared.

CHAPTER FOURTEEN

Sextidi, 26 Pluviôse, Year II

Methodically, desperately, de Born retraced his steps, plunging down every dim alleyway, combing every garden and patch of wasteland. As he was passing what in former days had been the house of the town's only doctor, he heard a noise coming from somewhere near an overgrown vegetable patch. On getting closer, he realized that the sound was coming from the far side of the well-head.

He found Louis crouched on the ground, his head in his hands as if to shut out the world, shoulders shuddering with staccato sobbing. At a loss, de Born stood looking down on the boy. Then he knelt on the damp earth and enfolded Louis in his arms until the sobbing had virtually ceased.

"Why didn't you tell me?" Louis asked, turning his tear-stained face up to his guardian.

"Because I didn't want to hurt you," de Born replied, taking his handkerchief from his sleeve and wiping the boy's tears.

"She was my only hope" the boy sobbed as he took the tattered scrap of engraving from his pocket and kissed it gently. "My guardian angel".

"Don't grieve for your her, Louis," de Born whispered. "She's in a far better place now."

"Do you - ?" Louis asked hopefully. "Do you really believe that?"

De Born hesitated, conscious of saying the words only out of a desire to comfort the boy. Who knows, he thought, perhaps she is.

"Yes, I really believe that," he replied with counterfeit conviction. The two hugged each other again, one seeking comfort, the other seeking faith.

De Born became aware of the convent bell tolling the Angelus and, taking the boy by the hand, made his way back to the convent steps.

"Hello, who's this fine young fellow?" said Laparre jovially, taking a dried plum out of his pocket and handing it to the boy.

"He's an orphan I'm taking care of for the moment," replied de Born, casting an anxious glance at the marketplace, where a few of the town idlers still stood about.

Sensing his mood and the direction of his glance, Laparre moved his not inconsiderable bulk to shield de Born and the boy from the public gaze.

"Where's your horse, Jean?"

"At the farriers, but it should be ready by now," replied de Born.

"Good," said his friend. "Leave the town as if you are going to Castillonès, but instead take the back road through Bournel, then go the long way to Pierre Niolle's house. I'll meet you there." Then he shook de Born's hand with some condescension, as if dismissing a petitioner, ruffled the boy's hair, gave him another prune and ambled off towards his cabriolet standing by the ruined fort at the side of the church.

*   *   *

Sleet was falling by the time de Born reached the farmstead of Gigouzac, the home of Pierre Niolle. His father's former gamekeeper lived alone in a handsome, three-storey house made of limestone that he rented from Laparre. It had been built earlier in the century on the hill-top site of a Roman villa and had the steep, hat-shaped roof typical of the region. It was here in the fields, woods and streams surrounding the house that de Born had learnt to shoot, fish and snare for the pot. About the healing herbs and plants of the forest and all the other useful arts and sciences of the countryman. Niolle himself was a hunchback and therefore a bachelor - no local woman could ever overcome their superstition. Thus no one ever discovered the gentle, learned man underneath the crippled body. This had not embittered the gamekeeper, who regarded his misfortune with fatalistic resignation, but living alone for so long had made him habitually silent and wholly self-sufficient. His only companions were his briard dog and a vixen, which he found as a motherless cub. De Born could see him now, framed against the farmhouse door, hat in hand, silently smiling his greeting. Even his old briard seemed to recognize the visitor and was delighted by the boy's enthusiastic petting.

Inside, Laparre was already comfortably ensconced on a settle beside the enormous fire blazing in the kitchen nook, full of pulleys and cranes and spits, trivets, coppers and cauldrons. Louis asked if he might course rabbits with the dog so Laparre, with only a look, signalled Niolle to follow and keep an eye on the boy.

De Born took the opposite settle and warmed himself.

"What would you like to know first, Jean?" asked Laparre quietly.

"Who killed him, Sieur?" came the quick response.

"Let me start at the beginning," said Laparre, in his slow careful way. "After the news of the Bastille the town went a little crazed. You can't really blame them. They were told that counter-revolutionary armies would cut their throats while they slept, seize their land and rape their wives. Anyone who had planted a liberty tree would have their hands cut off and so on - you know the sort of thing."

De Born nodded.

"The people became terrified of everything and everybody. The town's worst elements banded together and started to take advantage of the situation. The priests and nuns were their first target. They were robbed and beaten in the streets, so they fled to their homes and barred their gates." Laparre poked at a smoking log until it burst into flames. "The mob contented themselves with burning the manorial pews in the church and stealing the ciborium. Then in February '90 they started large-scale riots all over the district. Each parish was in its turn a target. Soon all the châteaux and churches had been sacked and only Born remained untouched.

"One Saturday, a large mob collected in the square and proceeded to get very drunk, encouraging each other to go to Born with stories of buried gold. When the market closed they all rushed off, intent on burning down the château and attacking the village, which they considered to be loyal to your father and full of counter-revolutionaries. I sent word to Villeneuve, where there was a detachment of National Guard militia, and then went to warn the marquis. By the time I arrived, they were already gathered before the gatehouse, shouting silly slogans and threatening those inside with all sorts of blood-curdling fates if they didn't open up. I went up to the church to get a better view and saw your father and Lasserre, the old carpenter - you remember him? - standing in front of the gatehouse. Your father fired off a shot over their heads to quiet them down and spoke a few words. I couldn't hear what he said.

"Then they swarmed all over him. I saw one man plunge a pitchfork into his chest and he went down. He never got up. They poured into the château, looting and despoiling what they couldn't carry off. The militia eventually arrived and arrested twenty-six of them, mostly the ones too drunk to escape, and took them off to Agen prison in chains."

De Born, who throughout the telling had not once glanced at Laparre, but just stared into the fire, now looked squarely at his friend.

"Who was it?"

"Who was what?"

"Who killed him?"

"Bissière, the big cowherd with the beard," replied Laparre, looking into the flames as if seeing the murder yet again in his mind's eye.

"Where is he?" asked de Born grimly.

"Oh, as for that," answered Laparre, "one dark night the *Aversier* got him. At least, that's what they say - the body was never found."

"And the old carpenter, Lasserre?" de Born asked, remembering his funny, buck-toothed grin and those slender, capable hands.

"They butchered him on the spot and hung his corpse from the weather-cock, poor old fellow," replied Laparre sadly, crossing himself.

De Born got up and paced around the kitchen for a while before halting before Laparre and shaking his hand.

"Thank you, Sieur," said de Born. "For four years I have been thinking about what I was going to do with my father's murderer. To find you've already taken care of him is, I admit, a relief."

"Better that way, Jean," said Laparre, who had been studying him anxiously. "Vengeance can eat away at a man like a canker, turn him sour. It's over. Best forget about it. And don't blame yourself for not being there to help your father. I assure you that you could not have saved him. No one - including me - could have. It would only have brought about the end of the house of Born. Now, what about you?" he said, changing the subject rather obviously. "What brings you here, and who on earth is that boy who calls you 'papa'?"

De Born told him everything. Everything, that is, except his feelings for Sophie and the answer to the second question. "As to the boy," he told Laparre, "his parents are dead, and I'm trying to get him to England. Chaumette has his reasons for trying to stop me."

"This Chaumette," said Laparre. "Does he have hair the colour of straw?"

"Yes," said de Born, his heart sinking, knowing with utter certainty what Laparre was going to say next.

"He's here, along with a foreigner and that lady who married

Etienne de Roquefère."

"Sophie," de Born muttered.

"Yes," replied Laparre, watching de Born closely. "That's the one. Attractive woman, eh?"

Seeing this elicited no response other than to provoke de Born to recommence his pacing up and down the *terre cuite* tiled floor, Laparre told him what had happened.

"A few days ago this fellow came to see me, with the lady and a foreign-looking man in tow. Said he was a friend of yours from Paris and asked to stay at the château to await your arrival. I didn't like the look of him but, seeing the marquise was with him, I gave him permission. I took the precaution of telling the servants to keep an eye on him and report to me daily on what he did and where he went. The next day six armed men arrived on horseback, all tough-looking fellows and obviously in his employ. Two are billeted in the village - they watch the crossroads constantly. Two sleep in the gatehouse and the others guard this Chaumette day and night. There may of course be others I don't know about."

"How does she look?" asked de Born, unable to concentrate on these details.

"The marquise? Oh, well enough. A bit tired, perhaps," replied Laparre, intensely curious at seeing the expression of relief on de Born's face, but knowing that he had to bide his time.

"You said you gave him permission," wondered de Born. "Do you own the château now?"

"No, Monsieur le marquis," Laparre said beaming. "You do."

De Born wheeled round to confront Laparre. "But uncle Philip was told by the Paris embassy that it was sold at auction. He even tried to buy it for me."

"It was," Laparre said, unable to contain his merriment at a secret joke. "And you bought it!

"What happened was this. After you were pronounced *émigré* and outlaw, an auction was arranged, as it had been for all the other properties around here the Jacobins could get their thieving hands on. I put the word out that no one should make any bids, so it was knocked down to me for a song. The auctioneers grumbled a bit, but I soon saw them off."

"I will, of course, repay every penny," said de Born, "but you have to understand that at the moment I'm virtually penniless."

"No need," said Laparre. "When I said you bought it, I meant just that. Your father came to me shortly after the Revolution started and said if anything were to happen to him, I was to tell you to look on the island."

"The island in the middle of the lake?" asked de Born,

remembering the place he used to go as a young man on quiet summer's days to read and dream his dreams of glory.

"That's it," replied Laparre, chuckling. "So, after his death, may he rest in peace, Niolle and I rowed out one night with a spade, dug up the floor of the ice-house and found an iron box containing no less than ten thousand gold louis. Those drunken fools were right about the buried treasure," he laughed. "They just didn't know where to look." And he burst out into another roar of laughter, wiping his eyes with a massive lawn handkerchief.

After he had recovered a measure of his usual composure, Laparre became more businesslike.

"So Jean, I suppose you've been foolish with that young lady and we're all supposed to rush the château and rescue her?"

"Something like that," de Born said, giving him a rueful grin. "But the key is to put Chaumette out of action, at least until I have the boy safely in London."

"This boy is even more important than the woman, then?" mused Laparre, determined to get to the bottom of the mystery.

"Sieur," replied de Born. "I have never lied to you before, but if you ask me about the boy I'll have to. My orders are to get him to London at any cost, including that of my own life."

Impressed by this solemn warning, Laparre gave up. "Very well,

Jean. Forgive me. It's just an old man's stupid curiosity. I won't ask again. What I will ask, however, is how do you intend putting this Chaumette out of action?"

"We'll do what my father always said one should do in these circumstances," said de Born, smiling for the first time in a long while.

"Time spent in reconnaissance is seldom wasted!" they chorused together, laughing at the memory of the old marquis' favourite maxim.

"For the moment we taste whatever Niolle has poached for the pot and then we sleep," said de Born. "Tomorrow we'll go and take a closer look at our straw-haired friend."

The three men and the boy spent a pleasant evening around the fire, eating Niolle's jugged hare with a slice from the ham that hung in the chimney, and smoking their pipes. Despite his desperate desire not to, Louis soon fell asleep and was put to bed in the corner. The briard immediately joined him, to Niolle's amazement, a dozing sentinel next to the boy.

*   *   *

Next morning they made their breakfast on the customary chestnut porridge of the Haut Agenais peasants. Outside, the valley bottom was obscured by a rolling mist, useful for concealment, but it would mean getting much closer to the château than was really safe.

Laparre was left behind, with strict instructions to hide Louis if strangers came, while de Born and Niolle set off to reconnoitre.

The château lay on top of a mound overlooked by the village of Born, itself atop a much higher hill. The village consisted of no more than the church and a few houses clustered around it, together with a forge and oxen lift, a baker's oven, a sabot-maker's atelier and a large barn. One road led south down the river valley to Gigouzac. The north road passed by the church and threaded its way through the farmsteads to Villeréal, while the track east led down to the château. No road could be built to the west as the land dropped away too sharply for the oxen to manage.

De Born and Niolle approached the village from the south but, even taking advantage of every bit of cover, soon realized that the man standing guard at the crossroads would be able to see them long before they could get close enough to spy on the château. After retreating to think things out, de Born decided that they should use the old goat track that wound its way up the steep incline from the west and emerged near the church. From there they should be able to slip from house to house.

Despite his physical disadvantages, Niolle proved the better climber. De Born was left scrambling and slipping up the muddy track, greasy with the previous night's rain. When he reached the top and had

recovered his breath, he turned left, crossed the road by the church and

stood by the baker's to get a clear look at the château through his spy-

glass. Everything seemed peaceful enough, the chimneys were smoking

furiously, a gaggle of geese cropped the grass near the lake as always,

and he could see one of the old servants tending the trees in the plum

orchard. As he swivelled the glass on to the gatehouse he saw that its

chimneys were likewise in action and two figures paced up and down,

stamping their feet to keep warm. As he was completing his sweep, the

side door of the baker's opened, releasing a fragrant blast of heat into the

chilly morning air. There was no time for de Born to move and the

baker's eyes widened when he recognized the intruder.

De Born hustled him back inside and told him briefly why he was

there.

"They're holding the marquise against her will?" the incredulous

baker asked. "How can I help?"

"Go to the other men, the ones you can trust," said de Born, "and

meet me at Niolle's house at six o'clock tonight. Tell them to bring what

weapons they have, together with some food for their supper, and come

out of the village at intervals, one by one. Use the goat track, not the

road."

The baker shook his hand eagerly and promised to do his best, saying that he himself only had his wooden oven-shovel, but it was heavy enough to crack a man's skull. De Born whistled up Niolle and gave him his instructions, then he sauntered up the street towards the crossroads. He hadn't gone very far when, hearing the noise of his boot-heels on the stone chippings, the sentry whirled round, musket at the ready, and began advancing on de Born.

"Get back inside and stay there until I tell you it's all right to leave your home," he shouted, unable to recognize de Born at first. He halted abruptly when the mist cleared enough for him to get a good look. His finger tightened on the trigger. De Born gambled that he could never fire without a direct order, too afraid of taking the responsibility for de Born's death on himself.

"Ah, it's you," said de Born cheerily as he walked up to the man, whom he recognized as the scribe from the Masonic Lodge. "How's the cheek?"

Instinctively the man put his hand up to touch the still livid mark of Chaumette's crop, and that movement coincided exactly with Niolle's short swing of the life-preserver. The sentry crumpled without a sound, de Born neatly catching his musket before it hit the ground.

Niolle hoisted the unconscious man onto his shoulders as if he were a bag of feathers and preceded de Born back down the goat track. As they approached Gigouzac, Niolle put out a warning hand to stop de

Born in his tracks. Lowering the still unconscious man onto the wet turf, he signed to de Born to stay with the prisoner while he went to investigate.

The front door was ajar and no smoke could be seen coming from the kitchen chimney. More ominously, there was no sign of the briard. Niolle edged up to the low dry-stone wall in front of the house that enclosed the kitchen garden, and then by degrees up to the kitchen window. One look was sufficient, for he instantly beckoned de Born to follow. The kitchen was a shambles. Shards of smashed pottery and glass were everywhere. A straw-bottomed chair lay on its side, both back legs neatly severed from the seat. Laparre was lying, semi-conscious, by the fire. While Niolle retrieved the still comatose figure of Chaumette's man, de Born endeavoured to bring Laparre round.

"Where's the boy?" asked de Born urgently as soon as he saw signs of life in Laparre's eyes.

"Hiding in the wood. The dog is guarding him," answered Laparre weakly.

De Born went to the track that led from the side of the house to a quarry at the bottom of the hill and shouted the boy's name. No answer. He advanced slowly into the wood, shouting distinctly every few yards, so that Louis might recognize his voice. As he passed the first bend in the track he thought he saw a clump of hazelnut quiver, although it was a perfectly still day. As he came closer, he heard the briard's deep warning growl and he paused to let the dog recognize his scent.

"Which hand, Louis, left or right?" he asked and, reassured, the boy clambered out of his hiding place.

"I wasn't frightened, you know," Louis confided, still trembling a little.

"Really?" said de Born. "I certainly would have been."

"Would you? Truly?" asked the boy, unwilling to believe such a slur, even one self-admitted.

"It's perfectly reasonable to be scared, Louis," said de Born as they marched back together to the house. "Brave men are simply those who are scared and still advance into danger because duty or honour demand it."

"Do freemen have to be brave?" asked Louis.

"Yes," replied de Born, studying the boy's face in an effort to read the motive for the question. "But it's a different kind of bravery. They must sometimes do what is unpopular, because it is the right thing to do."

"But how do freemen know it's the right thing to do?"

"They don't," replied de Born. "That's why it's brave to do it. Look, it may be a little difficult for you to understand now, but when you're free you will learn to be brave."

Louis frowned, as he always did when the subject of his future life came up.

"Will I be brave when I'm free?" he asked in a small voice.

De Born felt somehow they had reached the core of the boy's unease. He halted and turned to face him.

"Forget anything that people may tell you, Louis. Your father was honest and kind while he lived, and he went to the scaffold bravely."

The boy's relief was evident and immediate. He curled his hand inside his guardian's and they walked the last part of the track in a thoughtful silence.

*   *   *

When they entered the kitchen, Laparre was sitting on the settle drinking pear brandy and Chaumette's scribe was trussed to a chair.

"Oh, don't worry about me," Laparre said, waving away de Born's ministrations. "Just a tap on the head. I'll be perfectly well after another glass of Niolle's prune *eau de vie*."

"Who was it?" asked de Born.

"The foreigner and two bullies," replied Laparre. "The dog smelt them a quarter-mile off and I told Louis to run and hide, just as you ordered. They burst in, asked me where you were, smashed a few things and, when that didn't impress me, one of them gave me a taste of his cudgel. Unfortunately, from his point of view, he overdid it and I must have passed out. When I woke up they were gone. You must have arrived a few minutes after that."

"This foreigner," asked de Born, well aware of the locals' habit of calling everyone a foreigner who wasn't actually born within hearing of the Villeréal bells. "Was he a Frenchman or truly foreign?"

"Truly foreign," replied Laparre without hesitation. "I'm certain of it."

He must be from the comte de Provence's headquarters at Turin, thought de Born. Chaumette has reverted to his original patron's offer, which meant that he would kill the boy on sight; or perhaps, now there was the complication of the boy in the Temple, take the dauphin alive to his uncle for verification and then kill him.

All de Born's efforts at eliciting from the prisoner the facts about Chaumette's plans and the state of affairs at the château came to naught. Whatever technique he employed - friendliness, bribery, threats - all failed. The man was plainly more terrified of Chaumette than anything de Born had to offer. The briard circled the prisoner and, sensing de Born's hostility, growled at the man, who flinched visibly. De Born remembered a boy at school who had been badly bitten by a dog as a child and who, although normally fearless, was terrified of dogs. He watched the prisoner's reaction to the circling animal.

"Do you still have that large cupboard in the upstairs bedroom?" he asked Niolle, who nodded. "Has the dog been fed today?" This time Niolle shook his head.

"Take this man up there and lock him in with the briard," said de Born, as if out of all patience. "However loud he screams, you are not to open the door until ten minutes have passed."

Niolle moved towards the prisoner.

"Wait!" the man said in an unnaturally loud voice, beads of sweat standing out on his forehead. "What do you want to know?"

"Who is in the castle? Where are they? What are they planning to do?" rapped out de Born.

"Citizen Chaumette, a foreigner whose name I do not know, and the woman are in the main house, along with the servants. There are two men in the gatehouse. Me and another man guard the crossroads in turn. We are billeted at the sabot-maker's house," said the prisoner, licking his lips nervously, still watching the briard's every move.

"And what do they intend?" asked de Born.

"You know Chaumette," said the prisoner. "Do you think he takes me into his confidence?"

"Niolle, take him upstairs," ordered de Born.

"All right, all right," cried the man in a panic. "But if Chaumette ever finds out it was me it would be better you had killed me now."

De Born nodded to acknowledge both the truth of that and to indicate that his silence was assured.

"You are to be persuaded to hand over the boy in exchange for the woman," said the prisoner.

"And then?" asked de Born.

"The boy would be taken to Turin."

"And then?" asked de Born relentlessly.

Chaumette's man looked at the boy and shrugged expressively.

"I want him to hear you say it. Let him hear you say it," insisted de Born.

"After identification, he is to be killed," said the man finally.

De Born sensed he was holding something back.

"What else?"

"My God, Jean, what else could there be?" asked Laparre, who had been listening to the exchange with growing horror.

"He's holding something back," said de Born, staring into the man's eyes.

"The whole thing is just a trick," said the scribe. "You are both to be taken afterwards, but Chaumette says you have powerful friends and may not be killed. The woman, however, is to be ... " Here he hesitated.

" ... dealt with separately."

"And just what does 'dealt with' entail?" asked de Born icily.

"She is promised to the guards ... for their ... amusement. When they grow bored they are to take her to Roquefère and hang her from the great mulberry tree there."

De Born went and sat down on the settle, his hands trembling with rage. He had not forgotten that Chaumette had promised him just such a fate for Sophie at the masonic lodge. He knew his adversary intimately now and there was no doubt Chaumette would carry out his threat. He ruled by fear, and this would be a useful illustration of exactly what happened to those like de Born who double-crossed him.

"Take him upstairs, Niolle, and put him in the cupboard," ordered de Born and, as the cry of protest formed in the prisoner's mouth, added, "The briard stays down here for the moment.

As soon as the man was out of the room, Louis came over to de Born.

"Don't worry, Louis," said de Born before the boy could ask his question. "With the Sieur and your new friend with the big teeth here to protect you, no one is going to hurt you."

Content, the boy ran over to the dog and stroked his long matted coat. When de Born looked back to Laparre he saw that his friend was staring fixedly at the boy. Slowly he turned his gaze towards de Born.

His eyes revealed that he had guessed the truth. It was the mention of Turin that had started the process. He had suddenly remembered reading about the comte de Provence's court in exile at Turin. The foreigner was therefore Provence's servant. It was Provence who wanted to kill the boy. Only one boy in France was so important. His eight-year-old nephew. The boy who stood between Provence and the throne.

De Born stared back steadily and the look that passed between them was all the conversation they needed. Laparre knew all and would tell nothing.

*   *   *

Snowflakes began to appear on the window and, when de Born went to the door, he saw that the garden had already been covered with a fine white layer. Soon the sky was full of flakes swirling in the breeze and covering the valley.

De Born cursed his bad luck. They could not fight in a blizzard and, as soon as it ceased, they would stand out like scarecrows in a field of ripened wheat.

"We must do as the ermine does, Jean," said Laparre.

"Yes, yes," murmured de Born, only half listening. Here they had an insuperable problem and all the old fellow could do was witter on about stoats.

Laparre, seeing he was making no headway, went to the corner of the kitchen where Niolle slept in winter. He took a sheet from the bed and wrapped it around his broad shoulders.

"As the ermine do," he repeated. "Change to our winter coats."

"By the body of God, yes," de Born exclaimed. "Sieur, you are a veritable genius. White on white: that should get us close enough to the gatehouse so that we can deal with the guards there."

"But what if those people in the main house hear us?" asked Laparre. "They might kill the woman."

"They might," de Born admitted. "But I doubt whether Chaumette will throw away what he thinks of as his trump card. You see, Sieur, he judges that I will hand over the boy if the marquise is threatened, or at least hold to the original contract. Well, he's wrong. I will never hand over the boy, and what's more, Sophie - the marquise, that is - knows it. No, he thinks that if he kills her then his advantage over me disappears. I came here because I had no friends left in Paris to help me. Now I'm fighting on the ground I know, with people I can trust. Chaumette makes the mistake all arrogant men do: he is judging me by his own standards. We will finish all this, one way or the other, at dawn tomorrow."

It was not long before the men from the village began arriving in dribs and drabs. By half-past six, eight villagers stood, bare-headed, ranged around the walls of the kitchen, shuffling their clogs on the tiles and murmuring to each other in their harsh occitan twang. Each man carried a weapon of some sort. Most had knives. Four had their fowling-pieces; two had bill-hooks tied to long poles, and nearly all had the sling shots they used to kill birds. The baker, as promised, had brought his oven shovel. With the two barrels of Niolle's flintlock shot-gun and de Born's stick, plus the captured musket, their fire-power was now equal in strength to the enemy's. To the casual observer, however, this little army hardly looked like the right material for a crack regiment. Two were badly goitered, making it hard for them to move their heads; one had his leg missing from the calf down - the result of an accident with a scythe; one was blind in one eye; and most had suffered from rickets in childhood and now with rheumatism from constant exposure to cold and damp. Nevertheless, both the goitered, who were twin brothers, could bring down a red legged partridge in full flight at fifty yards. The amputee could and did climb his cherry trees to pick the fruit on the highest branches that others normally left to the birds. The smith, who had been blinded by a red-hot cinder from his forge, could bend an iron nail using only his thumb and forefinger. All were crack shots, all had learnt to move silently through the woods after game and, most important of all, every man had loved and respected de Born's father.

De Born sketched out the plan he had conceived on his reconnaissance. Laparre would stay as before with the boy and the dog. One man would be posted on the track half-way between Gigouzac and Château Born to fire a warning shot if Chaumette's men counter-attacked. The others would go by the road and use their camouflage to get close to the sentries at the gatehouse. They would use their sling shots to knock them out silently. Two men were detailed to drag them into the gatehouse and, taking up their muskets, resume their sentry duty, to fool anyone looking out from the castle windows.

While that was happening, de Born and Niolle, together with the smith, would use the goat track and disable the guard at the crossroads. There was no need to replace him, as he could not be seen from the castle. As soon as the gatehouse was taken, they would advance through it and surround the great hall. If necessary the smith would use his sledge-hammer to break down the heavy oak door. De Born, Niolle and the twins, who were the best shots, would enter. The others would guard the door. There was to be no shooting, de Born stressed, unless the marquise was directly threatened or a man felt his own life was in mortal danger. "These men are criminals," he said, "but that should not make us savages." All the men murmured their agreement. Most had wives and children, and supposed the guards did too, and anyway, they felt there had been too much blood spilt lately for them to add to the score.

"All clear?" asked de Born, looking at each man intently. "Now is the time to go home if you feel that would be best." No one moved.

"Excellent," said de Born. "Now let's all have some supper and get some sleep."

"What about the geese?" came a question from near the door. Astonishingly, it was Niolle who had spoken. Everyone stared at him in utter astonishment, unable to remember the last time he had uttered so much as a syllable to a living soul.

"What about the geese?" he repeated stolidly.

"By God, Jean," exclaimed Laparre. "He's right. They are bound to alert the castle to our coming."

"Then they will have to be distracted," said de Born, looking to the corner of the room. All eyes followed his gaze and a bout of chuckling and nudging broke out amongst the men. The fox, the subject of all this unusual attention, stirred uneasily.

"Bring her with us, Pierre," de Born said to Niolle. "Then release her amongst the geese. In this weather the sentries won't bother to investigate further as soon as they see what's causing the commotion. Any other questions?" he asked, looked around at each man. "Good. Let's eat and then rest. We start at first light."

Finding it difficult to sleep, de Born went out and plodded around the kitchen garden. He was soon joined by Laparre, similarly afflicted. When Niolle looked out around midnight, he saw them still deep in conversation.

*   *   *

The snow stopped during the night but, when one of the men went to the well for water, de Born noticed that his tracks were over three inches deep. Each of the men went in turn to the stone sink set into the kitchen wall and splashed themselves awake, then checked their weapons and put on their camouflage.

The main party set off up the road to the crossroads, while de Born, Niolle and the smith set off for the goat track. Before he went, de Born entrusted Louis to Laparre's care.

"If something should happen, Sieur, take the boy to England. This amulet will gain you entry to my uncle Philip at the Admiralty. Tell no one, absolutely no one, of the boy's identity. Trust no one, French or English, save Philip Stephens. You understand?" he asked the old man. "No one."

Laparre made no answer but simply shook hands, and then de Born was gone. At the top of the rise, where they stationed the lookout, he turned and cast one last, anxious look at Laparre and the boy, still standing at the farmhouse door. He raised his stick once in acknowledgement and then turned and trudged through the snow to Château Born.

The goat track was now almost impassable. The smith used his *masse* as a support to lever himself up and then pull de Born up with him. Niolle seemed to ignore the treacherous footing, even with a sack over his shoulder containing an obviously unhappy fox. The guard at the crossroads proved no more of a barrier than his colleague had been; the same life-preserver repeated its work of the previous day and with exactly the same result. The trio then worked their way to the lake, which lay at the side of the west wall of the château. As they moved nearer the geese became more and more agitated. By the time they had reached the wall, making themselves invisible to the castle's occupants, the geese were now in full cry and Niolle released the contents of his sack.

The fox stood still for a moment, getting her bearings. The geese froze when they realized what was facing them. Slowly the vixen's head turned and gazed on the luscious expanse of flesh and feathers. She took one pace forward, checked, and gave a sly, vulpine, backwards glance to her master, seeking his confirmation. Then pandemonium broke out. The fox, faced with such an *embarrass de richesses*, lunged at every inviting neck in sight. The gander attempted to defend his flock with hisses and attacking forays of his own. The rest of the flock fled to the safety of the lake, cackling and flapping their clipped wings.

De Born heard a window on the south side of the château open and a voice shout to the gatehouse for the sentries to investigate. The reply was not long in coming and he heard the window close again. He worked his way along the wall and was just in time to see two sentries being dragged by their boots into the gatehouse. Two men wearing their newly-acquired greatcoats and hats took their place.

At de Born's word, all five men ran as fast as the snow would allow through the gates and towards the door leading to the great hall. De Born, Niolle and the two marksmen positioned themselves under the window while the smith gingerly tried the door-handle. The door opened a fraction. The smith closed it to and retreated to join the others.

With the luxury of complete surprise, de Born whispered to the smith to go and guard the hall's only other exit, the servants' door which led to the well in the courtyard. Then little by little he poked his head up until he could look into the room. At first he could see nothing, as one of the guards was standing in his way, his back to the window. When at last he moved to one side, de Born saw three figures, also with their backs to him, sitting in front of the fire. Sophie and Chaumette were side by side and de Born could see that Chaumette was arguing with her. The other man, presumably the comte de Provence's envoy, sat slumped in his chair. As de Born watched, he got up and threw another log on the fire. As he turned to go back to his seat, de Born got a clear view of his face. It was Dick Ferris.

CHAPTER FIFTEEN

Septidi, 27 Pluviôse, Year II

De Born slid back down onto his haunches, his back scraping down the wall. For a moment he was tempted to get right back up and take another look inside the room, yet he knew it was pointless. There was no mistaking that pirate's beard, even when worn much shorter than before, or the way Ferris habitually sat with his hand cupped under his chin. The others looked at each other, bewildered by de Born's expression and a little afraid. They could not imagine what had shocked their leader so as to produce this sudden paleness and jerky breathing.

Niolle edged closer and had a quick look for himself. He saw the straw-haired man and the foreigner with the beard by the fire, recognizing them from Laparre's description. As far as he could see, the woman was not injured or tied, or even distressed. The guard looked exactly how Niolle expected the guard to look, solid and alert. Niolle ducked back down and shrugged at the twins, signalling that whatever de Born had seen was not obvious to him.

De Born sat for several minutes without moving, calmly trying to work out what his friend's astonishing resurrection meant. Why had Chaumette saved him from the scaffold? Had Ferris been working for Chaumette all along? Whose side was he on? Perhaps, he thought, Ferris is playing a double game. Perhaps he had been infiltrated into Chaumette's organisation by Whitehall. Maybe de Born was, by attacking the castle, ruining a carefully conceived plan. Then he remembered what had happened to Laparre. Perhaps Ferris had traded his life for complicity in Chaumette's scheme, presumably to replace de Born as the boy's courier. Perhaps. Time to discover the truth, he thought, and signalled to the men to get ready.

At first, when they burst through the door, only the guard reacted, quickly sizing up the intruders and letting his rifle fall to the ground with a loud metallic clatter in a gesture of surrender. It was this noise that roused the trio by the fire at the other end of the room.

"Sophie," de Born said, without taking his eyes off Chaumette. "Walk towards me, but keep to the wall. You," this was directed at the guard, "lie down on your stomach, hands clasped behind your head.

"Pierre, cover these gentlemen with your gun and if they move, shoot them," de Born ordered. "You two," he said to the twins, "take the guard over to the gatehouse and tie him up. Then find the other two sentries, disarm them and come straight back here."

The brothers beckoned the guard to leave with jerking motions of their muskets, while Niolle placed himself by the window so he had an uninterrupted line of fire to the fireplace. Sophie was now close enough for de Born to smell her scent. He still had not looked at her.

"Stand behind me," he said, lowering his voice until the others had to strain to hear him. "Near the wall. If there's shooting, fall to the ground and stay there.

"Now, gentlemen," he said, advancing towards them. "You will oblige me by turning your chairs to face me and sitting in them with your hands on the arm rests."

While Chaumette obeyed, Ferris took a step forward. Niolle cocked one of the barrels of his gun and the click made Ferris halt.

"Johnnie. By Christ, I'm glad to see you," he said with a great grin. De Born saw that his eyes weren't smiling.

"Do what I say, Dick," de Born said.

"But John - "

"Do it."

Ferris shrugged. "Of course, old cock. Anything you say. Just give me a chance to bloody well explain, won't you?"

"Explain what?" asked de Born.

"Explain what I've been up to," Ferris said. He still had not moved.

"Go and sit down, Dick" de Born said, swinging the stick up until it pointed at his chest. "You can do all the explaining you wish, just as long as you're seated with your hands in sight."

Ferris shrugged again and obeyed.

De Born looked back at Chaumette, who lounged in his chair, legs stretched out before him, seemingly relaxed.

"Of course, I knew you would come, de Born," he drawled with a triumphant smirk. "You're such a predictable creature."

"If you knew I was coming, why did you stay?" asked de Born sceptically.

"Why should I not?" responded Chaumette. "I wanted you to come. How else were we to come to an agreement? There was no need for this melodrama," he said, pointing to the sheets they still wore. "You only had to announce yourself at the gatehouse and I would have received you at any time."

There was something very wrong about Chaumette's demeanour, thought de Born. He was truly at ease, while Ferris had not stopped twitching and fidgeting since he sat down.

"As for this pathetic specimen," he indicated Ferris with an elegantly distasteful sweep of his hand. "He's been in my pay since '91, although Lord knows why I keep him on."

"That's a lie, John," Ferris said, breathing heavily, his face red with anger. Or fear. "I've been stringing him along since I persuaded him to stay my execution."

"And how exactly did you manage that?" asked de Born.

"By promising to betray you for money while I was secretly making plans to double-cross him and help you get away."

"How?" asked de Born.

"How what?"

"How were you going to help me?"

"Ah, well, difficult to say, old cock. Just thought I'd know the moment when it came."

His explanation, thought de Born, was so weak, yet so in character, it was almost plausible. Dare he trust Ferris? And where the hell were the twins?

"Let's stop all this nonsense," said Chaumette, "and progress to the arrangements concerning the boy. You don't trust Ferris? Fine. Nor do I. In any event, he's irrelevant to the main issue. The boy is the only thing that matters. What's your price?"

"I have none, Chaumette," said de Born. "You misjudge me yet again. In any event, you're in no position to bargain. Indeed, what do you have to bargain with? I have the boy."

"Are you sure?" Chaumette asked slyly. "Ah well, perhaps you have," he conceded. "For the moment at least. Let me, however, make you a proposition. In exchange for the passage to America, together with at least enough money to live on for, say, five years, I will tell all the secrets of the revolutionary government to your dear uncle Philip."

De Born did not need time to contemplate how important an offer this was. Chaumette undoubtedly had access to state secrets that could save many thousands of lives on the battlefield. He could certainly shorten the war and might conceivably even guarantee Britain victory.

Thinking his silence meant refusal, Chaumette added another prize. "I will also write out two lists. One will contain the names of all the British agents in France who are in fact in our pay. Ferris - which is not his real name by the way - will be at the top. The second will contain the names of all the agents sent by the Committee of General Security to London and Dublin since the war began."

"If you were so willing to make such an arrangement, why did you send Ferris and those bully-boys of yours to Gigouzac?" asked de Born.

"I didn't send him. I was briefly, er, shall we say incapacitated, and he used what he is pleased to call his own judgement in a pathetic attempt to ingratiate himself," sneered Chaumette.

"You're surely not going to believe that, John, are you?" De Born could see the desperation on Ferris' face and he could smell the fear. "While this bastard was crazy with ether, I went to find you. I just roughed up the old boy to make it look convincing."

"Where are the assignats?" asked de Born.

"Assignats?"

"Dick, don't make me repeat myself."

"I haven't the faintest idea, old cock."

Chaumette grunted in obvious scorn at this reply.

"All right," Ferris shrugged," look John, I admit I took some of the money, but I never would have countenanced killing the boy, you must know that." He put his hand in his coat pocket. "Here, I'll share what's left with you."

De Born wanted time to think.

"Can you handle a gun, Sophie?" he called over his shoulder, without his gaze leaving either of the two men.

"Yes, Jean," came the firm response.

"Then walk behind me and take Pierre's gun, and if they move suddenly, pull the trigger," said de Born. Niolle's shotgun was 16-bore, with a mixture of large shot and small nails. At that range it would be very nearly impossible to miss.

"Pierre, go and find out what has happened to the twins. They should have found the other guards by now."

Niolle moved a little towards Sophie, who put her hands out and clutched the barrel and the stock. At that exact moment, the door behind de Born opened and all hell broke loose in the room.

Chaumette's expression changed in an instant to one of shocked disbelief. Ferris jumped up, taking his hand out of his pocket and starting to point towards something at the end of the room. Niolle grabbed back the gun, shoving Sophie sprawling to the floor, and fired, filling the room with a dense, choking cloud of acrid smoke. Ferris took the full force of the shot in his face and chest, and jumped backwards as if a giant's hand had plucked him into the air and then suddenly let go. De Born's finger contracted automatically on the stick's trigger and the ball grazed Chaumette's temple and exited out through one of the window panes. As the smoke cleared, de Born saw that Ferris was lying in a crumpled bloody heap by the fireplace. Niolle had cocked the second trigger of his gun and was now standing, pointing it directly at Chaumette, who was clutching his brow with his hand. Between the fingers, rivulets of blood were beginning to show. De Born walked over to Ferris and turned the body over. He was blasted beyond recognition. A widening pool of blood was forming under him.

De Born looked across at Niolle.

"Look in his hand, Monsieur le marquis," Niolle said, still aiming at Chaumette.

De Born examined the hand. It was empty. In the other, the fist still clutching its prize even in death, was de Born's overcoat pistol. It was still cocked. He had never got the chance to fire.

"Who was he?" he asked Chaumette, who was now seated again,

wiping his forehead with a large cloth.

"Oh, some Irishman," muttered Chaumette vaguely. "I never found out his real name. He needed the money to pay off gambling debts. His only interest in you was that bundle of paper money you were carrying."

Looking down at that shattered face, de Born thought back to the night when he had caught Ferris secretly counting the assignats. Maybe Chaumette was speaking the truth.

"How do you think I knew you were heading here?" asked Chaumette, seeing that de Born's belief in his friend was crumbling. "It was Ferris who told me that in prison you swore that if you ever got out alive you would go back to Château Born and avenge your father."

De Born's mind went back to that conversation in the Conciergerie. Chaumette was speaking the truth. That's why he came to be at the bridge in Orléans.

All the other little incidents fell into place. That's why Ferris insisted that they dine at *Procope* - so that Chaumette would be able to appraise de Born for himself. That's why, in prison, Ferris was so absurdly optimistic about getting out. And that's why Ferris provoked Simon and then punched the slaughterman in the wine-shop, making their capture a certainty. Whenever de Born looked like succeeding in his task, Ferris had made sure that any chance of success was wrecked.

Laparre, the cause of this eruption of violence, came and stood by de Born.

"It was just as you predicted last night, Jean," Laparre said, staring at Ferris's mutilated face. "As soon as you had left, four of them approached the house. They tried a rush and our look-out man killed one and I wounded another. Then they tried to work round the back and come through the stable-yard, but I killed another from the rear *meutrière* and the fourth fellow retreated with the wounded. It only took a few minutes. The boy is in the gatehouse."

"What happened to the two men?" asked de Born.

"They met the twins coming from the castle. They're both dead," Laparre said, righting the chair Ferris had been using and slumping down into it.

"Have the bodies taken to the churchyard and buried. Open some old graves and double up each one," ordered de Born.

Wearily Laparre nodded his assent. "What about the men in the gatehouse? Do you want them killed?"

There was a gasp from Sophie and de Born looked directly at her for the first time.

"No, their loyalty is to money, not Chaumette," said de Born. "Pay them off and let them go."

"Well, if you're sure," said Laparre doubtfully. "And what about him?" he asked, jerking this thumb towards Chaumette. "Surely you can't let him live, given what he knows?"

De Born looked at Chaumette, who seemed to have recovered some of his colour, his bleeding now staunched. The thought of this creature sitting on that chest of money aboard ship for America sickened him.

"Citizen Chaumette is going to provide us with the list of agents he so generously promised me, together with a signed confession of his treachery in dealing with the Republic's enemies."

"And just why should I do that?" asked Chaumette.

"Because you will be dead if you don't," de Born replied.

"You wouldn't kill me in cold blood," Chaumette jeered. "I know you better than you know yourself. You haven't the stomach for it. You'd happily kill me in the heat of battle, but never in cold blood, never."

"Perhaps," said de Born. "But he has."

Chaumette looked in the direction of de Born's pointing finger. Niolle stared back at him impassively.

"Tell the Monsieur where you are from, Pierre," asked de Born. "That is, where you were born, before you came to live here."

"La Vendée." Niolle spat out the words as if they were a curse.

Chaumette's eyes widened and he licked his lips.

"And I have your word of honour you will let me go?" he asked de Born.

"No, you do not," said de Born. "If I think of a better plan that involves killing you, I'll probably do that."

This unexpected answer seemed to deflate the remainder of Chaumette's remaining self-confidence. Pen and paper were brought and slowly he began to write. De Born had no idea whether the lists of agents he produced were fiction or not, although he recognized one or two names on both. The 'confession' was a blatant attempt to conceal his part in the boy's escape from the Temple, only admitting that he had gone along with the plan in order to entrap elements of the English spy network. De Born tore it up.

"You are, I take it, tired of this earthly existence?" he said, "and wish to investigate further the possibilities of the afterlife?"

"Nothing is more certain in this life," countered Chaumette, "than the fact that Philip Stephens would make sure Robespierre received any confession of treason I wrote. The day after, I would be dead. That is another certainty. Compared to Robespierre, your peasant army," he gave a weary wave of his hand at Niolle, "is nothing."

De Born knew he was right and decided on a compromise.

"Write out an affidavit that the boy in the Temple is not the Dauphin, and sign it."

Then he took Sophie to the gatehouse, introduced her to the boy and told her who he was.

*   *   *

"For God's sake, Jean, kill him." Laparre's voice was urgent, pleading.

"No," said de Born sharply. "I've seen all the blood I want to see. There'll be no more of it."

Laparre stared at de Born in amazement. As a boy he had been silent, secretive and hard. No, not hard exactly, but fierce. Laparre could not imagine what on earth had happened to make him say a thing like that.

"But if you let him go, he'll hunt you both down, the woman too," continued Laparre. "At least think of the boy. What future has he with that madman on the rampage?"

"I am thinking of him," replied de Born impatiently. "If Chaumette disappears we'll have half the local militia down on us within days. Simon would then be questioned and it would only be a matter of time before he confessed to helping the boy escape. Louis only has one hope of surviving the journey to London. As long as no one ever suspects that the boy in the Temple is an impostor, he is safe. Chaumette is obviously the one person who can never reveal his part in the plot; he'd be signing his own death warrant."

"Maybe," Laparre said sceptically, shaking his massive head. "I still don't like the idea of that fellow at large."

"Oh, but he won't be for long," de Born said, looking pleased with himself. "Before we let him go, you're going to send this anonymously to Robespierre." He tossed an unsealed packet over to Laparre.

After he had read it, Laparre looked admiringly at his old friend's son. Perhaps, he thought, the ferocity of boyhood had been replaced with cunning.

"Where on earth did you get this?"

"One night in Paris," replied de Born, taking the letter back and sealing it with a wafer, "Chaumette was loquacious with ether and boasting of his golden future. He started to talk of how important he was going to be if Provence ever became king. How he would return from America in triumph. My scepticism enraged him. He showed me that letter as proof. It never left his side, so I knew he'd brought it down here with him. I found it sewn into the lining of his cloak."

"Are you sure it's from Provence himself?" asked Laparre.

"Certain," replied de Born. "That's his private seal. It's incontrovertible proof that they were plotting to kill the boy by neglect and that Chaumette was involved in a conspiracy to replace the Republican government and restore the Bourbons, with Provence as

King Louis XVIII."

"Chaumette is a dead man just as soon as Robespierre gets this," chuckled Laparre maliciously. "By Our Lady, Jean, it's damned clever."

"As soon as we've gone, let him 'escape'," said de Born. "But make sure he suspects nothing."

Laparre nodded.

"What are you going to do?"

"Go back to England, find the traitor who was working for Chaumette, and kill him."

"And the marquise?" asked Laparre.

De Born didn't answer.

"Why do you hesitate?" asked Laparre, scrutinizing him keenly. "Take an old man's advice, Jean. Bed the woman and get her out of your system, then take that boy back to London before her tears are dry."

De Born still didn't answer and, after a while, Laparre went off to see to the dead.

* * *

As de Born paced up and down the great hall, lost in thought, Sophie sat watching him, still seemingly getting over her shock at discovering the boy's identity -although she seemed to take it calmly enough. This should be a moment of triumph, thought de Born despondently. He had the boy. He had the means to end Jacobin attempts to stir up revolution in England. He owned Château de Born at last. And, most amazing and wonderful of all, to find this woman, now watching him so anxiously. So why, he asked himself, do I feel so sick at heart?

The answer, he knew, was unpleasantly obvious. The lists of agents forced out of Chaumette could well be fakes. The castle was in enemy territory. The woman was already married. Indeed, he was unlikely to see either ever again. And then there was the boy.

He thought back ruefully to all those dreams of glory he had dreamt on the walk back from Downing Street. Those fantasies of dramatic entrances into the throne room, of casually introducing the boy king to Cousin George. His Majesty - according to the more pleasing versions - knighting him on the spot in a fit of ecstatic gratitude, while Pitt applauded and Philip Stephens burst with avuncular pride. He had pictured himself receiving all the gilt-edged finery of the authentic hero: the Freedom of the City, medals, ceremonial swords, honours, celebration dinners, even newspaper articles which Aunt Anne would cut out and keep. And now everything was changed. The boy had seen to that.

'Live Free or Die,' read the brass button on the boy's coat. The Jacobins were right about that at any rate. God's blood, didn't the boy have as much right to his freedom as anyone else? Why shouldn't he just open the door on that gilded cage and let him fly free?

But this was just more stupid daydreaming, he thought, and a pointless waste of time. Stephens knew from the letter Sophie delivered that he had rescued the boy. So what choice had he but to fulfill his duty and deliver him, as ordered? What the hell else could he do?

"What do you mean, Jean?" asked Sophie.

De Born realized that he had asked the question aloud. He stopped and stood in front of her.

"I don't want to give the boy to the English, but I have no choice."

"Why not, if you don't want to?" asked Sophie. "All you have to tell them is that you failed to rescue Louis due to Ferris's treachery. They'll be so excited by the lists of agents Chaumette supplied that Louis will soon be forgotten."

"You forget the letter," said de Born, miserably. "You delivered it yourself. Stephens knows I have the boy: it was written secretly in the note I gave to you."

"That?" said Sophie, puzzled. "But that letter is destroyed."

De Born grabbed her by the shoulders. "What?" he shouted in his excitement. "What do you mean destroyed?"

"You gave me the note in that strange room at the Palais Royal," Sophie replied calmly. "I understood the part about sending it to Philip Stephens, although I couldn't work out why from its contents. Immediately after you left, Chaumette came to me and took the letter. Then he did a very strange thing. He went over to the fire and held the paper to it, just as if he was making toast, and then he read it again. He kept holding it to the flames and then reading it. After a while he just shrugged and, before I could stop him, he crumpled it up and threw it on the fire."

"By God!" de Born exclaimed. "London has no idea I have the boy. Chaumette must have thought I would use the usual Department issue ink," he explained. "It appears when heated. I didn't. I used a different type, that kind needs a reagent. By God!" he repeated fervently. "All this time I thought I had no choice but to hand the boy over."

"But why not hand him over, Jean?" asked Sophie. "Why would you want to keep him?"

"Live Free or Die," muttered de Born.

"I don't understand," said Sophie, taking his hand in hers.

"Oh, it's just a foolish, empty revolutionary motto," said de Born. "They don't mean it, of course, but for the boy it happens to be true. He's terrified of staying here - and who can blame him?"

"But why not keep him " Sophie insisted, "it's not as if he's the Dauphin".

De Born whirled around to face her. She was grinning at him.

"How long have you known" he asked incredulously.

Sophie shrugged. "Almost as soon as I saw him".

"But how on earth....?" continued De Born.

"Simple", explained Sophie, "the real dauphin would have recognized me instantly. I spent every day with him at Versailles. This boy looked at me without the slightest sign of recognition. In any event, although he does look quite like the dauphin it's not enough to fool anyone who had actually known the boy well. Who is he anyway?"

De Born explained who Louis' father was and how he had double crossed Chaumette and switched the boys in the Temple.

"But why not take this boy back to England" asked Sophie.

"Because neither boy deserves such a fate" replied De Born. "The Dauphin remains in the Temple where he will die soon enough -the first time I laid eyes on him I could tell he was dying, from tuberculosis I would say- and this one will escape the fate reserved for any son of Philippe Egalité".

"But your orders, Jean, and your duty," said Sophie with quiet irony. "What about those?"

"So it's perfectly all right to do what is wrong," asked de Born, "as long as one is ordered to do it?"

"Yet orders are orders," said Sophie, ignoring his question.

"Nothing you can say or do can change that."

"Maybe," said de Born. "Maybe." He dropped her hand. "I'm going for a walk. Take care of the boy while I'm gone. I won't be long."

Sophie looked after him uneasily. He seemed so changed since the Conciergerie. More serious, more careworn, as if he carried a burden even greater than waiting for death. He had said nothing of their future together. She stood for a moment at the window until he passed out of sight, a solitary figure climbing the twisting, stone road up to the church.

De Born walked slowly through the village until he came to the church yard. By the western wall was the family vault. Bare-handed, de Born wiped away the snow covering the tombstone, revealing his mother's inscription. And underneath, 'Beloved husband'. He remembered the day the news came. The urgent summons sent to his barracks. The nervous glances of the Admiralty clerks. His uncle Philip's tense formality and his aunt's tears. But it was only now, finally seeing the crisp-cut letters in the stone, that the reality of his father's death came home to him. The mixture of dull shock and deep emptiness felt only at the moment that a man realizes that he is no longer a son and therefore truly an adult. Always alone, he felt, for the first time in his life, truly lonely. It was as if his father had abandoned him. What would he have done in my place? de Born wondered. He could hear his father's voice and see those hooded eyes glaring at him sternly. 'Do what you know is right, boy. Follow your instincts. Do your duty - your duty to yourself.'

"Thank you, father," he replied out loud, and went back down the hill to the château. Now he knew what he had to do.

*   *   *

"Can you arrange passage for the boy and Madame la marquise from Bordeaux?" he asked Laparre.

"Certainly, but where to?"

"Philadelphia," de Born said, and went to face Sophie and the boy.

They were playing with the briard in the plum orchard, both yelling so excitedly in the heat of the game that they did not notice his coming. A lock of Sophie's hair had escaped her ribbon and de Born watched as she paused for a moment to tuck it back.

"I've made a decision," de Born said, as they both stopped and looked at him expectantly.

"Where are we going?" asked Sophie.

"Philadelphia."

"And you?"

"London."

She nodded, as if to show that she knew all along that would be his answer.

"You know, Jean," Sophie said, looking at him intently, "that I would stay with you - if that's what you wanted."

"Yes, I know."

"And?"

"And I want you to."

Sophie's eyes glittered with pleasure.

"But we both know," de Born continued, "it would be wrong."

"Wrong?"

"Dishonourable."

"Is honour stronger than this feeling?"

"The dishonour would poison it." De Born tried to discern from her expression whether she understood. He could see that she didn't.

"And me?" Louis interrupted, his face pale with apprehension.

De Born took the boy onto his lap. "You'll be safe in Philadelphia with Sophie and her husband."

"And will I be free there?" asked Louis, searching his eyes.

"Yes," smiled de Born. "You'll be free."

Louis nodded, to show he understood. "And will you join us later?" he asked, the tears starting to form.

"No," said de Born, searching for his handkerchief. "I have to go back to London."

"But why?" complained Louis, now unable to prevent the flood.

De Born did not answer, but held the boy and looked over his shoulder at Sophie, until both could bear to look no longer.

*   *   *

The days that followed were miserable for all three. Both de Born and Sophie tried their best to interest Louis in his new home over the sea, reading him books from the library showing coloured drawings of fierce Red Indians and famous trappers along the Missouri, but what was unsaid and could not be said weighed down on them all. De Born spent his nights alone at Gigouzac.

And then, finally, the moment came.

Sophie brought the boy over to him. "He wants to ask you something, Jean."

"Ask away, Louis," de Born said, smiling down at the boy.

"May I have a keepsake, papa?" Louis asked shyly. "If I have a keepsake I can kiss you every night when you're away."

De Born fumbled around his neck and put his hands behind his back.

"Left or right?"

Like his namesake Louis always chose left. The amulet lay gleaming in de Born's palm. The boy turned it round to puzzle over the inscription and then he kissed it. De Born ruffled his hair while the boy grinned and ducked his head out of reach, as he always did. De Born opened his arms and they embraced for the last time.

Sophie came close, close enough for de Born to reach out his hand and gently touch her hair, stroking it with the tips of his fingers.

She took de Born's hand and pressed something small and hard into his palm. Then she took the boy by the hand and walked quickly to the carriage. Just before she entered Sophie turned and gave a little wave, then she smiled, a small, sad, hurt smile.

De Born stood, not moving, for a long time, long after they had disappeared from view. Then he felt something in his fist. A small screw of paper. He opened it carefully, as if unfolding a rose's tight petals. Inside was a woman's garnet ring. As he picked it up to put it onto his little finger, the scrap of paper was lifted by the breeze and fluttered down to the ground. When he bent down to retrieve it, he saw that in the middle were written just two words.

'Remember me.'

AUTHOR'S NOTE

Most of the people, places and events described in this book existed. After the murder of the boy's parents, Hébert (Chaumette's deputy and a man who in another age would have been a guard at Belsen) had Louis XVII shut up permanently in a tiny cell, his meager rations passed through a hatch. The boy, by now wracked with pain from the untended sores and ulcers that covered his half naked body, lived in his own filth and excrement, amongst lice and rats, without company of any kind. After the Terror, when conditions were alleviated somewhat, it was far too late. His health had been irretrievably and deliberately destroyed by his revolutionary jailers.

Pierre-Gaspard Chaumette and Antoine Simon were both executed on 24 Germinal (13 April 1794). Maximilien de Robespierre followed them to the guillotine 10 Thermidor (28 July). Jacques Louis David survived to become court painter to Napoleon. Sir William Codrington was eventually released from the Conciergerie and returned to England. Philip Stephens retired from the Admiralty in 1806. Cléry died in Vienna in 1809, after completing his memoirs. The boy's uncle, the Comte de Provence became Louis XVIII de facto as well as de jure after the fall of the Corsican gangster.

Mme Simon died in 1819 at a home for incurables. She remains the one enduring mystery of this affair because to her final day -and despite all evidence to the contrary- she stoutly maintained that the boy who died in the Temple was not the Dauphin -who she claimed had been removed in a laundry basket.

In 2000 the only known remains of the Dauphin were subjected to a DNA analysis by scientists from the University of Leuven in Belgium and the University of Munster in Germany. By comparing fragments of the ten year old boy's mummified heart (cut out by a doctor during an autopsy before the rest of the body was dumped in a mass grave) with locks known to be of Marie Antoinette's hair, the DNA specialists proved once and for all that Louis XVII had in fact died in the Temple in 1795.

The orphanage boy's half brother Louis-Philippe became King of France in 1830, thus ending rule by the House of Bourbon, but was subsequently deposed in the 1848 revolution and died two years later in England as the last French king to actually rule France.

On the 25th of June, 1938, John de Roquefère -the scion of one of Philadelphia's oldest families- married his college sweetheart. The wedding photographer was asked discreetly not to photograph him from the right side as this would reveal a hereditary birth defect- his misshapen ear lobe.